THE BIG SUGARBUSH

A LESBIAN ROMANCE

A DEEPLY SUPERFICIAL TALE OF LEZZY, DYKE, QUEER GIRLS BEHAVING BADLY*

ANA B GOOD

If you are seeking something more substantial, we'd recommend Kafka.

Chick Lick Books, an Imprint of
Hot Pants Press, LLC
4 Carmichael Street, PMB #2160
Essex Junction, VT 05452
E-mail: thebigbush@thebigsugarbush.com
Web: *www.TheBigSugarBush.com*

First Print Edition: December, 2016

ISBN: 978-0-981-5678-1-5

Credits
Editor: Carolyn Haley, DocuMania
Cover Design: Dane Low, Ebook Launch

Acknowledgments

It takes a long time, and a lot of support, to *create* any creative work. I have a lot of people to thank in preparing this production. Please direct your applause to early readers of the effort. Cindy Yager, Linda Beal, Docie Woodward, Anne Stockwell, Suzanne Stofflet, bless your souls for reading the dirty first drafts and for your priceless suggestions. To the best friend ever, Gretchen Bryant, thank you, wherever you may be now, for all your love and deep understanding of the writer's soul. I miss you, goddamn it. Thanks also to Kim Fountain and Josie Leavitt of the Pride Center of Vermont, and all the good peeps who hang out there in Burlington, Vermont, working diligently to make Vermont a safe and happy place for the LGBT community. A portion of the proceeds from the sale of *The Big Sugarbush* go toward helping sustain the Pride Center of Vermont, so read often, and read a lot. If you like this novel, please review it online, and be sure and buy a copy for your mother.

The Cast

Ten power lezzies — A-gays at their best (and worst) — have thirty days to kick booze, drugs, and drama and get their lives back on track. Sugarbush, a Vermont rehab center, seems just the place. Quiet, tranquil, and therapeutic … until the dykes arrive, and the drama begins.

Prepare to fall in love with

~ *Dylan Redford:* An installation artist whose *Big Pink Pussy,* a mammoth sculpture of her own genitalia, has the art world in an uproar.

~ *Storm Waters:* Petite powerhouse of CNN's war correspondent team, and America's chain-smoking, gun-toting sweetheart.

~ *Candice Antwerp, M.D.:* Surgical mastermind behind the best-sculpted bodies in Hollywood, and a real closet case.

~ *Nan Goldberg:* Queen of the Bond Market, until the market crashes and she loses a fortune along with her professional verve.

~ *Bunny Van Randolph:* Aging only daughter of Senator Van Randolph, and a one-woman Welcome Wagon for the East Coast Butch Brigade.

~ *Poppy Zigfield:* Lead singer of the all-girl British band, Poppy and the Pop Tarts, and a woman who isn't shy about her sexual preferences.

~ *Wee Gee Judd:* America's best-selling writer of bodice-ripping romance for hetero housewives.

~ *Dirk and Thumper McGraw:* Stud-muffin Olympic snowboarding twins with six-pack abs and a special talent for pleasing the society ladies.

~ *Betty Frump:* Sergeant General of the Lesbian Thought Police, an icon of the feminist women of the 1960s and '70s, and a real pain in the ass for the fun-loving queers of today.

Part I

The Gang's All Here

1.

The Real Sugarbush

Nan Goldberg lit a Dunhill cigarette and inhaled until her lungs ached. She rubbed the foggy window of the limo with the tail of her Hermès scarf, hoping to see something other than the snotty sleet that had pelted the car since they'd left the airport in Burlington, Vermont, an hour ago.

No luck.

Nan Goldberg did not want to be fishtailing in a limo around Bumfuck, Vermont, in the middle of a snowstorm. She wanted to be in Manhattan, inside her cozy townhouse at Sixty-Seventh and Lexington, wrapped in soft, warm layers of angora. She missed her tiny, manicured bonsai trees. She longed for her toasty-warm, cedar sauna.

Plus, she could guzzle top-drawer gin in peace in her townhouse. A shot of Nolet's Reserve for breakfast - maybe five or six shots, as she'd enjoyed that very morning - who'd be the wiser?

Nan shot a glance across the limo's back seat. Her gaze fixed on the matronly woman in a tightly tailored blue tweed suit who'd forced her into another limo that very morning. Who'd be the wiser if Nan kept sucking on a gin bottle like the town drunk? *Birge Hathaway, that's who.*

Birge, Nan's partner of thirty years, tapped Nan's platinum cigarette case, which lay on the tufted red-leather seat between them. "Can't take those with you, dear."

Nan clawed for the case. "Ohhh no! Not on your life, baby! I agreed to give up drinking, *not* smoking. Drinking, *not* anything else." Nan fumed. She'd always had a short fuse, but this past year, with the stock market as flat as West Texas, and the bond market in the toilet, too, she'd dialed up to dynamite.

Ten years ago Nan Goldberg had been at the top of her game, the cover girl two times running for *Fortune*. Ten years ago The Motley Fool had sung her praises. Now the SEC had frozen her assets — not all, she still had over five million in Cayman cash accounts and her priceless Bar Harbor, Maine, estate — but she'd bet and lost a billion in bad bond calls. Her name was poison on Wall Street. Even Donald Trump, who had his own problems, was declining her calls.

Birge thought drying out might help Nan.

Nan thought the answer lay in switching drinks. The jewels of the juniper at seven hundred dollars a bottle were no longer sufficient. Maybe she should switch to Scotch with Prozac, an increasingly popular bear-market mix in the marble gutters of Wall Street.

Recognizing the desperation in her partner's eyes, Birge launched into a reminder of the purpose of the trip. "This place is a rehab center, dear. They frown on all addictions. Smoking is an addiction." Birge pried Nan's manicured fingers from the platinum case and pocketed it in the outer zipper compartment of her own briefcase. "No more Dunhills or you from here on in."

Nan locked her arms across her pink cashmere sweater and stared out the snow-pelted limo window. Sleet. Snow. Ice. No cocktail hour. And now no cigarettes? This rehab thing felt stale already. "Anything else you neglected to tell me about this little Vermont vacation?"

"Love you, dear," Birge said.

Nan popped open the limo bar and busied herself mixing what might be her last cocktail in perhaps forever. She didn't look at Birge. She didn't have to look. She could feel her disapproving glare across the cold canyon stretch of the back seat.

Nan sipped a puddle of golden gin and tried to remember why she had ever fallen in love with Birge. They'd met three decades ago in business school, at Cornell, in the after-hours smoking lounge of the library. Birge had cool moss-green eyes, the color of the granite seabed in Bar Harbor, where Nan's family had kept a summer home for three generations.

It wasn't Birge's eyes, though, that Nan had fallen in love with. It was her attitude. Her walk, more precisely, clipped, like a military cadet's. It drove Nan crazy with lust, the way Birge, eldest daughter of a steel worker, walked: with a confident swagger that typically only men of their generation enjoyed.

Once Nan had Birge's strident movement going wild deep inside her, she wanted more, much more. It had been a wonderfully wild thirty years. Hell, if Birge Hathaway, financial wizard of Wall Street, wanted her sober for thirty days, she supposed she could humor her. One day for each year they'd been together. Why the hell not. Humor her.

"We'll get through this," Birge murmured as she slipped a glossy lavender flier from her briefcase. She tapped the folder on the seat between them. "Sugarbush, Vermont. Run by a sassy old Yankee gal named Lily Rockworthy, who, for the record, has cured worse cases than you."

Nan snorted as she mixed a second triple Nolet's from the limo bar. "Sugarbush? You're kidding, right?" Nan had been on the Manhattan pro-lesbian circuit long enough to know that *sugarbush* was Seven Sisters lingo for an elderly trust fund dyke. In her line of work, as a Wall Street bond broker, Nan had serviced many a sugarbush.

"*Not* what you're thinking, dear," chastised Birge. "Get your mind out of the Wall Street gutter. This is Vermont. Up here, a sugarbush is a stand of maple trees."

Nan nursed her drink. "A stand of maple trees? Really?"

"Yes, really. Like those." Birge slid her fingers along the sleet-smeared window, tracing a thick, dark, smoothly barked line of trees as they whizzed by on the mountain road.

"Those," murmured Nan as she squinted through the storm, "are not maples. Those are oaks."

Birge adjusted her trifocals. "Oak? How in God's name can you tell?"

"I was a Girl Scout."

"A Girl Scout?" Birge grunted. "I don't think so. You hate camping. I've known you three decades and you hate camping."

"Who said anything about camping?"

"You said you were a Girl Scout."

"I was."

"I don't understand. No camping? How'd you become a Girl Scout?"

"The way we all did in the '70s, dear. I ate my fair share of Brownies."

Birge bellowed as the limo skidded to an uncertain stop.

Both women rubbed at the windows trying to see if they'd arrived at their destination.

Nan saw it first. A simple, white farmhouse materialized through swirling curtains of snow. The two-story structure was nestled in a snowbank, the wraparound porch drifted in white. Two Adirondack rocking chairs sat quietly on the porch like a pair of snow-covered turtles. Buttery light leaked from the windows. A faded wooden sign that read "Sugarbush" creaked in the winter wind.

Nan grasped the limo door handle and sprang it open, not waiting for the uniformed driver to tromp back through the snowdrifts to assist. She had to flee before Birge said something sentimental, something that would surely make them both cry. She was way too old to cry or to throw a temper tantrum, though at the moment she desperately wanted to do both.

Thirty days without alcohol? No problem. Hell, she was a middle-aged lesbian. She'd survived an East Coast Jewish upbringing. The Reagan administration. The Bee Gees. Big hair. A year in electrolysis. And three decades of blue-collar Christmas parties with Birge's cross-clutching, Catholic mother, Nona Francis Marie.

Nan Goldberg didn't need gin to survive; what she needed was for Birge Hathaway, the love of her life, to believe in her once again.

2.

The Big Pink Pussy

The *Big Pink Pussy*, San Francisco's hottest new museum art installation, was Dylan Redford's response to the Washington Monument. It bothered Dylan horribly that the father of the country had an five-hundred-foot erection dedicated to him in D.C., and that no one called the thing indecent. People paid, in fact, to climb it. But nowhere did American women have a public monument that celebrated the great nation they had literally birthed.

Precisely why Dylan Redford had spent two years hand-crafting her *Big Pink Pussy*. The Pussy, eighty-feet tall, was scientifically accurate, molded from liquid latex stretched around a giant cast of Dylan's own interior. Dylan had lovingly superglued a thousand steel-wool pads to the giant slit in representation of her own unruly pubic hair.

The day the *Big Pink Pussy* art installation opened at its permanent home in San Francisco's fashionable South of Market district, Dylan stood at the lipped entrance, handing out tour maps like it was a real estate open house. "Welcome to my pussy," she enjoyed saying to the more attractive ladies. The more uptight they appeared, the more she enjoyed saying it.

When museum visitors toured the *Big Pink Pussy*, Dylan encouraged them to stroke the wiry wool before stepping through the eight-foot pink slit into her throbbing uterus. One stroke and the installation moaned. More than that and it shook with the fervor of a San Francisco earthquake, tossing spectators side to side like a carnival ride.

For one dollar, Dylan gave Americans the chance to see the womanly side of the birth of this great nation. "This is what the Statue of Liberty *ought* to look like," she was quoted as saying in the arts and leisure section of the *San Francisco Examiner*. "The insides of a real woman, not that humble, horse-faced French lady they have parked outside New York harbor."

Art Today had not wanted to cover Dylan's new installation, but the damn thing was built with tax money, a National Humanities Grant. It was all the rage. No way to ignore it.

Dylan judged that the museum opening was going famously until Ginger Fitzgerald of *Art Today* had stepped inside the museum installation room in her red stilettos. Ginger had reviewed Dylan's installations twice before, neither time favorably. Tonight she was in a mad hurry. Her copy was due at the office at eight a.m. and she'd already toured three unbearably bad installations.

Dylan gnashed her teeth as Ginger clicked up the raised platform in her Prada heels to tour the *Big Pink Pussy*. Dylan had read, indeed memorized, Ginger's previous mudslinging reviews of her artwork.

Ginger squinted as she strolled inside the crinkly pink cervix. On the advice of her audio tour master, she peeled a paper tab off the slick pink walls. (The lick tabs were covered with a juicy ooze, which had been flavored peppermint for those bold enough to take a lick, which Dylan *always* encouraged.)

Unimpressed by the installation, Ginger brushed past Dylan, tossing a comment over her shoulder as she clicked out of the museum. "Disappointed, dear," she sneered, *"Très derivative of Judy Chicago."*

Dylan puffed up. "That bitch did suburban dinnerware. This is my vagina."

Ginger sniffed the air, recalling the odor inside the installation. Peppermint and warm latex were not a pleasant mix. "And it smells like it, too."

It took three rent-a-cops to pry Dylan Redford off Ginger Fitzgerald.

Not one to take physical assault lightly, Ginger pressed charges.

"Art bitch," grumbled Dylan in the courtroom the next week.

"What did you call me?" asked the San Francisco judge, who happened to be a lesbian, but also a Republican. Without waiting for an answer, she sentenced Dylan to six months in women's prison — this was her third felony assault charge — or one month in rehab with a year of pissing in plastic cups thereafter.

Dylan arrived in Vermont at Sugarbush two weeks later dragging her duffel bag in the snow. It was loaded with sculpting and welding tools. She was so high on coke she thought she was checking in at a queer art resort in Switzerland. She wondered for a moment when she saw the owner, Lily Rockworthy, manning the check-in. She'd never seen a seventy-six-year-old counter girl, dripping in diamonds, but heh, she dug older chicks, especially ones who were stacked, a term which clearly applied to Lily.

Only later, when Dylan awoke to find herself neatly tucked into a twin bed, wearing striped pink cotton pajamas, did she realize how dire her life had become.

"Oh fuck," Dylan moaned. "Not another psych ward!"

Nan Goldberg, the Manhattan bond broker who was booked in the bed across from Dylan, poked her head out from under the covers where she'd been enjoying a Lisa Scottoline novel (*Dirty Blonde*) and a smuggled pack of Dunhill cigarettes. She fanned away a halo of smoke before speaking. "Actually, dear, it's lezzy rehab."

Rehab? *Shit*, thought Dylan. This was worse than she'd thought. At least in the nuthouse they gave you drugs.

3.

Poppy and the Pop Tarts

They told Poppy Zigfield, lead singer for the British all-girl band, Poppy and the Pop Tarts, that she was going to perform at Disneyland alongside Taylor Swift. Poppy was understandably pissed when the private helicopter her mum had commandeered dropped her down at Sugarbush rehab, a veritable snow cone in the middle of an unimpressive pile of rocks called Vermont.

No Taylor Swift.

And not a Mickey Mouse in sight, either, just a monstrous brown-eyed creature, pawing the snow in search of an edible morsel. The moose stared sad-eyed, with icy smoke curling from his nostrils, as Poppy leaped from the helicopter that had shanghaied her from New York's Madison Square Garden, her last American gig.

The helicopter pilot tossed a tiny pink leather overnight bag out onto the snow at Poppy's feet and yelled, "Good luck, mate!" as she swirled away, back up into the clouds.

Poppy swallowed hard when she saw the moose ambling toward her. She'd never faced such a large, hairy, unruly creature up close — unless one counted her ex-girlfriend, Tubby McGuire, after three days on Ecstasy.

Fuck that moose.

Poppy had to get inside quickly or she was headed for a bad case of chapped quim. Ambling to one side, clutching her polka-dotted micro-mini in an effort to warm her stick-thin thighs, and grabbing her bag, Poppy slid across the ice field toward the front door of the farmhouse.

Poppy and the Pop Tarts were an awesome girl band. The global press had tagged them the hottest act ever to tread the boards in West London. Their global record sales made the Spice Girls and old broads like Lady Gaga look like warm-up stunts at Brighten Beach. But one split second of bad judgment had done poor Poppy in.

One effing mistake.

Poppy had gotten into a fight with her fuck buddy, B-Bo, Britain's star girl soccer player, and accidentally torched the superathlete's East Hampton mansion.

Big deal. Like B-Bo would miss a five-million-dollar beach shack. B-Bo made more than that standing around in a g-string looking good for European underwear ads.

But apparently arson was a big deal to the Americans, who seemed to have no empathy when it came to drug-induced crimes of passion that destroyed prime real estate. The Hamptons' district attorney's office charged Poppy with felony arson. Her mum had booked her into Sugarbush hoping to force her to abandon recreational drug use before she did a total Winehouse and popped off the planet for good.

Dear-old wanky Mum, in Poppy's estimation, was overreacting. Menopause — *mental pause* — or something like that, as near as Poppy could tell. She, Poppy Zigfield, lead Love Tart, did *not* have a problem with drugs. The only problem she had was with Dame Diane, her dear-old Victorian mum.

A multimillionaire by her twenty-first birthday, Poppy was managing just fine, thank you. Sure, she weighed less than her pet pug, King James, but thin was in. Her dark eyes popped from her head like a love-starved puppy. Her big red lips, plump with collagen, played kissy-face with the world.

On a good day her generous use of mascara made her look like a refugee from the *Twilight* trilogy. Poppy Zigfield thought of her blood-starved look as her trademark, like Dolly Parton's huge breasts and hay pile of hair.

Lily Rockworthy, owner of Sugarbush, eyed Poppy as she shivered toward the registration desk. Lily had been running Sugarbush for so long she could diagnosis a girl's favorite addiction with one glance. She held out a ziplock bag with Poppy's name stenciled across the front. "Laxatives," she demanded as she peered over the bridge of her turquoise half-glasses.

"What's that, love?" Poppy twisted her long black hair around her pinkie as she spoke. On stage she belted out her songs. In real life she spoke more softly, like the prep school princess her mother had hoped she'd become.

"Everything you're holding goes into the bag. Can't bring stash with you. If you still want that stuff at the end of your thirty days, we'll give it back."

Poppy puffed her cheeks. "Piss off, queenie. I don't belong here. I'm supposed to be performing with Swift at Disneyland. Call me a car service, a freakin' dogsled, whatever."

"No taxis up here. Next ride out not 'til next week."

Poppy rolled her eyes as she took in the shabby lobby. "What is this place, love? Hell on a budget?"

"Your mom arranged a winter vacation for you."

"Well, it smells like old-lady farts to me." Poppy fished through her micro-mesh bag and yanked out a finger-length cigarette flecked in gold dust, which she stuffed into a carved ivory holder.

Lily reached over and plucked the cigarette from her lips. "No smoking in the house, love. That'll be in the rule book come morning. Might as well warm up."

Pouting, Poppy plucked an ebony Montblanc pen from her purse and attacked the register with her trademark *P*. She slapped down the signature as large as she could in an act of defiance.

Sod it. I'll stay seven days. Get Mum off my back. What difference could a bloody week make, anyway?

She emptied her bag onto the registration desk, allowing Lily to brown-bag several bubble packs of laxatives, a vaporizer, an Altoids tin of Ecstasy, and a rainbow assortment of pills even she didn't recognize.

Must have been a party pack B-Bo slipped on her when the cops came.

Lily handed Poppy a nicely folded set of striped pink flannel pajamas. "You'll be toasty in these."

"You joking, doll? Who made these? The Queen Mum? I can't wear something freak-girl like these. What if my fans see me? Do you know who I am? *Do* you?"

"Yes."

Poppy's eyes brightened.

"You're a dyke. A fucked-up English one, from the sound of you."

4.

Dating Little Debbie

Lily Rockworthy raked back the long velvet curtains in the living room and studied the snow as it wrapped its plump, cold arms around the farmhouse. Several women had not yet checked in. Weather was causing some of the delays, but Lily knew that her guests were dragging their feet; insisting that they were not addicts; begging their families to let them detox on their own terms.

Few came to Sugarbush willingly. Most tried every trick in the book to persuade their loved ones that they absolutely did not need an intervention.

Lily ought to know. She'd be forty years sober come Christmas. Before that she'd spent a decade on Broadway slinging bourbon and breaking hearts. She still had the long, shapely legs of a Rockette. (And a library of little black books full of the phone numbers of women who adored her — drunk or sober.)

Yawning, Lily let the curtains fall into place. She called her partner, Babe Swenderson, to the front office. She was too tired to handle more intakes. Babe would be their chief therapist. Best if she met them up front, while they were putting their worst feet forward.

Babe strolled into the office and stashed a bottle of filtered water and a bag of organic rice crackers under the registration desk. She'd just finished braiding her flaxen hair, which was graying at the temples. She'd spent the day trying to get her head in place to begin a new group.

They came every thirty days, each group crazier than the last. Sometimes Babe missed the good-old days when dykes were dykes and they either drank too much beer or bourbon or couldn't leave the weed alone.

Nowadays lesbians (dykes? queers? chick-lickers?) came in all sizes and flavors. Their problems were likewise assorted and complex. It was crazy out there with drugs like synthetic marijuana and heroin and meth being manufactured and sold in Walmart bathrooms for less than a cartoon of Marlboros.

"Who's left?" Babe queried Lily as she glanced at the nearly blank registration book.

Lily peered over her turquoise half-glasses at the roster. "Most. I've only checked in Nan Goldberg, the broker; Poppy, the British rock star; and that foul-mouthed handsome thing that built the *Big Pink Pussy*."

Babe raised her eyebrows. "Dylan Redford?"

Lily nodded.

Babe had toured Dylan's pussy — professionally speaking, that is — she'd never met the woman in person. She'd toured the art installation during its road show in Boston. "I hear she's as wild as they come."

"Well, she didn't arrive sane or sober." Lily chuckled at the memory of how enthusiastically Dylan had trounced upstairs. She wondered if the young thing realized yet where she'd landed. Not the leather room at San Francisco Sal's, like she'd hoped, no doubt.

Lily was still meditating on her new group of clients when the farmhouse door blew open. Snow swirled into the foyer. A large black woman stumbled in, dumping her luggage and her hat, a red felt affair with white ostrich feathers, onto the polished wooden floor.

Lily smiled. "Wee Gee! Wee Gee Judd, you old dyke!"

"Who you calling old, girl?" Wee Gee laughed so loud the house shook. She clasped first Lily then Babe in her ample arms.

"Fall off the wagon?" Lily asked.

"Hell no!" boomed Wee Gee. "Damned wagon fell on me."

Babe chortled. While she hated to see clients return, if she had to see a repeat, Wee Gee Judd was among her favorites. "What's the problem, honey?"

Wee Gee sighed heavily as she slapped the keys to her Caddie SUV onto the desk and signed herself in — for the third time in a decade.

"Got booze licked. Not playing the ponies no more, either."

Babe shook her head. Cure one addiction; watch another pop up. Like Whac-a-Mole. Impossible to win, but they'd all die trying. "What's the problem now, dear?"

Wee Gee cupped her ample ass with both hands. "Got a new girlfriend: Little Debbie. Gained fifty pounds this fall. Blood sugar higher than my IQ. Doc says I need to get this weight thing under control or face sugar shock. Think you skinny white gals can help?"

Lily held open an extra-large baggie with Wee Gee Judd's name stenciled on it. "Third time's a charm. Hand over all you're holding to us and the good Goddess."

After signing in, and handing over all the candy she had in her purse, including her Tic Tacs, Wee Gee reached over the counter to squeeze Babe's pecs. "Damn, honey, you've gone all Arnold S."

"Pumping iron."

Wee Gee glanced over at Lily. "Still pumpin' you, too?"

"Nightly, with glee," said Lily.

The women were yucking it up about the good-old days, specifically the early 1970s, when the farmhouse door blew open and a duo frosted with snow and ice tripped into the lobby like a pair of gangly snow women. The two young women, mirror images of each other, traipsed into the foyer. Over six feet tall, they shook snow from their closely cropped, blonde heads as one of them lumbered toward the desk. The other moped behind, cradling a red snowboard flat against her chest. Their bleached-blonde hair glistened with gel and snowflakes.

"We're here," the front girl sighed sourly as she ran a tanned hand across her buzz cut.

"So you are," remarked Babe as she slid the register across the desk. "And who might you be?"

The girl sighed deeply, the way a teenager does when addressed by her mother. "Dirk McGraw." She jerked a thumb over her shoulder. "That's my sister, Thumper. Flunked our drug tests. U.S. Olympic snowboarding team. Gold medalists. Need to be clean by January. Anything else you need to know, ma'am?"

Babe eyed the girls as they shed their matching black down jackets. Sinewy muscles rippled through their black Levi's and T-shirts. The girls were buff, with butts as muscular as a cowboy's and jaws as square as Brad Pitt's.

God didn't make young women that buff. Not even lesbians.

Babe entered "Steroid addiction" on their treatment cards and handed them a pair of striped pink cotton pajamas.

The McGraw twins snatched the striped pink PJs and stared at each other like they'd just loped into an episode of *The Twilight Zone.*

5.

Bunny Yum-Yum

Dirk McGraw and her twin sister Thumper were bumping up the stairs to their bedroom, dragging their Olympic snowboards, when a ruckus in the lobby caused them to halt at the landing at the top of the stairs.

A tall woman with ass-length, honey-blonde hair had entered the lobby and was barking orders at an entourage of men who toted her Gucci leather luggage. Her dog, a white Westie, was barking, adding to the commotion.

"Justin!" the woman chastised the man who held the door open for her. "Icky snow on my feet. My Manolo Blahniks. Oh my God! These shoes are a work of art! Do somethinggg!"

Justin whipped off his tie and bent to buff the purple shoes whose straps wound around the woman's shapely calves like vines.

Inspecting her shoes, the woman made a clucking sound before kicking Justin out of the way and calling another man, Colt, to her rescue. Before long, both men were bowed at the woman's feet frantically attempting to scrape off the icy sludge.

"Welcome, honey," Lily called to the woman, who was busy shedding her white finger mink wrap and fluffing her yellow hair in the hallway mirror simultaneously. "Register here."

The woman frowned as she smoothed her red, silk cocktail dress over her long frame and checked her diamond earrings in the lobby mirror. The earrings sparkled like glass walnuts. Not paste. The real thing.

"Justin, be a doll. Register me." The woman waved one hand. "Colt, darling, find my black cashmere pashmina. It's chilly in this old barn. Brrr! Sending me to the mountains of Vermont this time of year. Really, what was Daddy dearest thinking?"

The woman pulled her Westie out of his plaid traveling bag and kissed him full on his little wet nose. "Mommy loves Mr. Yummy. Does Mr. Yummy love mommy? Does Mr. Yummy love his mommy?" She rubbed noses with the terrier.

Justin took the register and signed in Ms. Bunny Van Randolph.

"Of *the* Van Randolphs, Senator Van Randolph, from the Cape," he whispered discreetly to Lily. "Ms. Bunny needs special attention. The senator requests you spare no cost where his daughter is concerned. Are those your bellboys?" He gestured up the stairs, toward the McGraw twins.

"You, fellows, come here!" Justin snapped his fingers, beckoning the twins toward Bunny Van Randolph's monstrous pile of white leather luggage.

Dirk McGraw bounded eagerly down the stairs.

Justin snapped his fingers as Dirk approached. "More trunks en route, Ms. Van Randolph's evening wardrobe. Her luggage limo slid off the road. A large hairy creature has it cornered in an icy meadow three miles down."

"Moose," Babe offered quietly.

"Excuse me?"

"Our pet moose, Winkle."

"Pet?" the man looked incredulous. "What's wrong with hamsters or a nice little pussycat?"

Babe hooked her thumb toward Lily. "The old gal prefers moose."

Lily nodded. "Rather found of penguins, also, but it's too warm to keep them up here. I've tried."

Dirk McGraw spoke. "Which suite is Ms. Van Randolph's?" The well-muscled snowboarder glanced over her shoulder at the socialite, who was busy admiring her svelte profile in the mirror.

From a distance, Bunny looked thirty-five, tops. In reality, she was forty-five and freaked about her collapsing looks. Thus far she'd held on to her looks with the help of cosmetic surgery and a generous supply of Botox shots and anti-anxiety pills. (Her last two girlfriends had conveniently been physicians.)

Twenty years of amphetamines chased with downers had left Bunny with a tick in her right eye. She'd managed to work it into her repertoire as a flirtatious wink, but lately it was worsening. When someone or something excited her, her wink went wild. Her father, up for the Democratic nomination for the presidency, wanted her off the pills before the family hit the campaign trail. These days, having a gender-fluid family member was a political plus, but not if that family member kept showing up on YouTube muff-diving international women of ill repute.

The senator was hoping to rehab his daughter's image, if not her, so she looked more like a "family" kind of lesbian. A nice family-oriented lesbian who drives an SUV and adopts biracial children. Family lesbians tested very well in the polls.

Unfortunately Senator Van Randolph's daughter had recently been showing up in social media under #twinkletwat, and that handle did not test well in mid-America.

Recognizing a prime #twinkletwat when she saw one, Dirk pushed up the sleeves of her Olympic T-shirt and eagerly introduced herself to Bunny.

Bunny's nervous eye twitched uncontrollably as she drank in the snowboarder's thick muscles and lopsided grin. *Oh shit. I love Vermont already.*

Babe pushed a stack of papers across the desk toward Justin. "Ms. Van Randolph will have to read and sign these."

"Read?" Justin scoffed. "Ms. Van Randolph does not read."

"Well, she'll have to read. Treatment papers."

"Treatment?" Justin bent and whispered into Babe's ear. "Say, what kind of resort is this?"

Babe snorted. "The kind where we'll resort to anything to cure women of their addictions."

Justin paled. "Oh, well, the senator did not tell me. I thought we were going skiing at some rustic hippie lesbo family resort. I'm sure Ms. Van Randolph doesn't know … about the rehab thing." He uttered the last part softly.

"Guess you'll have to tell her."

But before Justin was done speaking, Bunny was sashaying around the lobby arm in arm with Dirk McGraw. She brushed by Justin, her valet, tossing Mr. Yummy, the terrier, to him for safekeeping. The dog yapped his head off, but Bunny ignored him, her attention fixed squarely on the tall, muscle-bound snowboarder.

"Dirk is going to show me to my room," Bunny said as she snatched the key from Babe's outstretched hand and climbed the stairs arm in arm with Dirk.

6.

Storm Ho

Sometimes Sugarbush guests arrived in such a state they had to be literally tied down and sedated. Babe Swenderson was used to this by now. She kept a tranquilizer gun under the front desk for rabid wildlife and surly drug-crazed lezzies.

And she knew how to use it, just in case.

Three a.m. Babe was asleep at the registration desk, snoring deeply. A loud *boom!* brought her out of her sleep along with a blast of arctic air rushing through the wide-open front door. A tornado of snow swirled into the lobby as Babe's head popped up.

As the snow settled, a petite woman dressed in desert fatigues and a hooded orange parka appeared. Pale icy-blue eyes appraised Babe from under a fur-lined parka hood. The eyes were mesmerizing, almost as captivating as the steel machine gun the woman shouldered.

"We expecting you?" Babe yelled across the snow-blown lobby. She squinted hard, hoping to make out the woman's face. She'd never had a guest arrive wearing a machine gun ensemble before. Her right hand shot under the desk and located the tranquilizer gun, just in case. There had been a rash of break-ins on the western slopes, kids looking for drugs, so Babe and Lily had decided to be prepared.

The woman in desert fatigues unzipped her parka and let the machine gun drop from her shoulder as easily as if it were a purse. She smiled as she stepped into the bright light of the foyer, sweeping her dark pageboy back from her eyes. "Military airlift was late. Damn Brits. Hell of a time getting out of Baghdad."

"Storm Waters?" Babe gasped as she caught sight of the woman's face.

"And you?"

"Babe Swenderson. My partner, Lily Rockworthy, and I run this place."

Storm cast her gaze around the farmhouse. "You gals dry me out? Got forty days before I'm due back on tour in the Middle East."

"What's the problem?" Babe was amazed at how beautiful Storm was in person. She'd read somewhere that the war correspondent had a Japanese father and a Swedish mother. Her unusual parentage gave her skin a delicate creamy sheen, like porcelain. Her dark hair was straight, jet-black Japanese. Her voice was strong, raspy from cheap foreign cigarettes and too many late nights crawling around in desert foxholes.

"Can't sleep. I'll suck down anything that helps me calm down when the job's done. Sleep on my job, get your throat slit." Storm made a cutting motion with two fingers under her chin as she spoke. Then she grinned, as if enjoying the daily danger of her job.

Babe could imagine. At least twenty war correspondents worked the danger zones of the world for CNN, but Storm was the only woman who reported live from the front lines. She looked so fragile, yet her voice had a deep, sexy quality. She wasn't even five feet tall, but her personality was huge, electric, alive. She never sat behind a desk and read the news. She always reported live from the war zone, from the site of the latest natural disaster, always dangling from some dangerous place, looking cool as a cucumber as bullets and bombs whizzed around her beautiful head in halos of iron and fire.

America was in love with the woman.

(Babe, too, but she'd never, ever cheat on Lily.)

Storm pulled a pack of cheap French cigarettes from her parka pocket and lit one. "Hooked on painkillers, Percocet, blah, blah, blah, and these," she said, blowing the words out in a puff of smoke. "But I ain't giving these away. These are legal far as the network suit boys are concerned. I flunked my last drug test for opioids. Network won't renew my contract if I can't pass the next one in January."

Babe could imagine Storm's incentive. She'd read in *People* that Storm earned two million a year, plus bonuses for any story she broke right out of the gate. For two million a year, most gals would give sobriety a try.

"Doesn't matter you're late. We saved you a room."

Storm laughed, a rich, deep laughter that came out in a cloud of smoke. "Where do I sign, sugar?"

Babe slid the big book across the desk. "Hand over the smokes and sign here," she said.

Anchoring her fine black hair behind her ears, Storm scrawled her name boldly across the page. She squinted at the name above hers. "OMG. What the fuck. Bunny? Bunny Van Randolph? She's here? *Really?*"

"You know her?"

Storm sucked her cheeks. "Yeah, I know her. Sort of. We had a fling this past summer on the Cape. Frankly it was screwing her that convinced me I might have a little judgment problem. I mean, have you ever seen such a princess?"

Storm rolled her eyes before lowering her voice. "She alone?"

Babe squirmed. She wasn't sure how to respond. Bunny wasn't really alone, not the way Dirk McGraw, the snowboarder, had been hanging off her when they disappeared upstairs. "Er. More or less."

Storm chortled. She had a feeling she knew what *that* meant. Bunny was never alone if she could help it. There wasn't a butch on the East Coast social circuit who hadn't pearl-probed the Princess of Cape Cod.

"Well," murmured Storm, "she's such a pill hound, probably won't even remember me."

Studying Storm as she walked up the stairs, Babe seriously doubted any woman who'd slept with Storm could forget the experience. The woman didn't walk, she swaggered. Put a swagger like that in a dress instead of military fatigues and Babe bet most women wouldn't be able to decide if they wanted to be Storm or bed her.

Babe thought about shouting up the stairs after Storm, warning her that her assigned roommate the next thirty days would be no other than Bunny Van Randolph, but then decided to let it slide.

They could deal with the issue in group therapy, every day for the next thirty days.

7.

The Midnight Sound of a Satisfied Woman

Babe was sound asleep, head buried in folded arms, snoring at the front desk, when all hell broke loose upstairs. She glanced at the grandfather clock in the foyer: four a.m. "Not already!" she groaned as she rubbed her eyes. Shaking off sleep, she bounded the stairs two at a time toward the second story, where the women shared bedrooms.

Heads popped out of doors as Babe strode the corridor searching for the source of the commotion. Wee Gee had her hair, which she'd treated with a conditioner, stuffed into a flowered nightcap. She was sharing a room with Poppy, the rock star. Both women had been fast asleep when the odd yodeling had begun.

"Not me!" Wee Gee called after Babe. "Not this time! Old Wee Gee was fast asleep in her own damned bed."

Babe scanned the heads as they popped out the doors up and down the hall. Who was missing?

Thumper McGraw, the snowboarder, stepped into the hallway. She was wearing black silk boxer shorts and a skintight sleeveless black silk T-shirt (causing Poppy to gasp). Thumper had been alone in her room watching a training tape of the

Kyoto snowboarding trials where she and her sister had taken gold last month. She didn't have to do a head check for her twin sister. She'd heard yodeling like what was happening now before, lots of times. Her twin, Dirk, had a peculiar talent for pleasing society ladies. Unless she was mistaken, Dirk had just scored some grade-A East Coast pussy.

The yodeling was coming from Bunny Van Randolph's room at the end of the hall. Indeed, it was the only room where the door remained shut. Bunny's clipped Cape Cod accent had turned into an orgasmic yodel — *yes, baby, yes baby, oh yes, please, yes!* — that shook the rafters of the farmhouse as Babe quickened her pace toward the closed door.

"What in bloody hell was that?" inquired Poppy, wide eyed, her ebony hair swept up in a Pebbles Flintstone ponytail.

Wee Gee, Poppy's roommate, snorted. "That, girl, was the midnight sound of one very satisfied woman."

Babe stepped over Storm Waters, who was sprawled atop her parka outside Bunny's door, chewing on the butt of a French cigarette. She stuffed the cigarette in her pocket when she saw Babe raging up the hallway. "Not me," Storm murmured. "Soon as I saw you'd put me in a room with the Princess of Cape Cod, I backed out and crashed in a pile here."

Babe squared her shoulders. "Bunny have company in there?"

"Uh-huh."

"Who?"

"Dunno. When I went in about an hour ago, I caught sight of one very muscular ass poised midair, not the princess, either, if you know what I mean."

Babe tried the door, but it was locked, which was impossible because she and Lily had removed all the locks eons ago since no one could ever trust an addict not to get embroiled in ridiculously stupid adventures.

Bunny or Dirk must have dragged something up against the door.

Babe banged on the door with both fists. "Open up, ladies! Open this door now or I'll use Storm's machine gun to blast my way in!"

Before long Dirk McGraw was standing at the door, grinning. She was dressed exactly like her twin sister, in black silk skivvies. Her thick thighs strained against the flimsy material. (Poppy fainted and had to be propped up by Wee Gee.)

"What?" Dirk smirked. "Something wrong? What's wrong?" She rubbed her hand across her spiked blonde hair as she spoke. One hand hiked up her tight boxers.

"Is Bunny Van Randolph in there?"

Dirk glanced back over her shoulder. "I'd have to check, but yes, I think so."

"What are you two doing in there?"

"Talking. About stuff. We're going to be roommates, Bunny and me. Her assigned roommate" — Dirk pointed to Storm on the floor of the hallway — "wants to, er, be reassigned. Seems they have a past conflict of interest."

"No," said Babe, arms crossed. "You can't room with Bunny."

"Why?" Another lopsided grin.

"You're in treatment. You're not allowed to have sex with each other."

"Why?"

"We'll go over that later, in group."

Dirk shrugged. "Bummer. But okay, I guess." She walked across the hall and slid into the room her sister occupied, quietly shutting the door behind her.

Babe turned and stared at the women who lined the hallway, their eyes focused on her. "You guys are not allowed to have sex with each other. No sex. It's part of your treatment.

Some of you are here because of sex addictions." She stared overlong at Dylan Redford, the artist, making her flinch. "No sex. Nada. You girls got that?"

Nan Goldberg, the bond broker, stepped into the hallway, clutching at her monogrammed silk overcoat. "Excuse me. Not even with ourselves?"

"Not even!" cautioned Babe with a wag of her finger.

Wee Gee pulled the still-stunned Poppy back into their room as Babe stormed downstairs, where someone was pounding on the door begging for harbor against the storm.

8.

Eye Candy

Wee Gee Judd was secretly delighted the bed-hopping had begun. She wrote steamy romance novels and was dead out of bodice-ripping ideas. If her luck held, she might be able to ditch Little Debbie and get a slutty new novel out of this whole rehab thing.

Her fertile imagination was already casting Dirk and Bunny in starring roles. She'd have to change Dirk's sex. No biggy, since Dirk was already halfway to Trannytown. Many of Wee Gee's best-selling novels were based on lesbian relationships she'd had to "edit" into straight novels for the Midwestern mainstream.

She was out of the closet with close friends but her professional peers in Romance Writers of America thought of her as hair-raisingly straight. She conveniently had two ex-husbands and seven grown kids to back up her hetero image: more than enough "family" to throw your average Republican housewife off track.

Only her agent, Jackie Perkins, knew otherwise, and that was only because Wee Gee and Jackie had enjoyed too many Wicked Blonde ales together when Wee Gee's last book hit the million-dollar mark. Author and agent had ended up hopelessly entangled in flowered silk sheets at the Atlanta Hilton.

One night only; that had been enough for Wee Gee. Her agent was a little mouthy for her long-term liking; also, her agent had a scary husband, a thick-necked fellow from Nashville who could literally belch the alphabet.

"Was that a girl?" the stunned Poppy asked Wee Gee about Dirk McGraw as they climbed back into their respective beds.

"Why you asking?" asked Wee Gee as she tucked the covers over her ample body and turned out the bedside lamp. Her mind was already busy creating a lurid plot line. "You got nothing like that in England, girl?"

Poppy didn't reply. In her head she was busy thinking maybe a Vermont holiday might not be so glum after all. Sure, that Bunny chick, whoever she was, seemed to have dibs on sexy Dirk. But she'd gone hand to hand with Yankee princesses before and won.

Of course Dirk did have that identical sister, Thumper (which had already translated into "thump her" in Poppy's sordid young mind). Poppy could set her sights on Thumper, thus avoiding a messy fight with that Bunny chick.

But hey, why not have *both* Dirk and Thumper.

Poppy fluffed up her pillow, dead certain what her dreams would be about tonight.

Downstairs, Babe unlocked the door and stood back as a tall, stately woman stumbled head first into the foyer. The woman was wrapped in what Babe recognized as a finely cut plaid English Burberry coat with fur cuffs that must have cost a mint. Her ears were wrapped in matching plaid with fur-lined earmuffs. She slid off the earmuffs and tucked them neatly into a side slit on her Gucci overnight bag before peeling off her form-fitting Italian leather gloves and sliding out of her coat.

"Bellhop?" the new arrival trilled as she shook snow from her carefully clipped red hair and stepped toward the desk. Emerald earrings glistened on the lobes of her alabaster ears. An emerald teardrop pendant framed in diamonds beckoned from her creamy bosom.

Babe slid the registration book toward the redhead's outstretched hand, which held the Montblanc pen as if it were an extension of her fine porcelain fingers.

"Candice Antwerp, M.D.," read the woman's signature in an eloquent script.

"Bellboy?" the doctor asked again, clearly impatient.

"No bellboy."

"All right," she sighed, assuming she'd been caught in yet another feminist faux pas. "Bell*girl?*"

"None of those, either."

Dr. Antwerp tapped her foot, which was clad in custom knee-high, Italian riding boots. "How will my bags get upstairs?"

"You might carry them, Candy."

Dr. Antwerp's fine nostrils flared. She leaned over until her surgically assisted aristocratic nose almost touched Babe's much larger snout. "Don't ever call me Candy," she hissed. "It's Dr. Antwerp. Candice, if you *must* get familiar." She straightened the collar on her form-fitting, jade-green Armani jacket as she spoke. "Never Candy."

"All right, then, *Candice*. I'm Babe and I'll be the official guide to your darker side while you're here. Care to tell me why you're here?"

Candice unwound a scarf from her elegant neck. She folded the scarf carefully before sliding it into the outer zipper compartment on her overnighter. "I'm off my game. My surgical precision," she sniveled, "seems to be suffering. A friend of mine recommended your place to help me refresh myself."

Babe narrowed her eyes. "Your treatment card says your malpractice insurance carrier ordered your stay due to a fondness for prescription downers and anti-anxiety meds. Seems the AMA is about to yank your license to practice as a plastic surgeon, *Candice*."

"That too," she sighed.

Babe recognized Candice — "don't call me Candy" — Antwerp from her monthly thrill reading *People* magazine at the massage therapist's in Stowe. Dr. Candy was the surgical mastermind behind the best-sculpted bods in Hollywood. She'd given Cher the ass (and nerve) necessary to appear on stage in spandex after the age of sixty. She was rumored to be the woman who'd done Madonna's vaginal rejuvenation.

Babe guessed the good doctor to be just past forty: the age professional women often started losing control over what began as a recreational taste for easily obtainable drugs that helped them wind down after a hard day at the office.

Candice studied Babe. "You recognize me?"

"Don't worry, honey. Your secret's safe. Lots of famous dykes vacation here."

Intrigued, Candice tried to sneak a peek inside the registration book, but Babe snapped it shut. "You'll meet your partners in crime come morning. Seven a.m. sharp, in the kitchen."

She handed Dr. Antwerp a key. "Room at the end of the hall. You'll be bunking with Bunny Van Randolph."

Dr. Antwerp caught her breath. "The senator's daughter?"

"Uh-huh."

Candice caught the key in her hand and held it tightly. So it was true, the rumors she'd heard out West about the East Coast senator's daughter. While she hated the idea of sharing a room — good lord, she hadn't had to endure that particular hell since her college days — it was comforting to know she'd be rooming with a woman of her own ilk. Thank God she'd brought along business cards. Bunny, a true A-gay, would be a stellar client. The woman was just the right age for everything to be giving out.

And not someone Dr. Antwerp would mind seeing butt naked on her operating table, either.

Dr. Antwerp grumbled under her breath as she toted her own bags up the stairs. She wasn't even sure she was a lesbian. She loathed that word, but not as much as she loathed the word *homosexual*.

Queer did little for her, either.

She'd spent her life cultivating a respectable professional veneer; the whole lesbian thing did little to advance that.

The A-gay Hollywood lesbians, Ellen and Rosie, would never lie down for a major nip-tuck. Sure, they'd endure chemical peels, and Botox, but they'd never order the big-ticket items. Hell, Dr. Antwerp had bought a private island in the Caribbean on Cher's ass-lift alone. God bless insecure straight girls.

"Lesbians should be more looks conscious," she grumbled to herself as she mounted the stairs.

9.

The Lesbian Thought Police

Babe was brewing a pot of lemongrass green tea at the registration desk when the farmhouse door banged open and a winter blast slapped her full body. She shivered. A large woman, shaped suspiciously like a purple tent, tumbled toward her.

Babe rubbed her eyes. "Betty Frump?" she asked, recognizing the woman from her photo on the editorial pages of *LesFam Magazine*, the monthly non-glossy magazine Betty and her partner, Alice Everwright, had founded three decades ago to further the political rights of gay families.

Frump approached Babe, hand outstretched. The activist wore black-rimmed plastic glasses and a scowl that grade school teachers everywhere would envy. Her frizzy hair was swept back from her face, braided in thick salt-and-pepper ropes that coiled like a crown around her head. She was wearing snow-clad black canvas slippers, the type Chairman Mao used to sneak about in. Her purple caftan whooshed as she walked.

"Sister." Betty pumped the hell out of Babe's hand.

This was the first time Babe had met Betty in person, but she knew all about her from the press. Betty Frump had been fighting for lesbian rights since Stonewall, where, barely a pimply-faced tween, she'd been arrested. Betty was an icon of the feminist women of her generation; and a constant pain in the ass for the fun-loving, gender-fluid queers of today.

"Being gay is not a lifestyle," Frump was fond of saying. "It's a political struggle."

These days not everyone agreed. These days, much to Betty's chagrin, many lesbians just wanted to have fun. They dressed like sluts and humped like hormone-crazed weasels. They joined the PTA and did hot yoga in sparkly barrettes like life was some sort of sorority picnic. Betty blamed the whole thing on Madonna.

That and the drug Ecstasy.

Betty Frump and her un-merry gang of political pranksters, glumly known as the Lesbian Thought Police, had recently come under scrutiny for issuing what was now known as Frump's Ten Commandments. The first commandment was no woman ought to penetrate another woman during sex.

Never.

Not ever.

No matter what.

Penetration was seen as violence. Phallocentric. What men did to women.

Frump had organized a dildo reclamation program at the last national Gay Day march on Washington. Every lesbian who turned in a dildo was eligible to receive a free subscription to *LesFam* and a discount coupon for a family fun pack of tofurkey.

The event raised a lot of eyebrows but only three dildos, two of which had clearly been chewed on by pets and were way past their prime, anyway.

Babe herself was not in favor of the no-penetration com-mandment — Lily demanded (and enjoyed) a good bit of invasive action — still, some of Betty's old-fashioned commandments sat right with Babe.

Betty had the registration book in hand and was signing in before Babe could give her the ten-cent tour. Betty grunted. "Sorry about being late. This place was hell to find. To conserve greenhouse gases I took an electric Uber from the airport. Driver was a Jamaican brother. Got lost quite a few times."

"We own fifty acres up here. Nice and quiet, deliberately not easy to find."

Betty dumped the contents of her canvas co-op tote onto the registration desk. "My luggage should come later. This is all I have." She stretched out her arms and twirled in a circle. "Frisk me?"

"Take you at your word. What's your addiction?"

"Dope. Smoke it to relax."

"Any on you?"

"Certainly not. I'm here to get clean. Need the Mary Jane monkey off my back." Frump glanced back at her rounded shoulders as if something really were sitting there.

"I the only crone here?" she asked as she repacked her canvas tote.

"Nope. Wee Gee Judd is about your age. From Kentucky. Writes those best-selling romance novels under the pen name Foxy Hot Pants."

Frump frowned. "Hetero trash?"

"I think they're all hetero. Not much of a market for lesbian romance, it seems."

"Romance is a weapon of the patriarchy."

Babe twisted her lips. "You don't think lesbians enjoy romance?"

"They might, but they ought not. You read my commandments?"

Wishing to avoid being Bible-thumped, Babe changed the subject and handed Betty a list of house rules along with the key to room number two, where Storm Waters, the war correspondent, was already ensconced. "You can smoke tobacco, but not in the house beginning in the morning. Once treatment begins you have to smoke outside."

"Don't smoke poisoned commercial stuff. Causes lung cancer." Frump grabbed her tote and headed for the stairs. "I have a room to myself?" she shouted over her shoulder when she'd gone halfway up.

"Everyone shares. Part of treatment."

"Who am I bunking with?"

"Storm Waters."

"The war correspondent?"

"The same."

Betty bumped up the stairs, thinking, *So the rumors are true.* Storm Waters was a sister and big-media connected, to boot. Betty's mind banged and buzzed with a plan to recruit the famous war correspondent for the sisterhood.

10.

Breakfast Not at Tiffany's

Poppy awoke disappointed to find neither Dirk nor Thumper McGraw in her bed, as she'd been dreaming, but that old goat, Babe. Babe was barking orders, something to the effect that it was time for Poppy to get her ass up and make breakfast.

"Breakfast!" Poppy squealed. "Sod off, you old bag!"

Babe pulled the covers off Poppy for the third time and grabbed her by a pretzel-thin ankle. She dragged her to the edge of the twin bed. "You'll be cooking our meals. You and Wee Gee. Up and at 'em!"

"Huh?"

Wee Gee loomed behind Babe. "You and me, baby girl, we got food issues. That's why we're on kitchen duty. It'll help us face our food issues. Me, I eat too much. You, well, I'm guessing from your looks you eat your fist every chance you get."

"Sod off!" Poppy repeated. She liked Wee Gee. The woman had spunk. And she was a straight shooter, but Poppy tended to loathe women her mum's age on principle.

"You better get your skinny English ass outa that bed, sister," warned Wee Gee again.

Poppy burrowed deeper into the down comforter. She hadn't become Britain's leading pop music diva by buckling under to old badgers. She had no intention of giving in now. Her normal time to get out of bed was … noonish. Furthermore, if and when she did get out of bed she certainly was *not* cooking breakfast.

Poppy thought she'd won the covers tug-of-war until she felt a bucket of ice slide up under her pajamas. A cold cube shot across her bum.

"Yooo!" she screamed as she leaped out of bed.

Babe stood there grinning. Her blonde hair, which had been braided the night before, was hanging loose in a large floppy ponytail now. She was wearing a plum spandex workout suite and a triumphant smirk.

"What the bloody hell!" barked Poppy.

"Get dressed, dear," said Babe.

Wee Gee took Poppy by an elbow. "You better do what that crazy old cracker says. If you don't, you'll end up on moose duty."

"Huh?"

"Moose duty. If you don't want to cook, you have to do another chore."

"Moose duty," echoed Babe. "We keep Lil's pet moose, Winkle, in the barn at night all this time of year because of the snow. The shit gets deep in there. Someone has to shovel it out."

"Me?" Poppy was sitting up in bed now, her wet PJ shirt ripped off. She pointed at her emaciated chest with her index finger. Her nipples were red and puckered from the ice. "Me, the bloody Queen of British Pop? Work for you?"

Poppy was so thin Babe could almost see through her. "What's your objection, dear? You telling me you never shoveled shit before?"

Wee Gee roared with laughter. "Oh, she's shoveled it before. She's shoveling it now!"

Poppy stormed into the bathroom. She turned to lock the door but the door had no lock.

Wee Gee shrugged in Babe's direction. "Don't worry. I'll get her downstairs. We'll make everyone a mighty fine meal. Just don't go expecting breakfast at Tiffany's."

In the room next door, Dirk McGraw rubbed her eyes and sat up in bed. Someone was pounding on the door to her room. Thumper was asleep, a motionless lump in the twin bed next to her.

"Coming," Dirk muttered as she stumbled to the door. It was that old chick from the night before. Lily, she seemed to recall. She was dressed in a lime-green bell-bottom jumpsuit, still dripping in diamonds.

"What?" asked Dirk as she raked a hand through her gel-stiffened hair. "What is it?" Dirk wrapped her arms around herself and rocked in the doorway, her brown eyes bloodshot. She was still trying to remember where she was. Not the Olympic training bunker. Too freezing-ass cold for that.

"Breakfast in half an hour."

"Uh, okay, I guess."

"Wake your sister up?" Lily peered into the room at the massive flannel lump.

"Yeah, sure. Probably."

"Fine," said Lily. "See you downstairs in the kitchen."

Thumper poked her head from under the covers. "What's up?"

"That old chick. Says we have to get up. Breakfast in half an hour."

Thumper blinked. "Who was that blonde chick you nailed last night?"

Dirk grinned. "Bunny Van Randolph."

"The senator's daughter? Cool!"

"She was okay. No biggy."

"Dirk?"

"Yeah," her sister said as she unzipped her duffel and searched for her toothbrush.

"Do we have to stay here?"

"Yeah, we have to get clean. If we flunk another drug test, we're history." Dirk plugged in her Sonicare and began to vibrate it against her perfectly white front teeth.

Her sister rolled out of bed straight into a baggy pair of jeans. She pulled on a black ski sweater, which form-fit to her muscular chest. "We stopped the 'roids last month."

"I know," Dirk mumbled as she spat brightening toothpaste into the sink. "But the Olympic board doesn't know. Until they're sure, we have to keep peeing in a cup. It's the way things are done. Play along with these old chicks. We'll be fine."

"Okay," muttered Thumper as she slipped on some woolen socks and shoved her feet into a pair of hiking boots. What she hadn't yet told her sister was she hadn't stopped using steroids. Not yet. She was scared that if she did she'd lose her edge. She hoped nobody at this weird lesbo farmhouse was going to make her piss in a cup anytime soon.

11.

Candy Irons Her Underwear

Bunny Van Randolph was certain she was having a lucid dream or an outright hallucination. A beautiful redheaded woman with skin as smooth as butter cream was knocking about in her room. The tall, stately woman was dressed in expensive Italian lingerie: a green silk bustier with matching lace panties that barely covered her impeccably waxed woo-woo.

The odd thing, thought Bunny, wasn't the lingerie. The odd thing was that the woman was standing at an ironing board, demonically pressing pair after pair of silk panties as if her life depended on the arduous task. She had an inch-high pile of underwear stacked on a ladder chair next to the ironing board.

Bunny gulped as she clutched the down covers tight to her breasts. Surely she hadn't picked up this woman in the lobby last night. Femme on femme was not her style. Bunny always wore the lingerie.

Always.

"Excuse me," she said, clearing her throat. "Have we met, honey?"

Dr. Candice Antwerp set the iron on end. "I'm your roommate. Arrived late. You were asleep." Candice offered Bunny her carefully manicured hand.

Bunny wrapped the flannel top sheet around her naked body and swung her waxed legs out of bed, relieved she hadn't crossed the dark line into doing femmes.

"Bunny Van Randolph," she said.

"Dr. Candice Antwerp."

"Doctor?"

"Plastic surgeon."

Bunny's face lit up, at least as much as it could, given her fondness for Botox. "Oh yummy!" she declared.

Downstairs Babe and Lily were setting the table for breakfast, making sure Poppy and Wee Gee knew where everything was located in the kitchen. As a two-time rehab veteran and mother of seven grown kids, all born while she was struggling to make subminimum wage as a writer of torrid romance, Wee Gee knew her way around a stove.

Poppy was still grumbling about having to work. Wee Gee handed her young sous-chef an electric mixer and instructed her to shut her gums and beat the hell out of the blueberry pancake batter instead.

Yellow batter splattered Poppy's cheeks and her inky-black Pebbles ponytail. Following Wee Gee's urging, she licked batter off her fingers, not stopping to worry about the calorie-laden treat.

Cooking with Wee Gee was almost fun, Poppy decided. She just hoped no paparazzi got a shot of her, Poppy Zigfield, pop diva extraordinaire, doing domestic duty.

Poppy stopped licking batter when the snowboarding twins loped into the dining room, their blonde hair mussed from sleep. She tried unsuccessfully to catch either of the twins' attention; which one, she didn't care.

It pissed Poppy off when Bunny arrived in the room wearing too little skirt and too much makeup. She watched the senator's daughter make an ass of herself around the McGraw stud-muffin snowboarders. Her only consolation was that the twins seemed bored with Bunny's yak-yak. It didn't take them long to shoulder their snowboards and dart out the back door for an early-morning run in the snow.

Several other women sauntered into the dining room. Poppy didn't recognize any of them. All older. Blimey, she had no idea old dykes had so many problems. She thought only cool young people did drugs. She was relieved when one woman under the age of thirty erupted into the dining room. She heard one of the other women address her as "Dylan."

Dylan looked promising. Tomboy. Tall and deliciously rangy. Her raven hair was unevenly sliced, streaked auburn in a patch or two. A thatch of black hair hung like a flag of bad-girl honor over Dylan's right eye. She was delightfully loud. Her black, paint-splattered jeans were ripped at both knees. She wore a red T-shirt that proclaimed: "Ask Me About My Big Pink Pussy."

Dylan had been in the room less than ten seconds when a verbal joust broke out between her and some elderly dyke who floated around the table wearing what looked to be an oversized purple tent.

"Who's that?" Poppy whispered to Wee Gee as Wee Gee poured the pancake batter onto a sizzling iron griddle.

"Child, you don't know anything, do you? That old goat is Betty Frump. Sergeant General of the Lesbian Thought Police. Helped Clinton win the gay vote. One hard-assed, nail-spitting lesbian. Got hair on her chest, and proud of it. Better not mess with the likes of her."

"Who's the woman she's yelling at?"

Wee Gee chuckled. "That's Dylan Redford herself. Girl, she's the artist who made that piece of monumental art what has the White House so upset. The *Big Pink Pussy*. You've heard of that, no?"

Actually Poppy had heard of that. She hadn't seen it, but poster-sized photos of the artwork had been all the rage in London's Soho the last few weeks.

"She's, like, steaming hot," whispered Poppy, feeling like she was confessing lurid desires to her grandmother.

"I'll say," agreed Wee Gee. "Now put your tongue back in your mouth and mix us more batter."

Across the room Betty Frump was not backing down.

Neither, unfortunately, was Dylan Redford.

The two had gone face to face before. On public TV last month. They had debated whether Dylan's *Big Pink Pussy* glorified women or defiled them. Dylan had insisted her art was meant to force people into honoring the existence of female genitalia.

Frump had argued that women like Dylan, shock dykes, were doing more harm than good by making America think all feminist lesbians were little more than loudmouthed pornographers.

"I am not a pornographer!" shouted Dylan.

Betty came at Dylan, puffed up. At almost six feet and three hundred pounds, Betty rolled like a lavender stone across the room. Her thick glasses were fogged with anger. Her Amazonian hatchet earrings threatened to fly off her head and impale Dylan in the heart. Her long, frizzy salt-and-pepper hair couldn't help but put everyone in mind of a witch.

Lily was the only one brave enough to step between the two women. "Time out!" she boomed. "Back to your corners, both of you."

Lily grabbed a cowbell from the table and rang it loudly in both their ears. "Breakfast!" she yelled as she motioned to Wee Gee to bring steaming stacks of blueberry pancakes to the table before all-out war erupted.

12.

Grumpy Group

Storm Waters sprawled atop a stack of fluorescent hippie pillows on the floor of the group therapy room. Sullen, she studied the steel-toe tips of her khaki commando boots. She was happily stuffed with pancakes and maple syrup, but pissed that she had to attend a group. The schedule sheet she'd been given at breakfast stated that every day would begin and end with a group.

Yucko.

Storm hated groups. Of all kinds. She hated teams, too, unless she was the captain. She loved being a war correspondent because all the candy-assed freaks who enjoyed playing boss were way too scared to go into battle.

Alone on the battlefield. God, how she loved that.

"Do you have trust issues?" asked Babe, who was sitting cross-legged in the middle of the group, looking painfully empathic.

Storm shrugged as she brushed the ebony bangs back from her brilliant blue eyes. "No problem. I've been clear on that issue since grade school. People ought not be trusted. To think otherwise is insane."

"I don't think that," countered Betty as she smoothed her frizzed hair. "In fact, I think only collective action will free us."

Dylan leaned over to Wee Gee and whispered, "I think someone ought to tell her she needs to iron that hair."

Babe spoke up: "Dylan, would you like to say something to Betty? To the group?"

Dylan stretched across two pillows, her knees poking playfully through her ripped black jeans. "Yes, I would." She turned to face her nemesis. "1972 called and wants that hair back."

The group broke into howling laughter. It took Babe several minutes to calm them. She eyed Dylan sternly. "You have to speak to each other with respect. It's a rule. Always treat each other with respect."

Dylan shrugged. "I'll try."

"Now try talking to Betty again. Try an apology."

Dylan smirked.

"Dylan …?"

"Okay! Okay!"

Dylan turned to face Betty, who was drawn up into one very ugly hulk. "I'm sorry."

Betty deflated. "Apology accepted, sister."

Babe nodded. "That wasn't so hard, was it?"

Actually, thought Dylan, it had been damned hard. Like swallowing a lump of horseshit, but she needed this place to sign off on her treatment papers, either that or face prison for the felony assault charges on that art review bitch.

"We're all sisters," said Betty. "And to show my point, I wish to apologize to Dylan. I have said some very unpleasant things about her *Big Pink Pussy* and I want her to know that while I may disagree with her politically, I still think of her as my sister."

"Thanks," mumbled Dylan. "Ditto." *Like swallowing horse shit again.*

Storm leaned back and listened as the group went on to discuss trust. Maybe she ought to trust people, but the trust thing had never quite worked for her. Her father had abandoned her at birth. At the age of five, her mother had said she was taking her to McDonald's for a Happy Meal then dumped her, still hungry, at the social services department in Oakland, California. When, at the age of thirteen, she'd come out as a lezzie to her Republican foster family in the Valley, they'd returned her to social services, complaining she was a freak.

You could trust people, sure, but brother oh brother, get ready for some serious heartbreak.

Noticing how quiet Storm had become, Poppy scooted close to her. "Seen you on the telly." She popped her gum. "Caught my eye."

"Excuse me?"

"The telly. Television, as you Yanks say. Never knew you were a lesbo."

"Well, I am."

"Single?"

"Very, it seems."

"You up for some fun?"

Storm's eyebrows shot up. "Like?"

"Later. After group. Kitchen pantry."

Babe cleared her throat. "Poppy, did you have something to share with the group about trust?"

"Yeah. I trusted my old mum and she sent me here."

"You don't know why?"

"I got wasted and torched my fuck-buddy's house."

"You don't see that as a problem."

"She cheated on me."

"So?"

"With a bloke."

"So?"

"I trusted her."

Silence.

"Anyone care to say anything to Poppy about that?" Babe turned to the snowboarding twins, who'd been quiet the entire group.

Dirk cleared her throat. "Uh, yeah. Sure. Never trust a chick. Especially a naked one."

Babe sighed. "Does anyone in this group other than Betty trust anyone?"

Not a soul raised her hand.

13.

Packed Pants

After group came an hour of "private time." The women scattered to their respective rooms. Dr. Candice Antwerp, who'd remained mute throughout group, approached the twins. She'd been admiring their physiques all morning. Even Brad Pitt didn't have an ass like those twins did, and that was after he'd invested a hundred thousand in what could only be termed *strategically placed butt pads.*

Candice sidled up to Dirk, who was setting a sock cap on her head, getting ready to go outside and catch some air in a snowboarding practice session with her sister. The twins had stepped into a pair of matching red snow pants with black racing stripes down each leg.

"Can I touch it?" asked Candice as she glanced admirably at Dirk's ass.

Dirk twisted her head around. "I guess. Sure. If you want." Dirk had never had a girl ask before. She felt flattered. True, she and her sister had taken designer steroids for the last two years, but a lot of what they had packed into their pants was the real thing. They exercised five hours a day. A lot of Dirk's ass was hard won. Snowboarders needed strong butt muscles. It took a robust butt to finesse that half-pipe.

"Silicone?" asked Dr. Antwerp as she fingered first Dirk's posterior, then her sister's.

"Huh?"

"Implants? Have you girls had any implants?"

Dirk reddened. "Not there, no ma'am."

Candice straightened. "Where?"

"Dirk," her sister cautioned. "We can't talk about that. Our agent said we can't talk about that, not after that thing in Aspen with that Australian chick."

Dirk shook her head. "Uh, she's right, ma'am. We gotta practice now. Catch ya later."

Candice was left at the farmhouse door, intrigued about where the twins might have had fleshy endowments added. If she were their surgeon, she could think of a few places …

Bunny Van Randolph appeared at Candice's elbow. "I know."

"Pardon?"

"Where Dirk has, er, added a little something special for us ladies." Bunny rolled her eyes. "She nailed me last night."

"Where?"

"In my bed. On the floor. In the shower."

"No," said Candice, obviously irritated. "I mean, where has Dirk added endowments?"

"No way," mewed Bunny. "A lady never speaks of her sexual adventures. You'll just have to discover what's so special about Dirk all on your own."

After the twins had disappeared over the hillside with their snowboards, Nan Goldberg decided to take a walk. Alone. The snow outside looked deep. Luckily the old gals had a pile of wooden snowshoes oiled and ready to go sitting at the back door of the farmhouse. Knowing she ought to ask someone to be her buddy — the rules they had been given that morning demanded they buddy up if they went outside — Nan decided she'd rather go solo.

All the women of Sugarbush seemed fine to her. No more crazy than your average roomful of overachieving career-drunk lesbos. But she really wanted to be alone. Not so much for her soul as for her lungs. She was dying for a cigarette.

Babe appeared at Nan's elbow by the back door. She touched her arm in an empathic manner. "Need alone time?"

"Uh-huh."

"I understand, dear. Don't go too far, though, okay? Things live in those woods. And take a buddy with you, just to be safe."

Nan seriously doubted that anything scarier than the SEC review board or Betty Frump on a bad hair day lurked in those shadowy woods. And she definitely was not in any mood to buddy-up. She strapped on the snowshoes and thumped across the wooden kitchen floor feeling like Bozo the Clown on crack. She arrived at the back door and jumped out into the sugary snow, which was almost a foot deep.

Her lungs sucked in the freezing air. A relief. Not sure where to go, she spotted a ramshackle gray barn across the field and decided to hike for it. Once inside the barn, she reasoned, she could sit and enjoy a smoke.

Also, if her cell worked she'd give Birge a call. They weren't supposed to have outside contact for a week. But Nan missed her partner; more so, in fact, than she missed cigarettes. Birge was her anchor. And at the moment Nan was feeling very much adrift.

Keeping her eye on the barn in the distance, Nan propelled herself forward on the giant webbed shoes. Her ski poles dug into the sugary snow helping her to keep balanced while falling forward toward her destination.

Out of breath, she traipsed into the barn and plopped down on a high pile of hay. It was warmer in the barn than outside. She kept her snowshoes on, uncertain how to release them. She sat with her legs far apart, admiring her huge snow-clad feet.

Walking in snowshoes had turned out to be fun. Maybe she'd do it every day just for the hell of it. She'd worked so hard her entire life she'd forgotten about fun. Bond brokers weren't fun; lesbian bond brokers in particular were a snorefest.

Nan pulled off her fuzzy angora mittens with her teeth and dug her cell phone out of the back pocket of her L. L. Bean snow pants. She hit the speed dial for Birge and was happy as a clam when the woman answered.

Birge yawned. "Hi, honey. Funny you should call. I was dreaming we were retired, living in Florida, one of those retirement villages like the ones my parents are holed up in."

"That wasn't a dream," said Nan as she stuck a cigarette in her mouth and inhaled deeply. "That was a nightmare."

Birge laughed. "The odd part was that Lauren Bacall was there and she was lounging on a chaise poolside, coming on to me."

"Should I be worried?"

"Only if Lauren Bacall comes to town."

Nan laughed. She wanted to hear more from Birge. Reassurances. Words of love. But something had just popped up in the hay. Something large and brown with hunks of hair hanging off its humpy backside. The thing snorted. It smiled, showing big cheesy teeth that boasted of an apparent lack of a dental plan.

"Nice moose," purred Nan. "Good boy."

The moose, however, seemed miffed that Nan had fallen into his bed. Winkle was up on all legs charging Nan in a matter of seconds.

"Crap!" said Nan as she pocketed her cell, and shuffled on snowshoes like a drunken goose toward the farmhouse.

14.

Out of the Closet — Into the Pantry

Storm eyed the paint-splattered pine door that led to a recessed nook under the kitchen stairs. She wasn't sure this door led to the pantry, but it was the only door she could find other than the back door that led into the yard.

And the door under the stairs looked like it had been left open a crack. Suggestive, to say the least.

Poppy — what the hell kind of name was that for a lesbian? — had asked Storm to meet her in the kitchen pantry. Storm had assumed Poppy wanted a friendly fuck; at least she hoped so. Several days without prescription opioids had left the war correspondent wired, eager to burn energy in any legal way. Poppy was young, but certainly over twenty-one. At the moment that was sufficient fuck-buddy criteria for Storm.

Sex always made Storm edgy. It made her juices flow the same weird way that popping across a battlefield got her energized. Storm felt having sex with a woman was more dangerous than crawling across a battlefield. War had rules of engagement. A semblance of order. Nothing could, in Storm's estimation, be less predictable, and therefore more dangerous, than two women intertwined in utter nakedness.

Her heart pounding with anticipation, Storm creaked open the pantry door. She could see the shadowy suggestion of vegetable bins along the far wall: apples, potatoes, and an assortment of odd root vegetables jutted from the bins. Aprons hung on brass hooks along the bead-board interior.

Oh wait. She was deep into the dark pantry now. She couldn't see anything, but she did feel something.

Lips, soft as heated velvet, slid along the back of her neck.

Shivers danced up Storm's spine.

"Blimey, I thought you'd never get here."

Storm took the lead, slipping her tongue into Poppy's soft, warm mouth. Feeling bold, she slid her hand up under the pop star's lacy white teddy. Her clit throbbed as she felt Poppy's nipples harden under her thumbs. Storm preferred women with small breasts. Poppy's breasts were teacup sized, very responsive. Perfect. Unable to control herself, Storm began flicking her tongue across the pebble-hard nipples before teasing one taut bud between her teeth.

Eager for more, Poppy unbuckled Storm's fatigues. She slid her hand sideways through the sharp metal teeth of the zipper and cupped the war correspondent's mound. "Got something for me, baby?" Poppy purred in her delicious English accent.

"Not yet, you little tart," rasped Storm in her deepest voice as she pulled Poppy's hand out of her pants and rezipped. "Work for it."

Poppy fell to her knees.

Things were reaching a frenzy when a slice of light fell across the two women. Storm had her shirt off, but was still wearing her unbuckled fatigues and her combat boots. Poppy was on her back, up against a crate of McIntosh apples, naked from the waist up, her nipples as purple as mauve roses.

Storm turned and squinted into the light.

Something hulked there. Large. Wavering. With hair like tumbleweed.

Betty Frump, who'd entered the pantry looking for a safe place to light up her portable mini bong, dropped her flashlight on Storm's head and screamed.

Storm scrambled to pull up her fatigues. She grabbed the vegetable bin to get her balance but the thing came loose from the wall, raining potatoes on the mostly naked and writhing Poppy.

Hearing the clatter, Babe ran downstairs and flung open the pantry door. Storm waved Babe away with one hand as she scrambled to pull on her scoop-necked T-shirt.

Poppy pulled a pair of large sweet potatoes over her breasts.

Babe turned to face the horror-stricken Frump, who'd had enough presence of mind to squirrel away her mini bong in a fanny pack hidden under the outer layer of her caftan when she heard Babe trounce down the stairs.

"And what were you doing?" Babe asked Frump. "*Watching?*"

* * *

Afternoon group began with silence.

Wee Gee studied the glum faces. "I took a nap," she whispered to Poppy. "I miss something?"

Babe began the group. "Can anyone tell me why we're not supposed to have sex with each other?"

Storm's cheeks reddened. She hated being called on the carpet. But at least Babe wasn't pointing a finger directly at her. Besides, Bunny and Dirk had broken that rule first.

Wee Gee spoke up. "Who had sex? Someone have sex while old Wee Gee was sleeping?" Her gaze spun around the circle looking for a guilty face. Or two.

Dirk shrugged. "Not me."

"Me neither," said Thumper. "Me and Dirk were outside, practicing our wheelies."

Nan shook her head. "Don't look at me. That moose tried, but I gave her a slip. Besides, I'm happily married. Monogamous. Old. Satisfied."

"Not me, girls," said Bunny, who'd brought her manicure kit to group and was busy buffing her cuticles. "I mean, Dirk and I had a tumble last night, but that was before I knew there was a rule. I've been very good since." She smiled at Dirk, who averted her gaze.

No one gave Betty an accusatory look.

"Oh for chrissake!" cried Storm. "It was me! Okay?"

Poppy rolled her eyes as she twirled at a clutch of rainbow beads that hung on her chest like a breastplate. "Me too, I guess."

Babe nodded. "It's good you two are confessing."

Storm was on her feet. "It's not a confession. You asked, I'm telling. It was me. In the pantry. With Poppy. I barely got to second base. No one got screwed."

Betty held up a hand.

"What? What is it?" Storm grumped as she plopped down on some pillows and grabbed a foam bat she desperately wanted to use to club Frump.

"Women don't screw each other."

Poppy: "Oh, love, I think you've got that wrong. I mean, let's just say I've been around the mulberry bush a time or two and I was in that pantry and I'm pretty sure Storm was about to screw me. Right, Storm?"

Storm rubbed her forehead with the heel of her hand, flipping back her dark bangs. "Like I said, no one got screwed. The Lesbian Thought Police interrupted."

Everyone stared at Frump.

Frump looked alarmed. "What? I wasn't watching. Really, I wasn't. I heard a noise and I was worried someone might need help."

"Who'd you think might be in that pantry?" sneered Storm. "The Taliban?"

Poppy snickered.

"Okay! Enough ladies," said Babe. "I need an answer to my question. Why the no-sex rule?"

Poppy chewed on a fingernail.

Wee Gee held up her hand. "Because some of us have sex addictions. We shouldn't have sex while we're here because we're very vulnerable."

"And?" asked Babe.

Wee Gee heaved a sigh. "Sex distracts from the work at hand. We need to stay present. Sex creates a false intimacy. It makes us feel we know each other when in fact we do not. Sex is a drug."

Babe nodded. "Precisely. Now, does everyone think they can keep their panties on?"

Everyone murmured yes.

Everyone except Dr. Candice Antwerp, who was busy studying Dirk, still wondering about those hidden enhancements.

15.

Pumping Iron

By the end of the first day, Babe was exhausted. She lay next to Lily in their massive cherry sleigh bed and moaned.

"That bad?"

"My God, the worst yet!"

Lily rolled over and kissed Babe on the forehead before drawing her close, nuzzling her face deep into her cleavage.

"Much better," crooned Babe as she nuzzled into the warmth of her partner's large, soft breasts.

"Relax. Have a little fun. The children are asleep. Sound asleep." Lily slid off her diamond rings and ran her hand gently across her partner's lean hips, raking her flannel pants down a suggestive distance.

Understanding the meaning of this gesture, Babe rolled over and slipped off her pants, completely. When she jumped back into bed, she wasn't wearing underwear, only one very large grin.

Downstairs, Dirk and her sister, unable to sleep, invaded the basement exercise room. Not Olympic quality, but all the basic gear. Rowing machine. StairMaster. Full set of weights. Two recumbent bikes.

Dirk climbed onto the larger bike. "Race you," she jeered at her sister.

"You're on!"

Both Dirk and her sister were in tip-top shape. They pounded the pedals trying to better each other for more than half an hour. The bike gave out before Dirk, the chain jumping the wheel. Dirk cursed as she stopped pedaling and leaned back to gulp air. Sweat soaked both the girls' tight T-shirts.

Dirk stripped off her T-shirt and tossed it to the floor.

"I win!" proclaimed Thumper, who slumped off the bike and grabbed a red microfiber towel. She mopped her face, then her shoulders.

"No way!" cried Dirk, who'd loped to the corner. She pulled a bottle of vitamin water from the mini fridge. "That old bike gave up, not me," she protested as she gulped down the bottle.

"Sore loser."

Dirk grabbed her sister's towel and flipped her.

Horseplay broke out. Dirk had Thumper pinned to the floor when Candice strolled into the room.

The twins rolled off each other.

"Hi," said Dirk, who seemed not at all bashful about the fact that she was bare-chested. Sweat glistened on her sinewy pectoral muscles. Her nipples were the palest pink.

"Hi, yourself," said Candice. "Don't let me interrupt your fun, girls. I have a routine. Can't sleep unless I've done at least an hour on the StairMaster."

"They got one," said Dirk with a nod of her head.

"So I see," said Candice as she sashayed past the twins in her designer silk yoga pants and matching waist jacket. She mounted the StairMaster, fully aware the twins were watching.

Their stares didn't bother her. In fact, she enjoyed them. Though Dr. Candice Antwerp was past forty, and a worldly woman, she'd not had all that much girl sex. She hated to lose control. And make a mess. She was, however, amazingly practiced at the art of teasing. "Watch if you want," she threw over her shoulder at the muscle-bound twins.

"Okay," said Dirk, who sat on a weight bench facing Candice's StairMaster and began to pump iron as the doctor quickened her pace on the machine.

Thumper shrugged. "All yours," she whispered to her sister as she left the cellar to go upstairs and study practice tapes. She hadn't shot up all day. She had a feeling she'd make it this time. Fuck the Olympic review committee. Her sister was counting on her and there was no one in the world she'd rather not disappoint.

Upstairs, in bedroom number two, Storm marched over to Betty Frump's twin bed and peeled back the covers. She coughed as clouds of smoke rolled from under the covers and spread like a fog over the dimly lit room.

Betty peered up from her bong, her chapped lips pressed tightly together. She'd been trying, unsuccessfully, to swallow the dope smoke.

Storm picked up her fatigues from the floor and waved them around the room. "You can't smoke that stuff in here. Against the rules. Besides, isn't that stuff why you're here?"

Betty coughed, then shrugged. "My partner's idea, not mine. Want some? California Dream Potion. Very mellow." Betty held out the mini bong.

Storm eyed the device. She hadn't been stoned in eons. Since college. It was the legal pharmaceutical stuff, Percocet in particular, that had her hooked. She had to be clean for the station's drug test but that wasn't for another four weeks. Marijuana, she seemed to recall, cleared the system in seven days.

Sighing, she grabbed the bong and sucked a big hit.

"Sorry about today," coughed Betty. "But don't you think that Pop Tart is a little young for you?"

"Who's looking to marry?" The bong had gone out so Storm relit it before handing it back to Betty.

"Free and single. Lucky gal. I've been with the same girl almost thirty years."

"I thought you preached that monogamy stuff."

Betty giggled. "I do, but that's the public me. Deep down I'm one wild chick."

Storm studied Betty's face. Without glasses she didn't look nearly so unapproachable. God knew what kind of body she kept hidden under those triple-X-sized caftans. "So, that penetration thing. You really don't believe that nonsense, do you?"

Betty giggled. "That's for me to know" — she palmed the bong to Storm — "and for you to find out."

16.

Shoveling Shit

Group the next morning began with dead silence.

Good, thought Babe, as she rolled a squeaky-wheeled white board into the center of the room. She'd been doing therapy long enough to know silence meant the girls were beginning to realize they were on the edge of some very deep shit.

Slowly, in large block letters, Babe wrote on the board: "ADMIT TO MYSELF AND OTHERS THAT I AM POWERLESS OVER MY ADDICTION. THAT MY LIFE HAS BECOME UNMANAGEABLE."

Babe underlined the last word, "unmanageable," twice.

Babe faced the group. "What does this mean?"

Dirk shrugged. Her sister, too.

Bunny, who was creaming the backs of her hands with a two-hundred-dollar tube of Parisian skin revitalizer, followed suit.

Candice sat motionless, arms locked against her pink Armani jacket.

Nan knew precisely what the words meant, but refused to volunteer an answer. If Dr. Phil of Dykeville wanted her vulnerable, let the old bitch work for it.

Dylan Redford was busy thinking about what she was going to do to Ginger Fitzgerald, the art critic, for getting her sentenced to this icy hellhole. Like she needed to waste a month of her life listening to a bunch of drug-addicted lesbo losers.

Wee Gee's hand shot into the air.

Babe ignored Wee Gee for a minute, hoping one of the newcomers might take a crack. When no one volunteered, she pointed a finger at Wee Gee, who burst out, "That's the first step to recovery. First, we have to admit we have a problem, and that it's screwing us up. If we can't admit this, we can't get better."

Babe turned to Storm. "What does this first step mean to you, Storm?"

The war correspondent chewed her bottom lip. "It means … I have a problem. I take drugs to sleep. I take drugs to wake up." She stopped, a pained look on her face.

No one said a word.

Babe continued. "How has that affected your life?"

"I could lose my job. My boss, my agent, sent me here to get clean."

"You like your job?"

Storm's face brightened. "Love it."

"Pays well?"

"Couple of million a year, plus bonuses."

Poppy gasped. "For talking on the telly?"

Storm reared back. "Yeah, for talking on the telly … with bullets whizzing past my precious little ass. See this?" Storm rolled up the right leg of her fatigues tight to her knee. A white scar ran the perimeter of her knee before taking off like jagged lightening up her thigh.

"Bugger!" Poppy fingered the wound.

"That," said Storm, "came from a mortar shell that ripped through the side of my Hummer. Damned lucky. Guy next to me got cut in half. I ended up with his brains leaking into my lap."

Babe spoke. "So, Storm, do you think you can control yourself, stop taking drugs when you want?"

"Sometimes," Storm said, busy rolling down her fatigues.

"You're sure about that?"

Storm lifted her eyes and met Babe's gaze. "Okay. Maybe I lied. Truth is, if I could have stopped by myself I would have. Not to insult any of you, but I fucking hate groups."

Several people giggled.

Babe thanked Storm for her honesty then addressed each woman in turn with the same question she put to Storm. Things went smoothly until she hit Dr. Candice.

Candice was sitting so upright on her therapy pillow Babe thought her spine might crack. She'd never met anyone with such rigid posture. She made a mental note to try some deep breathing work with the good doctor. "Candice," she said, "what does this first step mean to you?"

"I've never been out of control in my life. Never. Not once." Candice locked her arms tighter against her bosom. "I didn't physically assault anyone, like you." She narrowed her eyes in accusation at Dylan and Poppy. "And I'm not killing myself with gluttony." She shot a nasty cold gaze at Wee Gee.

Babe twisted her lips. "Candice, are you breathing?"

"Pardon?"

"Breathing. Are you?"

The doctor exhaled. "Of course."

Babe turned to the group. "Anyone have anything to say to Candice?"

Poppy gave it a try. "It's okay, love. We're all in the same sinking boat."

The tiny lines at the edge of Dr. Antwerp's eyes jumped. "You still live with your mother, correct?"

It was Poppy's turn to stiffen now. "Sometimes. But I have my own place in Chelsea. A townhouse used to belong to Winston Churchill. Say, what are you saying? That I'm too young to know anything? That it?"

"If the slipper fits, Spice Girl."

Poppy was on her feet now.

Storm intervened, dragging Poppy back to her pillow. "She's scared," she advised Poppy. "Give her some room."

Poppy sat back, allowing Storm to quiet her.

Babe spoke. "I want everyone to think about this first step. Especially you, Candice. We'll come back to it tonight. In the meantime, I've listed your job assignments for the week. The list is on the refrigerator. You start your chores this afternoon. You will be rated on how well you perform your work. I expect you to do your best. You'll get points for everything you do. Earn enough points and you can have things, like phone privileges."

The group broke apart, everyone in a glum mood.

Flipping hair out of her eyes, Dylan figured she might as well get her chores done. She needed to call her agent, but Babe held her cell phone hostage. She hoped she'd drawn something interesting, not some girly thing, like dishes. She wasn't happy when she read the list. Her job was to shovel out the barn.

Shovel moose poop.

And she had to work in partnership with Bunny Van Randolph.

17.

Gay and Disgruntled

Bunny placed her hands on her hips as she read the posted chore list over Dylan's shoulder. "No way!" she whined.

Dylan shrugged as she swept a mop of hair from her right eye. "Snowshoes in the corner. Let's go. Get this over with, Bun Bun."

Bunny's face fell into a pout. "No."

Ignoring her, Dylan sprawled on a bench by the back door and began strapping on a pair of snowshoes. "Come on!" she gruffed, grabbing Bunny by a hand. "Let's get this crap over with. I need to call my agent, and those weirdo old ladies have my cell."

Bunny stood her ground. "Go ahead, if you want. I'm taking a hot tub." Serious, Bunny trounced toward the stairs determined to immerse herself in a hot pot of water.

Dylan grabbed the tail of Bunny's Italian lace blouse. "Hold on, sister."

Bunny bounced backward into Dylan's arms. "Let go!"

"No."

Bunny tried to bite Dylan, but Dylan was quicker and dodged the danger. "I said we're cleaning that barn. I need my cell. Understand?" Dylan ground out the words. She squeezed Bunny's forearm and held on like a demon vise grip.

"That hurts!"

"Good."

Bunny spun around to face Dylan. "Oh boohoo! Big mean art dyke, are you?"

Dylan let go of Bunny's arm. "Look," she proclaimed as she yanked her black jean jacket from a hook near the back door, "you gonna help clean this barn or not?"

Bunny studied Dylan's jacket. The back yoke bore a pink, stenciled message: "Gay & Disgruntled." The right sleeve read, "Chick with a Dick." The left one read, "Lucy was gay. Just ask Ethel."

"Who does your wardrobe?"

"What?"

"Your clothes. Who designs your clothes?"

"I do. I believe clothes are art. They should reveal who you are."

"Yeah, I can see that. But why turn yourself into a freaking public-service billboard?"

"Isn't that what you do? Short dresses, high heels." Dylan backed away and slapped a finger frame around Bunny as though sizing her up for a photo shoot. "I mean, you're like a freaking femme highway sign. Your clothes scream *slut!*"

Bunny stuck out her tongue.

"Sorry, you'll have to get someone else to suck that for you. I've got work to do."

Dylan stumbled uncertainly toward the back door, her right hand steadying herself against the wall as she progressed, her left hand fruitlessly shoving the hair out of her eyes. The huge webbed shoes made her walk bowlegged. She shot a glance over her shoulder at Bunny, who was now sitting on the bench, struggling to strap her thigh-high red velvet Prada snow boots into a pair of snowshoes.

Bunny tried to stand, but wobbled and fell.

Again, same result.

Dylan clattered back to the bench. "Spread your thighs!" she growled at Bunny. "Just a little."

"Is that a come on? Because if it is, I've heard better, like, a bazillion times, Ms. Dykey Pants." Bunny stuffed herself into a pink silk down jacket and matching fur-trimmed mittens.

"Just trying to help."

Bunny raised her chin in defiance. "Trying to cop a feel, more like it."

"Whatever, Bun Bun."

"Stop calling me that!"

"Stop acting like some sort of freakin' airhead and I'll consider it."

Brushing Dylan aside, Bunny stood firm. One huge step. Two. "I'll help shovel your old barn. But just this once. Understand? And it's not for you. It's for me. I want my phone back, too."

"Whatever you say, Bun Bun." Dylan eyed the backyard through the glass in the door. Snowdrifts snuggled tightly against one another. She shivered. Unlike Bunny, she didn't have gloves. No hat or earmuffs, either.

Dylan turned to face Bunny. "You got another pair of those you could loan me?"

"What? These?" Bunny held up her fur-frosted hands.

"Yeah, those."

"Sure. I've got, like, a gazillon pairs. What's in it for me?"

Dylan raked the hair from her eyes. "I've got stuff."

"Stuff?" Bunny's eyes widened.

"Yeah. Pills."

"What?"

Dylan looked nervously around the kitchen, then the backyard. "Ecstasy. Pure. Loads of the stuff."

"Get out of here. You do not!"

"Do." Dylan whispered.

"Okay, I'll loan you a pair of my gloves. But you better not be lying."

"I'm not. Just get the gloves, Muffy."

18.

Failure Not an Option

Upstairs, Dr. Candice was trying to decipher which end of the vacuum cleaner hose went into the cleaning canister, and which end should stay free to suck dirt. At home, a gang of Dominican domestics dealt with such daily issues for her.

Dirk was leaning against the wall of the hallway, arms locked against her chest, scrutinizing the doctor. They'd been assigned to vacuum the upstairs together. They'd been trying for half an hour to bring the vacuum cleaner, a pot-bellied chrome creature that rolled uncertainly on a set of wobbly wheels, to life.

Dirk leaned down, hands on knees, and squinted. "That's gotta be wrong. That looks all wrong to me."

Candice, who was on her knees in the broom closet, glanced up. "Really? And you have like, what ... a doctorate degree in vacuumology? Well, how about you try running this thing?"

"Sure. Why not." Dirk fell on one knee besides Dr. Antwerp. She reconnected the hose and depressed the mammoth red On button.

Nothing happened.

The two women eyed each other.

"What now?" sneered Candice.

"Call one of those old chicks for help?"

Candice made a face. She'd not become Hollywood's top plastic surgeon by whining for help every time she hit a hard spot. "Oh, give me that! I'm sure we can figure this out." She disassembled the vacuum and rearranged the hoses and adjusted a nozzle or two. She flipped the switch, but the machine sat lifeless.

"We need help," muttered Dirk.

"We do not need help. *I* do not need help."

"Look, it doesn't work. *We* need help."

"Did you check the bag? These things have bags, right?" Candice fumbled with what appeared to be a latch on the butt end of the canister. A metal door sprang open, spewing out a cloud of dust and debris.

"Aghhh!" cried Candice, dust cutting her eyes. "Get me a towel! Something! Now!"

Dirk stripped off her T-shirt and used it to gently mop Candice's face. In the process, a good deal of Candice's makeup came off, too.

"Is my mascara smudged?" Candice asked, looking like a redheaded raccoon with dust balls in its hair.

"Nah. Uh, you look great."

Candice squinted at her reflection in the butt end of the chrome canister. "Liar." She wetted her finger and used it to smooth her eyeliner. Slowly, she began raking dust bunnies from her hair.

Dirk rubbed her chin. "Look, we only got half an hour to finish this vacuuming thing. We need help."

"I have a medical degree. I can do this."

"The thing won't work." Dirk kicked it with the toe of her boot, as if that might encourage the monstrosity to move. "The thing's dead as dead. How we going to vacuum? What are we supposed to do? Put soap on our tongues and lick the carpet clean?"

"You'd like that, wouldn't you?"

"Get real."

"Maybe if we tried cleaning out the hose and putting it back in." Candice shoved two fingers inside the mesh hose apparatus and rimmed the interior vigorously.

"What is it with you? Why not ask for help? You can't do everything yourself. Life's not like that."

"Mine is."

"Yeah, well maybe that's why you're in this hellhole."

"What does that mean?"

Dirk shrugged. "You're the one with the medical degree. You figure it out. I'm just a dumb jock."

"You're talking about those twelve steps? Aren't you?"

"Sorta."

"You think I need some sort of Higher Power to fix the vacuum cleaner."

"That or a mechanic."

"You're butch. Fix this thing?"

"Nope. There's lots of stuff I can't do. Same for you. Why not just admit that? Look, you may be a doctor but seems to me your skills are limited. You do ass lifts. Nose jobs. Maybe, just maybe, these old psycho chicks know a thing or two about how heads are screwed on. Maybe they're right about asking for help; about turning our lives over to a Higher Power. Why not give it a try? What's the worst that could happen?"

Candice bit her tongue. She knew the answer deep in her heart. To ask for help would mean she was failing. And failure was not an option. Never had been. It riled her even more that a jock with a wonder ass was the one pointing this out to her.

"You know," she said, shooting Dirk a cold look, "you're a lot cuter when you keep your mouth shut."

19.

Daniel Boone Was a Dyke

Storm trudged through the deep snowdrifts in the backyard, a yellow-handled ax slung over her left shoulder.

"You know how to handle that thing, love?" Poppy inquired as she trudged beside Storm, using her teeth to pull on a pair of insulated mittens.

Storm snorted, icy breath curling out her nose. "Think I can figure it out."

"How come I don't get to swing the ax? Seems like the bloody fun part to me."

The pair stopped in front of a cord of stacked birch logs. It was their job to chop the rounds for tomorrow's firewood. Storm peeled back the hood on her parka. The snow had stopped and the sun spun like a thin dime in the afternoon sky. "To be honest, Poppy, I don't see any of this as fun."

"It's sorta fun. Like pioneers. You know, like that Yank Daniel Boone."

Storm peeled off her gloves and clutched the ax with both hands. "You think every American is a pioneer who wears a coonskin cap?"

"Don't be silly. Some of you are cowboys."

Storm roared with laughter. Poppy wasn't as ditzy as she let on. The girl had substance. After rolling a butt onto the chopping block, Storm backed up and took a swing. She missed, slashing a thick hole in the snow. Black dirt and blue soapstone bled through the gash.

"Jolly good job, Danny," muttered Poppy.

"You try, Pop Tart." Storm swung the ax into Poppy's hands and stepped back.

Poppy circled the chopping block. She stopped, studied the angle, and circled again.

"What the *H-E-double-hockey-sticks* are you doing?" raged Storm. "We've only got an hour to get this done. No wood, no fire. Babe was clear about that. And I hate being cold."

"Don't get your knickers in a twist. I'm studying angles."

"Angles?"

"Yes, angles." Poppy planted both booted feet firmly in the trodden snow. She raised the ax and let it fly. She missed the chopping block entirely. Losing her balance, she landed face first in the snow.

Storm clutched Poppy around the waist from behind and hefted her up out of the snow.

The pop star struggled to her feet, the tip of her nose frosted in snow.

"That was impressive," chided Storm. "Think you might actually hit the log this time?"

Poppy made a face. "You think you're the only competent one?"

"Most of the time."

"Well, get over yourself. You may make a couple of million a year but I'm worth five times that. Plus girls everywhere cream their panties when I take the stage." Poppy thrust her chest out.

Storm rolled her eyes. "Well, Ms. Tart, I'm as famous as you, except I report hard news, not trot around a stage with my ass hanging out."

"Seems to me you liked my ass just fine when it was hanging in your direction."

"I was desperate. Sobriety does that to a girl."

"Sod off!" said Poppy, and this time when she turned to chop wood she scored. Splinters rained through the air.

Sobered by the petite pop star's swing (and dead-on accuracy), Storm fell quiet. She waited until Poppy had split more than a dozen logs before beginning to gather the wood. She studied the pop star's wiry body as it writhed and lunged, biting the hard wood into ever smaller pieces. Storm would never have thought that a femme fluff like Poppy could plow through an arduous task like chopping firewood.

But Poppy was no fluff. More like a wiry English lumberjack with a closet full of lace teddies.

When Poppy had chopped enough wood to fill the sled, she threw the ax aside and plopped down in the snow. Sweat streamed down her face. She used a mitten to wipe her cheeks, then her brow. "Think that's enough?"

Storm eyed the mountain of wood. "Yeah, unless you want to heat New York State, too."

Poppy laughed. "Thought I'd femme out, didn't you?"

"Maybe."

"No bloody maybe. You were sure. Admit it."

Storm tossed more wood onto the sled. "Yeah. Sure. I mean, my parents left me when I was a kid. Now, anyone says they'll do something I figure I'll get more of the same. No offense, but I much prefer to paddle my own canoe. That way I always make it to shore."

Poppy halted gathering the wood. "That's bloody awful. Your parents left you?"

Storm shrugged. "To me it's just normal."

"It's not *normal,* Storm. I mean, my mum is a pain in the bum. But no matter what I do she'd never leave me."

"You sure about that?"

"Yep."

Ignoring Poppy, Storm grabbed the rope tied to the front of the sled. Throwing the rope over her shoulder, she struggled to tug the sled toward the house.

The sled was so heavy it bogged down in the snow. Storm struggled with the sled, determined to slide it back to the house without assistance. But Storm's impatient jerks and kicks only caused the wood to tumble to the front, making the sled bite down harder into the snow. "Crap!"

Poppy stood next to Storm. "Slow learner, aren't you?"

"Excuse me?" Frustrated, Storm straddled the sled of wood. She fumbled in her parka pocket for a cigarette.

"Help, love. You need my help."

"You know, you're starting to get on my nerves." Storm took her time lighting the stubby cigarette. She blew smoke circles in the frosty air. Then toward Poppy.

Poppy stood her ground. "Are you going to ask me to help you with this sled?"

"Would that please you?" Another smoke ring.

"No, but it would make it possible for us to get the wood to the house."

"How practical of you."

Poppy sighed. "I think part of what we're supposed to learn here is how to ask for help."

"That what you think?" Another frosty smoke ring.

"Yes."

Storm crushed her cigarette deep into the snow with the toe of her combat boot. Poppy was right, of course, they'd never get the sled to the farmhouse unless they worked together. Babe had battered into their heads that morning that they needed to admit they weren't God; that they had issues; needed help.

Babe's sweatshirt that morning had read: "There's a God, and You're Not Her."

Storm rolled her eyes. "Fine. Maybe I need … help."

Poppy's face lit up. She grabbed the front of the sled while motioning for Storm to take the back.

Together, they lifted the heavy sled out of its slushy rut. Like magic, the sled slid cleanly toward the farmhouse.

20.

The Dyke Next Door

Wee Gee crawled into the cramped broom closet and yanked out a pair of dented metal buckets, swish brushes, and a bottle of mountain-rain-scented bleach. She shoved one bucket and set of cleaning tools across the floor to Thumper, who stood looking glum, hands tucked under her armpits.

"You know how to use this stuff? How to clean?" asked Wee Gee.

"Sure," Thumper sniffled. "Grew up on a dairy farm. Did all the chores."

Wee Gee and Thumper had been assigned to clean the bathrooms.

Wee Gee stuffed her hands into a pair of long yellow-rubber gloves that hugged her forearms and Thumper followed suit. "You grew up here in Vermont?"

"Just over the hill. Northeast Kingdom," replied Thumper.

"Kingdom?"

"That's what folks call the northeast corner of Vermont. The French fur trappers called it that a long time ago, back when the French claimed that part of Vermont. Not a lot of people up in that corner of Vermont even today. Nice. Quiet."

The two women traipsed upstairs, entering Wee Gee's room first. Thumper fell quiet. Wee Gee turned to her as they entered the bathroom. "Not much for chitchat, are you?"

Thumper shrugged. "Leave that to my sister. She likes being around people more than me."

Wee Gee rolled her eyes. "Girls, certainly."

"Yeah. That's true."

"How you want to do this?" Wee Gee asked.

"Dunno."

"How about I do one bathroom, you do the next?"

"Cool."

Wee Gee sloshed bleach into the toilet and scrubbed as Thumper perched on the edge of the sink vanity and watched.

"You like doing the Olympic thing?" Wee Gee asked as she flipped down the lid on the first toilet and inspected her work.

"It's okay."

"Okay? Girl, you're an Olympic medalist and all you can say is it's okay?"

"It was my sister's idea. I mean, she started the snowboarding thing. To pick up chicks, mostly. I sorta went along."

"And the steroids?"

"Accident. Sort of. We needed money to get to the snowboarding events out West and our dad is dead. Our mom, she stills runs the family dairy farm. We didn't have any money and they'd only give prize money and a free ride to the winners. We had a coach we ran into in upstate New York. Uncle Jerry, we called him, though he wasn't really related to us. He started giving us these injections. Vitamins, he said."

"Vitamins? Girl, you believed that?"

"We were, like, fourteen at the time. Fresh off the farm. We believed adults. I mean, we were kinda raised like that. Church. Respect for your elders. That sort of thing." Thumper ran a rubber-gloved hand across her blonde buzz cut. "We kinda suspected something was funny because like we both grew, like, little mustaches. Then muscles started popping out on our chests, but the coach said it was okay. Normal for athletes our age."

Wee Gee eyed Thumper. "Church? Your mama know about you and your sister?"

"The 'roids?"

"No, the girls."

"Yeah. Sure. I mean, we've always liked girls. Like, in second grade we both had girlfriends. Gave them valentines. Let 'em have the Twinkies out of our lunch bags. That kind of stuff." Thumper rested her chin in the cup of her rubber-coated hand.

"No one told you not to do that?"

"Nah. I mean, it didn't really become an issue until we started living in the Olympic training camp. About half the jock girls are queer. But the other half, they really don't like the whole queer thing. They feel they have to work really hard to be accepted as feminine. The queer thing is hard on them. I mean, most guys don't like muscle-bound chicks. And the straight chicks really want guys to like them. Just the way it is."

Wee Gee picked up her bucket and motioned for Thumper to follow as they went into Dirk and Thumper's room. Curious, Wee Gee turned to face Thumper. "You got a girl?"

Thumper's cheeks flushed.

"Come on, give. Who is she? What's she like?"

Thumper shook her head. "Never said I had a girl."

"Don't have to. Your face gave you away, Ms. Cherry Cheeks. Give, already. She a snowboarder?"

Thumper cracked her knuckles before grabbing the brush and vigorously rimming the toilet. "Nah." She looked up to face Wee Gee when she was done cleaning. "Don't like athletes all that much."

"Society chick?"

Thumper ruffled her own hair as they headed to the next room. "Nah, that's Dirk's thing. She likes party girls. Me, I like the girl next door."

"You mean the sweet type?"

"Nah, I mean the girl next door. Mary Lou. She lives on the dairy farm next to our mom in East Hardwick. Been there her whole life."

"She know you're sweet on her?"

"She let me kiss her once."

"Once?"

Thumper's face flamed. "Okay, maybe like a few times."

"Seems to me you like this little farm girl a lot."

"Maybe."

Wee Gee rolled her eyes.

Picking up her bucket and heading to the next room, Thumper changed the topic. "You always been into chicks?"

"More or less. I've been doing the ladies since Stonewall."

"But you had a husband?"

"We all did back in the day, honey. I mean, back in the '60s you could land in jail for kissing a girl."

"That must have been awful."

"It was."

"When did you have your first girlfriend?"

"When I was thirteen."

"No shit?"

"No shit. She was a lot older than me. Mrs. Ruth Ruck-house, the piano player at our church. She was giving me piano lessons. For free. Said I was gifted. One day we were working on a hymn together, "When the Saints Go Marching In," and in the middle she put her hand atop mine and stopped me playing and reached over and kissed me full on the lips. When she was done she asked me, 'Well, how did you like that, Ms. William Jean? William Jean, that's my real given name, got shortened to Wee Gee by my little sister back when we were babies.'"

"Holy smokes, Wee Gee. What did you say?"

"I said I liked that just fine, ma'am."

"Then what happened?"

"She did it again. And again. We were an item all that summer. Which, if anyone asks, is why I can't play the piano worth diddle despite a good bit of private lesson time."

"Then what happened?"

"Her husband. He came back from the war. Vietnam. He was like a master sergeant and he got transferred to Fort Drum, in New York. They left at the end of the summer and I never saw or heard from her again."

"You still remember her?"

"Remember her? Honey, to this day I'm the only woman, white or black, who orgasms to church hymns."

21.

Coming Clean

Nan Goldberg eyed Betty Frump. She was trying to understand how any woman could live with so much self-righteousness and not explode. Or just get plain sick of listening to herself.

Betty was supposed to be helping Nan gather the bed sheets and other public laundry and tote them to the cellar laundry room, but instead she was reading Nan the P.C. riot act. "You don't penetrate your woman, do you?"

"Pardon?" Nan asked, peering over a mound of flannel sheets she'd just struggled to gather into her arms.

"Penetration. You know." Betty made a circle of her right thumb and forefinger and jabbed in her left thumb, a gesture Nan found distasteful, not at all like the real thing, at least not like she and Birge practiced it. Other women she couldn't speak for.

Nan tossed the sheets down the first flight of stairs, onto a heap she'd already stripped from Bunny and Candice's room. "Of course I penetrate my girlfriend. But we don't do *that*. Whatever that was that you just indicated with that obscene little finger gesture of yours."

Betty appeared unfazed. "Why?"

"Why what?"

"Why penetrate."

Nan reflected for a moment. "Because I *like* it. It makes me moan."

Betty snorted. "Imitating the patriarchy."

"I don't think so. Birge never had a boyfriend. She's gay with a capital *G*. Came out in kindergarten."

"Doesn't make any difference. The culture tells us sex is phallocentric penetration."

"I like penetration!" Nan said, feeling oddly defensive as she tossed the last load of sheets down the stairs. "In fact, I like it a lot. Don't you?"

Frump shrugged.

"What, you've never had a woman deep inside you? You're kidding, right?"

"Look, it's up to us to re-create the experience of being womyn."

Nan grimaced. "I don't want to re-create anything. Life is okay with me, mostly. If you're different you have to deal with it. Makes no difference how you're different. The way I see it we're all queer in one way or another."

"And you're completely happy with the capitalistic, phallo-centric, patriarchal way you make your living?"

"Mostly."

"So why drink?"

Nan kicked the load of laundry off the landing down the steps that led to the back cellar. She jumped onto the landing and kicked the pile downward again. Like playing soccer, a game she'd excelled at in college. Her aim, as always, was dead on. "If you must know," she said as she scored a goal, "my father was an alcoholic."

"Ah, see! The patriarchy at work."

Nan snorted. "More like economics. My dad inherited wealth and kept up appearances but he was an angry drunk and reckless with money. It was hard on my mom. On everyone."

They were in the basement now and Nan, who was was stuffing sheets into the industrial-sized purple washing machine, was finding Frump an increasing irritant. Nan had worked her entire life to reclaim the family reputation and wealth, to get to where she was now, socially speaking. She had no desire to revert to a communist state.

And in case Frump hadn't noticed, most of the rest of the world had given up on that silly notion, also.

Nan Goldberg didn't want to change the world; she wanted to be a part of the world. For the life of her she couldn't cipher why Frump didn't put down her arms and join with the rest of the imperfect world.

Moreover, she was sick to death of the notion that just because she was a lesbian she should ride a bicycle to work and live inside a yurt or an earthern hut.

Definitely not her idea of lesbianism.

The machine loaded, Nan hauled down a box of detergent from the shelf and read the instructions to decipher how much detergent was needed for a machine the size of the thing she'd just fed. Not an easy task, considering she'd left her reading glasses upstairs and the bare-bulb light in the cellar was dim.

"Here," she grunted at last, thrusting the box toward Betty. "Make yourself useful. Read the instructions. How much detergent do you think we need?"

Betty frowned as she read the label. "Can't use this."

"Huh?"

"It's loaded with antibacterial agents. Poison of the patriarchy."

"We have to do the laundry. I want cell phone privileges. I *need* cell phone privileges. *Need.* Understand?"

Frump stuck the detergent box under her caftan. "Can't use this. I forbid it. Planet Earth is our sister."

"All right. How are we going to finish the effing laundry?"

Betty mused.

Nan folded her arms. It was almost five o'clock and she'd promised Birge she'd call. "Look, I need to get this done so I can get phone time. Can't we just move forward for the moment? Ask Babe to get us a different detergent next time?"

"Individuals have to surrender personal privilege to help the common good."

"Give me that detergent." Nan dove for the box.

Betty blocked Nan's advance with one thrust of her arm.

Nan considered her options. Normally someone like Betty would be a pushover for her. She'd not risen to the pinnacle of Wall Street by letting someone like Potluck Lucy here set her personal agenda.

"I need that freaking detergent." She held out her hands.

"No."

"You're really starting to piss me off." Nan's bottom lip quivered.

"You can't bully me. Babe said we have to work together. Learn to ask for help. Let others assist."

"Fine. So you tell me how we're going to do laundry without any freaking detergent?"

"I have a bar of soap, upstairs. Virgin glycerin. No dyes. No perfumes. No pollutants. It's handmade of organic materials by a collective of land mine amputees in Sudan. We can shave it down. Use that to do the wash."

"Fine. Get it."

As soon as Betty was gone, Nan grabbed the detergent box and emptied half the contents into the washing machine. She set the dial to large load with hot water and slapped shut the lid. The she raced upstairs. The grandfather clock in the foyer read twenty minutes after five. Nan, feeling frazzled, raced to Babe's office in quest of her cell phone.

Nan's fingers shot across the speed-dial button as soon as Babe handed her the phone. She needed to hear Birge's voice. She'd be okay as soon as she touched base with her partner.

Birge was her anchor. If she could just reach Birge. Hear her voice.

The cell rang for the longest time before Birge's answering service picked up to inform Nan that Birge had gone to the Hamptons for the weekend, and would not be accepting calls until Monday at nine a.m.

"Tell her it's me!" cried Nan at the bland-voiced operator. "Nan Goldberg. Her partner of twenty-nine-plus years."

"Sorry, ma'am, but Ms. Hathaway left strict instructions. No calls. Not even emergencies. You'll have to call back Monday at nine."

Throwing the phone against the wall, Nan swallowed hard to keep her heart from leaping out of her throat. Something wasn't right. Birge knew she was supposed to call. They hadn't spoken for three days. This call ought to be special for both of them. Birge should have waited. Since when couldn't — *wouldn't?* — Birge wait a few extra minutes for a call from Nan?

Where the hell is Birge? Where the fucking hell is my partner of all these years?

For the first time in days, Nan craved a drink.

Part II

Days of Wretched Reckoning

Interlude

Any addict will tell you the first week in rehab is the worst; that is, until the second week comes. Then the third. Well, you get my drift.

The first week is indeed bad. But somehow the utter shock of it wraps you in insulating cotton, protecting you as you realize full force that your life has been unmanageable for quite some time.

In truth, most addicts find relief the moment they stop hiding. The moment they publicly admit they have a problem. For most high-functioning addicts, the moment they realize there's a God and it's not them, relief floods into their tortured hearts.

Then comes a moment of quiet peace.

Unless you're Dr. Candice Antwerp.

At the end of the first week in rehab, everyone had managed to admit, some with more mumbling than others, that their lives had become unmanageable, and that they needed to learn new ways to handle stress.

Everyone except Dr. Antwerp. Her response to the question "Are you an addict?" had progressed from a steely "No" to a half-whimpered "Undecided."

Babe finally had to accept Candice's "undecided" as progress. She signed off on Dr. Antwerp's insurance treatment papers, allowing her to stay another week.

The doctor returned the favor with an icy blue stare.

As Wee Gee carried the celebratory chocolate cake (made with stevia and gluten-free flower) into the kitchen and slid it onto the oak table, everyone clapped.

One week sober. Now it was time for the group to begin step four: make a fearless moral inventory. Babe handed each woman a tablet of yellow paper along with a slice of cake.

"Get to work!" she bellowed as she left them in the kitchen, eating cake, hugging one another in a congratulatory circle.

22.

Nose Out of Joint

Candice squinted at the list of personality traits Babe had given them to study. They were supposed to start their fearless moral inventory by circling the adjectives they believed applied to themselves. Then they were supposed to hand their sheets to their assigned partners for a discussion about how those traits helped insulate them from feeling while simultaneously allowing them to hurt others.

Candice squinted across the room at Poppy, who was sitting cross-legged on the floor in front of a blazing fire. Poppy's black ponytail was bopping up and down in time to a tune she was listening to on her iPod.

Dr. Antwerp couldn't hear the tune but she could follow the beat from Poppy's head bops. Catching Poppy's eye, she yelled across the room, "Do you think I'm a nice person?"

Poppy pulled the sound bud from her right ear. "Definitely not, love!"

"You could think about that statement for a moment or two."

"Don't need to." Poppy plucked the remaining headphone bud from her ear as she continued circling items about herself on her own sheet. "You're not nice. You're selfish. And cold. And not a little bit rude."

"You don't know me."

"Don't care to, either."

Candice's brows clouded into one dark wrinkle. "Am I really that bad?"

Looking up, and seeing the distress on Candice's face, Poppy went to sit next to her on the sofa. "Can't lie to you, love. You're bloody awful. A real piece of poop."

"Why? Why do you say that?" The distress was evident in Candice's voice.

"Because it's true. I mean, you walk around with your perfectly shaped fake little nose in the air like we all smell bad. Never a hello, mate. Never a wish for a good day."

"Silly social contrivances. Waste of time."

"Not to me. I mean, you don't have to play kissy-face but you could practice being pleasant. Smile every now and then. Ask a question or two. At least *pretend* to be interested in something other than yourself."

"But," protested Candice, "I am interested. Like, in you."

"In me? You're interested in me?" Poppy screwed a fingertip into her own bosom.

"Yes. Like how is it you've got the guts to strut around half naked up there on stage then see all those magazine pieces about yourself plastered with those awful words: Poppy the Pussy-Licker."

Poppy threw back her head and roared in laughter. "It's good they write about me. I want them talking about me. Gossip sells tunes. Big time." She leaned down and whispered in the doctor's ear, "Besides, love, that last part, well, it's kinda true."

Dr. Antwerp stiffened.

"See, now look, you could have laughed at that statement but instead you coiled like you was the Queen Mum and I was a fishmonger. Lighten up!"

"I don't know how."

"You don't know how to laugh?"

"Not really."

"What? Your folks were missionaries or something?"

Candice frowned. "Let's leave them out of this, shall we?"

"Fine by me. I'm done with my list, want to trade?"

"I suppose."

The two fell quiet. Dr. Antwerp spoke first. "Your list seems okay to me. I mean, for as well as I know you."

Poppy had circled about a dozen terms. Some of them were traits she liked about herself, others less so. For instance, she liked that she was fun-loving and kindhearted, but she loathed that she was often irresponsible, especially around promises to her mum. She'd circled stubborn twice. A good trait in her work, but a trait that led her to never forget and rarely forgive.

"You think of yourself as irresponsible?" asked Dr. Antwerp.

"Kind of. I mean, people tell me that a lot. Mostly when I do drugs. I get carried away. And since I got famous, everyone is afraid to confront me if I behave badly. They treat me with kid gloves, like I might bite their little heads off if they dare upset me."

"Might you?"

"I can act pretty rotten, especially if I'm sodded. I don't like myself then. It's all about me. Me. Me. Me. I feel like a giant two-year-old with a bad tummy. I think that's why my mum sent me here. She wanted me to pay attention and clean up my act."

"You don't think you belong here?"

Poppy chewed the eraser tip of her pencil. "Not at first, but now I think maybe it's okay. I mean, I got wasted and burned down a house. What if there had been someone home at the time?" Poppy averted her eyes. "I didn't even check."

Poppy worried Candice's list in her hand. The doctor had circled only two traits: hardworking and perfectionist. "You work all the time?"

The doctor nodded.

"And you never make mistakes?"

"Can't afford to, not in my line of work. I mean, if you're a secretary and misspell a word in a letter, it's no big deal. You know what would happen if I did a nose job and placed the break even a centimeter off kilter?"

Poppy shook her head.

"Well, it could well mean the difference between looking like Paris Hilton or Pinocchio. Given that, wouldn't you want me to be as perfect as possible?"

"See your point. Definitely. But what about outside work? Like your personal relationships. Your girlfriend, for instance. I mean, you're not perfectionist then, are you?"

No answer.

"Oh come on," coaxed Poppy. "Don't go zip lip, Doc. I told you the truth about me. Give a little. You're got a steady bird, right?"

"No, I do not have a bird, steady or otherwise."

"But you used to have one, right?"

Candice folded her arms across her chest.

Scooting across the couch, Poppy pried the doctor's arms open. "When you're talking to someone, open your arms. Open your heart. Invite them in."

Dr. Antwerp's arms lay limp, looking broken at her side.

"Talk to me," encouraged Poppy.

Resisting the urge to lock her arms again, Candice admitted she'd had a steady girlfriend until recently.

"Go on."

"She's a makeup artist. Hallie. Owns her own company: Face Off. Does big-budget movies. That sort of stuff."

"Cool. And?" Poppy made a beckoning motion with her fingers. "More!"

"And she's hardworking."

Poppy groaned as she slapped both palms to her cheeks.

"Why? What did I say?"

"Sounds like you're describing an employee, not the love of your life."

"Fine. Let's see. She's a beautiful blonde. A talker. Like you."

"Beautiful as in hot?"

"Sizzling."

They both laughed.

"She know you're in the dyke drunk tank?"

Candice's face clouded. "She knows I took an East Coast spa vacation."

"She the reason you're here?"

Candice crossed her arms. Then uncrossed them. She strolled to the window where she pinned back a curtain. Dirk and her sister had tramped down a ramp in the snow bank at the side of the farmhouse. They were practicing flips and turns, laughing and jostling like kids.

Candice grew sad that she'd never really had a childhood. She'd been hardworking even in kindergarten. Even her grade school teachers had found her a perfectionist. Poppy was right: If she hoped to set her life aright, she needed to open herself up. Take a dare or two. Start making some mistakes.

Dirk turned a somersault in the snow, landing unsuccessfully on her back. Nonetheless she came up laughing, her feet bound together in the air on her blazing yellow snowboard.

Poppy came to stand by the window. "You fancy Dirk?"

Candice started to shrug but instead let her shoulders drop. "She's cute. But, um, rather dykey."

"That's putting it mildly." Poppy stole another look at Dirk. "Yeah, if you want a girl that can pass at family get-togethers, best to mark that stud muffin off your list. You're in the closet, yes?"

"I don't broadcast my sexual orientation, if that's what you mean."

"Not quite, love. I mean, you don't have to put it on page one, like I do, or be known on Twitter as #twinkletwat like Bunny. But, like, your parents, do they know about you?"

Candice locked her arms. "No, and for the record I have never asked them about their sex lives, either."

"Come on, love, that's not really the same, is it?"

"I think it is."

"I think you're in denial."

Candice made a face.

"Look," said Poppy, "did you tell Dirk you think she's cute?"

Dr. Antwerp thought back to their misadventures with the vacuum cleaner. "Sort of."

Poppy made a sound like a buzzer going off. "No good. You have to say it. Clearly. Out loud."

At that moment Babe rang the bell announcing evening group. Dr. Antwerp plucked her jacket from the couch but instead of buttoning it tightly across her bosom, as was her habit, she slung it casually across one shoulder.

"You go, girl!" Poppy whispered as they entered the hush of the group room.

23.

Little Bunny's Woo-Woo

Hearing the clang of the group bell downstairs, Bunny rolled over in bed and squinted at her glow-in-the-dark, diamond-studded Cartier wristwatch.

Seven p.m. Yucka-doodle. Time for group.

The lump under the sheets next to Bunny rolled over, revealing a sweaty face and a mob of dark, uneven hair. Dylan was butt naked, same as Bunny. They'd gone to Bunny's room to do a fearless moral inventory of their bad traits and ended up sharing some Ecstasy.

After that they'd shared everything.

Dylan wasn't sure, but she seemed to remember Bunny's woo-woo was dyed a lovely shade of lavender with mauve highlights. A first for her. Somewhat freaky, too, because for a split second while under the influence of E, Dylan had thought she was licking out her deceased grandmother's Evening in Paris powder-puff ensemble.

"Shit!" groaned Dylan as, sweeping the hair from her eyes, she fished around the foot of Bunny's disheveled bed for her jeans. She hadn't worn any underwear. She rarely did. She'd decided long ago that it was easier this way. Took less time to suit up and sneak away.

But Bunny, who was a twenty-year veteran at postcoital escapes, grabbed the back loop of Dylan's jeans, spinning her backward onto the bed, and into her arms.

"Hold on a minute, cowgirl!" Bunny murmured as she nibbled Dylan's tattooed earlobe. "What's the big rush? Relax. Have a cigarette."

Grabbing the offered cigarette, Dylan took a hard drag before remembering they weren't supposed to smoke in the house. Or take drugs. Or miss group. She took another drag, anyway. What would those old dykes do? Kick her out?

I should be so lucky!

Bunny plucked the lit cigarette from Dylan's lips and slipped it between her own. "Always offer a lady a cigarette after sex. It's polite."

"I look like Miss Manners to you?" Dylan grumbled as she yanked on her ribbed white wife-beater. She stubbed her bare feet in the darkness around the bed in search of her boots.

Christ, she couldn't believe she'd slept with Bunny. She didn't even like the woman. And now, on top of everything, she had a raging headache and a tongue as dry as a stick of salt. E was a great drug while it lasted, but coming off it could be one bumpy ride.

Sprawled on her belly in bed, Bunny furtively tucked one of Dylan's ankle boots under her abdomen. "Relax. We had sex. I'm not going to ask you to marry me. No biggy."

"Yeah, right. That's for sure."

"Okay, no need to be rude. It was fun. Don't get twisted up and think I'm in love with you or anything weird like that."

"You seen my boots?"

"You weren't wearing boots, darling."

Dylan held up the one boot she'd found under the bed and shook it. The brass buckle rattled. "Of course I was, Muffy. Here's one. Where's the other?"

Bunny shrugged.

By the time Bunny and Dylan were dressed and down-stairs, group was ready to disband, but Bunny insisted they go, anyway. "If we show up it counts. There's no rule against coming late. Late is okay. We can show up late and there's nothing they can do to us."

Dylan shuffled into the therapy room first. Her hair was disheveled, per usual.

Bunny bounced in next, looking as made-up as ever.

Babe scolded them both. "You girls are late." She gestured at her wristwatch. "Very late."

"Sorry," grumbled Dylan.

"Won't happen again," promised Bunny.

Babe eyed them both. "Where were you two?"

Bunny smiled as she took a seat. "Working together on our fearless moral inventory."

"Really?" Babe appeared skeptical.

"Yes," said Bunny. "Dylan got very upset. She started to cry when she realized how selfish she's been most of her life. I was trying to comfort her."

Babe circled Dylan, who sat, head hung, hair flagged across her eyes. She was busy trying to ignore Babe in favor of peeling the cuticles off her left fingers. "Yeah. I got, like, really upset. My fault we're late."

"Look at me." Babe instructed as she took Dylan's chin in her hand and raised it upward. "I said look at me."

"What?" sneered Dylan as she looked up.

"Your neck?"

Dylan slapped a hand to her neck. "What?"

"Hickey."

Wee Gee scooted over to get a closer look. "Girl, what was sucking on you?"

Dylan clamped both hands over her neck. "I do *not* have a hickey."

Bunny patted Dylan's neck. "Afraid you do, dear. Huge. Size of a pork chop."

Babe stared at Bunny. "Anything you want to confess to group?"

Bunny shrugged.

Dylan did the same.

"Fine," said Babe, as she dismissed the group. "You can all go."

But as Dylan tried to dart out of the room, Babe blocked her way. "Not you, stud muffin. I want you in my office. Pronto."

24.

Real Dykes Don't Cry

"I didn't do anything," mumbled Dylan. She was standing in front of Babe's massive oak rolltop desk, head hung, gaze glued to the floor. She kicked at an imaginary dust ball with one boot.

"You did Bunny."

Dylan shuffled in a little circle. Saying nothing, she slid over to a bookcase and yanked out a title. She squinted as she read the title: *Women Who Love Too Much*.

"Not your problem," stated Babe drily.

Dylan shrugged. "I dunno, I get my share."

"Of sex. Not love."

"Who says there's a difference?"

"Me."

"You're not God."

"To you, right now, I kinda am."

Dylan plopped into an oversized armchair. She slung both legs over an arm. Her knees jutted out the artful rips on each pant leg. "I'm not listening to your yak. I'm only gonna be here another three weeks."

"If you're lucky."

"Hey, what's that supposed to mean?"

"It means I decide each week who stays and who goes. Right now, girlfriend, I'm thinking maybe come Monday you pack your duffel bag."

"You'd kick me out?"

"You broke a rule. A very important rule." Babe rose and walked from behind the desk over to Dylan.

Dylan was sitting scrunched up in the armchair, peeling her cuticles again.

"Look at me!" commanded Babe.

In response, Dylan twisted in the chair, moving as far away from Babe as possible.

"Just look at me. Okay?"

Dylan raised her face.

Babe raked the hair from her eyes and studied Dylan's pupils, which shone like fiery black moons. "You're stoned. What the hell did you take?"

"Nothing. Allergies. My eyes get like this." Dylan sniffled.

"In the dead of winter?"

Dylan shook off Babe's hand. "Why pick on me? That old girlfriend of yours not putting out?"

"You have so much talent and potential."

Dylan rolled her eyes. "That's what my high school guidance counselor said. Man, was she wrong. Stupid bitch."

"You know why I say you have potential?"

"Don't care."

"I think you do."

"Fine. You can read minds? Go ahead and read mine now." Dylan glared at Babe. To punctuate the effect, she stuck out her pierced tongue.

Babe returned to her seat behind the desk. She placed both hands on the desk. "It's your anger. Your anger shows me you care."

"What the hell does that mean?"

"You're angry. At me. At the world. At life. Someone hurt you big time. You're stuck there. A long time ago. You want an apology. That's why you keep attacking people. You hope eventually someone might show you they care."

Dylan slid to an upright position in the chair and crossed her arms tightly to her chest. "Who died and made you Oprah?"

"What I said is true. Why not admit it?"

Dylan went back to studying her cuticles.

"Okay. Let's try another way. Your husband called me this afternoon."

Dylan groaned as she shrank further into the chair. She clutched a pillow to her chest before throwing it hard against a bookcase. "What the fuck did that fucking asshole want?"

"To ask if you were okay, and to confirm he's coming to see you this weekend."

Dylan swiped the hair from her eyes. "He's not *really* my husband, you know."

"Not my business. The court sent you here, and they say he's your legal next of kin." Babe slid on a pair of reading glasses and squinted at a piece of paper on her desk. "What happened to your parents?"

"Dead."

"I'm sorry."

"Don't be. Happens to all of us."

"Who raised you?"

"Crazy aunt and uncle."

"The uncle the one who abused you?"

Dylan drew into a tighter ball in the chair. "No one abused me. I ran away from that dump of a trailer park when I was seventeen."

"Why?"

"I wanted to be an artist. They wanted me to be a waitress at the Bob Evans. The uniform didn't fit," Dylan sneered.

"Do you want a better life?"

"Like what? Kids? Station wagon?"

"That's for you to define."

Dylan glared. She stood up and angled around the room. "Okay. Maybe I was abused as a kid, but that shit happens. No one abuses me now."

"I understand that. I'd say your *Big Pink Pussy* speaks to that regard."

Dylan stopped fidgeting. "You get that?"

Babe nodded. "I love your work," she continued. "Most women who are abused hide in shame. You're doing the opposite. You're making the world look at what they do to women's bodies."

Dylan plopped back into the chair. "You don't think my work is pornographic?" Her eyes narrowed in suspicion.

"The exact opposite. I think your work is full of anger and defiance, and that that anger is the first step in healing yourself. The first step, though. You don't want to get stuck there."

"Stuck?" Dylan looked puzzled.

"Yes, stuck." Babe consulted her wristwatch. "But that's enough for tonight. Think about what might come after anger."

"Huh?"

Babe stood and opened the door. "Just think about what else might be inside you, just underneath that anger."

"Huh?"

"This weekend. We'll talk more about it when your husband is here. One more thing," Babe added, catching Dylan by the elbow.

"What?"

"Flush the drugs down the toilet."

Dylan mumbled.

"Down the toilet, if you want to stay. Understand?"

Dylan mumbled, "Yeah. Sure. Okay, I guess."

"And don't sleep with Bunny again. Don't even so much as look at her in a way that might make her panties slippery. Understand?"

Dylan stopped abruptly in the hallway. "Why? Give me one good reason."

"Because you want to be loved, and every time you're not loved you feel worse about yourself. And Bunny is definitely not going to love you."

Dylan loped up the stairs. The lights were already out in the hallway. She ached to hurl something smart and disrespectful over her shoulder at Babe, but she felt tired as she climbed, like she'd just survived the worst day of her life.

For the first time in her adult life, Dylan felt trapped. She had this odd unpleasant feeling that she was about to cry.

Instead, she went to Bunny's room and popped another Ecstasy.

25.

Missing: One Pop Tart

That night, when Babe came to bed, Lily could tell she was at her wit's end. "Kids acting up?"

"To the max! Bunny and Dylan blew off group. I think they blew off group to have meaningless sex with each other."

Lily chuckled. "Like me and you in our baby dyke days?"

Babe and Lily had met through AA. In fact, Babe had barely been thirty days sober when Lily had approached her and offered to be her sponsor. An hour later they'd been wrapped around each other in Lily's Soho loft. They'd broken a sacred rule (sleeping together), and lived not to regret it, but they both knew this wouldn't hold true for most women struggling to remain sober.

"I don't think Bunny will make it. Dylan, either."

"Why not?"

"They don't think they have a problem — other than me."

"Did they admit to the group they have a problem?"

"Yes."

"Give them some time. It's scary. You know that. They may catch on. Some of the worst cases end up being the best at staying sober. You know you can't predict that."

"I know, but it's depressing, this time for the group, I mean. I won't know for another week if anything's taking with these guys."

"How's Wee Gee?"

"Fine. She's sailing right along."

"Well, maybe one of them may make it. Sometimes that's the best we can do."

Babe rolled over in bed. "Only one?"

"Don't get depressed. You know most of them will make it. They're tough. It takes a lot of courage to be a lesbian. Our kind doesn't roll over easily. You of all people ought to know that."

Grumbling, Babe tossed to one side and snapped off the light. She started to roll out of bed when she thought she heard a noise below their bedroom, in the kitchen, but she was so tired she fell asleep before her hand could find the light switch again.

Downstairs, Wee Gee inched along the wall in the dark. All the lights were out, save a lavender nightlight of Artemis, Greek goddess of the hunt, that leaked a weak light at the foot of the stairs. Wee Gee crept slowly toward her target: the industrial-sized refrigerator. Arriving at the tall, shiny box, she sprang open the door and began to shove things aside in search of the good stuff. Unfortunately, because Babe and Lily were vegetarians, little of what Wee Gee uncovered in the fridge would make for memorable binge eating.

Optimistic when her hand hit a hidden bag in the back of the crisper, Wee Gee pulled the bag onto the floor and ripped it open, only to have cucumbers roll in every direction.

"Damn!" she huffed.

Kicking the bag of cucumbers aside, Wee Gee decided to try the cupboards. There she found oatmeal and bran flakes. Canned soup, too.

By the time Wee Gee had ransacked the upper cupboards, her urge to binge eat had passed. She shuffled over to the table with the bag of cucumbers and a knife. When she was a child in Kentucky, her grandmother had given her peeled cucumbers in the summer as snacks. They tasted great in the heat of the Southern summer. Less so, she now discovered, in December in Vermont.

Nonetheless, munching on a giant salted cucumber soothed Wee Gee's desire to devour anything more destructive. While the cucumbers didn't fill her up, the memory of her grandmother did.

It was nice to remember she'd once been truly loved.

Sometimes Wee Gee thought sex was the worst thing in the world. Most of the time she was certain it had little to do with love. Certainly young people thought sex *was* love. But most every woman Wee Gee knew over the age of forty had figured out otherwise. Dating Little Debbie was the most satisfying period of most postmenopausal women's lives as far as Wee Gee could decipher.

With two cucumbers devoured, Wee Gee returned the paper bag to the fridge and climbed upstairs to her bedroom. She opened the door slowly so as not to wake Poppy, but as soon as she was inside the room she felt the rock star's absence. She walked over to the girl's bed and wasn't surprised when she peeled back the covers to find a pair of towels rolled up in imitation of Poppy's thin little body.

Wee Gee wondered where her roommate had gotten off to so late at night but figured it was none of her business. She liked Poppy, but Poppy was a grown woman. She had a mom who loved her. No use Wee Gee trying out for that same thankless position.

26.

Moonlight in Vermont

Following Storm's lead, Poppy relaxed her knees and fell backward into the snow. She landed with a thud, sinking into the softness until her arms and legs were embedded in a mold of cold.

"Flap your arms up and down," instructed Storm. "Like a goose. Try to fly." Storm made sound effects, which sounded to Poppy like a sick goose.

Freshly fallen snow flew everywhere as Poppy cranked her arms.

Alone in the backyard, the two women giggled. A full moon spun in and out of dark winter clouds. Poppy and Storm were lying side by side in the snow, staring up at the moon.

"Next," instructed Storm, "spread your legs in and out, fast, like you're flapping them also."

Poppy did as instructed.

"On the count of three," said Storm, "we have to grasp hands and rise straight up out of the snow. Together. Don't hesitate. Get up fast!"

At the count of three, the two women locked hands and jumped up. Still holding hands Storm and Poppy turned to face the place they'd been lying together. The snow was fanned into the shape of two angels, one clearly wearing combat boots.

"Snow angels!" proclaimed Storm proudly.

Poppy didn't know what to say. It had been a long time since anyone had invited her to do anything as patently silly as making snow angels. People talked to her all the time: about record deals, concert bookings, financial investments. About scoring a lot of whatever drug was popular on the club circuit.

Tears came to Poppy's eyes as the moon slid from behind a cloud, bathing the ground in a silvery light that made the angels appear to dance together in the darkness of the frozen night.

"Hey," chided Storm, squeezing Poppy's mitten-clad hand, "why so quiet? This is supposed to be fun." At dinner Poppy had confessed to Storm she was feeling depressed. Storm had suggested they sneak out after lights-out and have "a little fun."

Poppy had assumed Storm would be taking her somewhere private to have wild weasel sex.

But instead they'd come out into the backyard to hold hands and make snow angels. Standing hand in hand in the snow with Storm made Poppy feel warm, full of wonder. The area around her heart glowed with a happiness she'd rarely felt since childhood.

When the moon slid behind a stand of pine trees, leaving the yard dark again, Poppy suggested they go back inside. "Maybe have some hot chocolate?" she murmured.

The two women held hands as long as possible, right up to the time they absolutely had to let go to strip off their coats at the back door.

The next evening in group, Poppy started by asking if they might talk about a topic that was on her mind.

"Shoot," said Babe, glad to have someone finally suggest a topic.

"Sex —"

"Count me in," sneered Dylan.

Everyone laughed.

As soon as the room fell quiet, Poppy began again. "I was thinking maybe sometimes sex gets in the way of intimacy. Is that possible?"

Bunny rolled her eyes.

Catching Bunny's eye motion, Babe invited her to respond to Poppy.

"Well," began Bunny, "I rolled my eyes because what Poppy said seems silly. I mean, come on, sex *is* intimacy."

"Is it?" Babe turned the question back to the group.

Wee Gee's hand shot up. "As you guys know, I write romance novels."

"Patriarchal poison!" Betty bellowed.

"And," continued Wee Gee, ignoring Betty, "there's a lot of sex in the stuff I write. Girls love to be sexed up these days. They want their heroes well hung. They want to know he's packing to please."

"Oh please!" protested Betty. "Do we have to listen to this hetero garbage?"

"Yes, you do," said Babe. "Be quiet. Everyone will get a turn. Let Wee Gee finish."

"Well, as I was saying, the hero has to be well hung, but he also has to have a huge heart. I mean, it's the huge heart that snags the girl in the end."

"And what does this have to do with us?" asked Candice, who was somewhat suspicious of the huge heart theory of everlasting love since she made more than three million a year endowing other anatomical features.

Storm raised her hand. "I think I know." She turned to face Poppy. "What is it we really want from sex?" she asked.

"Orgasm?" offered Bunny.

Laughter again.

"Okay, I can go for that," said Storm, "but deep down I think what we all want, at least what I want, is to feel loved. Warm. Safe. Think about it for a moment. It's like the most intimate thing in the world, to invite someone deep inside you. Inside you, for chrissake. That's not like something you want everyone to experience. Is it?"

Silence.

Babe waited a long while before adding a comment. When she did speak, the room was deathly quiet. "I think Poppy brought up a good question. And some of you added items of value. Everyone here will have to find their own answer to this question, but I'd ask you to think about this one idea."

Babe hesitated. The group leaned in, all ears. "Think about the possibility that you may often use sex as a substitute for communication. Maybe you use sex because it's the only way you know to reach out. But maybe there are other ways to be intimate."

"God, I don't get that at all," said Bunny.

Dylan raked hair from her eyes. "Is this, like, some sort of moral thing? Like, I mean, are you telling you us sex is bad? Because, if you are, I'm here to tell you I kinda like it, myself."

"Ditto," said Dirk.

Babe held up a hand. "Just think about it, girls. Think about the possibilities. Think about the idea that maybe there are other ways to be close besides sex. Try and imagine it. Try and practice it just for one day. That's all I'm asking."

27.

Seven Sisters Fur Pie

Nan didn't contribute to the discussion on sex and love. Not because she didn't have an opinion on the topic. In fact, as of the last few days her heart was brimming with questions about both. She'd left message after message with Birge's answering service. In return she'd received only silence.

She and Birge had been together since college. She'd never once doubted Birge's fidelity. Oh sure, once or twice she'd seen the old gal's eye wonder. Lesbians today were a hot lot. More sexually explosive than her and Birge's generation of bang-ridden, guitar-playing, Girl Scout dykes. More than one young Wall Street thing had tried to latch on to Birge as a Sugarbush over the years. But Nan had always been there.

Or had she?

Hell, Birge couldn't leave her now. She and Birge had history. Almost thirty years. To her knowledge they were a content couple, maybe not deliriously happy, but solidly content. They knew each other inside out. Birge had insisted on rehab for Nan; Nan was now willing to admit Birge had been dead on about the rehab thing.

That's why Nan was trying to reach Birge: to let her know she was changing. That she was dedicated to this sobriety thing.

Doing a fearless moral inventory had led Nan to see a lot of ways she'd made Birge's life fairly miserable, especially this last year.

"Answer. Oh please answer," Nan begged the cell phone she had stolen without permission from Babe's desk.

After about a minute, a voice answered. But it wasn't Birge. Someone much younger. Someone with a sleepy, sexy voice. A Lauren Bacall voice.

"Put Birge on," demanded Nan.

Rustling in the background. Maybe covers. Then the sexy-voiced woman was back on the phone, speaking louder. "Who is this?"

"Who is *this*?" demanded Nan. "It's after midnight. Who the fuck are you?"

"Don't talk to me like that." The woman no longer sounded sleepy, she sounded offended.

"Put Birge on."

"I can't. She's not here."

"This is her cell phone?"

"Yes, it is. I'm house sitting. I work for her service. She's gone."

"Gone where?"

"I don't know. I can take a message, though. Wait. Let me find a pencil."

More rustling. Then the woman again. "Okay, your name."

But the line was dead. Nan had already hung up.

Nan fled down the stairs, barely stopping to pull on a jacket and her boots. The jacket wasn't even hers; it was Betty's, several sizes too large, made of native Peruvian wool, horridly itchy. The gloves were the same, wildly prickly. Nan yanked the keys to Babe's Subaru Forester off the pegboard by the front door and ran into the night.

To hell with sobriety. She was an adult. A woman worth millions of dollars. If she damn well craved a gin and tonic nightcap every now and then, she deserved at least that much.

Fuck Birge Hathaway. If that woman was leaving her for some young Wall Street chippie, the least she could do was muster up the courage to say so.

Fuck Birge. Double fuck that old lady.

Nan could find a replacement for Birge easy enough. And by God it wouldn't be another Catholic. She'd had it with sexually screwed-up Christian girls. This time she'd find a nice Jewish girl. A doctor. No, strike that: a surgeon. Manhattan was lousy with lesbian surgeons these days. They all came to her to invest their nest eggs. All she had to do was bat an eyelash. Cross her legs in a suggestive manner. A few cocktails later, she'd be eating Seven Sisters fur pie, big time.

28.

End of the Road Bar and Grill

Nan jammed the key into the Subaru's ignition. The auto roared to life despite the temperature, which the dashboard gauge reported as minus twenty degrees. Putting the car in gear, Nan slid down the driveway backward. Only one direction was plowed at the end of the driveway so Nan steered that way.

There had to be a town somewhere down the road. And every town had at least one bar. If not that, then an all-night Liquor Barn.

The noise from the spinning wheels of the Subaru alerted Wee Gee that something was up. She got up from her laptop, where she was struggling with the prologue to a torrid new novel, and ran to the window. She arrived in time to see the Subaru slide down the road, and to see Nan's curly head at the wheel as she slid past the security light at the bottom of the driveway.

"Not good," Wee Gee murmured. "Not good at all."

Poppy, who'd been proofreading some of Wee Gee's pages, ran to the window. "Nan?" she gasped.

"Afraid so. Our first escapee."

"Nan? But she's always seemed so quiet, so stable compared to the rest of us."

"That," said Wee Gee, "should have been our first clue."

"What should we do?" asked Poppy, biting her lip.

"Follow the girl. She needs our help whether she's sane enough to know it or not."

Poppy had her coat on in a second. The two ran downstairs to the front door. Babe and Lily had apparently already gone to bed for the night. All lights were off.

"Grab those keys," Poppy whispered. She was pointing to a set of keys on a rack near the front door. The keys were emblazoned with a Toyota insignia.

Wee Gee thought about taking her Caddie SUV, which was parked out back, but remembered that she'd given Babe the keys for safe keeping, just in case she felt compelled to make a midnight snack run.

Wee Gee took Poppy's suggestion and grabbed the Toyota keys from the rack. At the far end of the driveway, close to the snowdrifted pole barn, sat Babe's ancient, rusty Toyota Land Cruiser. "Thataway!" cried Wee Gee.

The Toyota choked and sputtered as Poppy twisted the key in the ignition. Both women cheered when the engine turned over. Poppy had to sit up in the seat to see over the dashboard. Wee Gee found a cardboard box in the back seat and stuck it under Poppy's ass when she bounced up to shift gears.

"Thanks, mate. That helps," said the music star.

Poppy, as it turned out, was an excellent stick-shift driver. The road was slick with a skiff of freshly fallen snow, but luckily so much snow had fallen that banks of it hugged the dirt road, making it impossible for them to slide off into the rocky ravines that lined each side of the road. It was like riding in a bobsled.

A feeling Poppy enjoyed tremendously.

Wee Gee less so.

They caught up with Nan the same time they reached the edge of what appeared to be nowhere. A simple crossroads. The only thing open this time of night was a bar, aptly named the End of the Road.

Nan was out of the Subaru and into the bar by the time Poppy and Wee Gee spotted her and veered in to park the Toyota.

The bar was dark when the women entered. A jukebox was blaring out a song about a redneck yacht club.

Nan was sitting at the bar next to the only person in the establishment, a man.

"Worse than I thought," gasped Wee Gee. "Drinking *and* flirting with the enemy. Definitely time for an intervention."

Wee Gee plopped down on the barstool next to Nan, who looked up, her eyes wide with surprise.

"Evenin', ladies," said the man as he tipped his green John Deere hat. "You girls like a drink?"

While Poppy was thinking about that kind offer, Wee Gee offered a heartfelt, "No, thanks. We don't drink. Terrible alcoholics."

"Suit yourselves, ladies." He grinned.

Nan already had a drink. A double gin and tonic with a twist of lime, Wee Gee thought, by the look of the frosted glass.

Wee Gee made a *tsk-tsk* sound.

Nan leaned toward Wee Gee. "Get lost, you old dyke! Leave me alone. I mean it!"

Wee Gee looked around Nan to the man. He was drinking Samuel Adams. "Excuse me, sir, but this woman belongs to me."

Then man stopped mid-sip. "That so?"

"Afraid so."

The man looked at Nan. "That right?"

"No," Nan huffed. "I don't know this woman."

"Honey!" Wee Gee pleaded convincingly. "I want you back! Don't make me grovel." Wee Gee gave Nan an amazingly loud smack on the lips, sucking the partially formed words of rebuke right out of her.

The man lifted his ale. "Okay. Don't want no fights here. I mean, if she's your woman, you had her first. That queer stuff, it's all good and legal up here in the great state of Vermont."

"Thank you, sir," said Wee Gee, who, rising, hoisted Nan, who was much smaller, off the barstool and toward the door. "Be quiet, you skinny little white girl!" she hissed in Nan's ear, "or this time I'll suck the life right out of you."

Nan did not resist, mostly because she was stunned, but also because she'd never in her life been French kissed with so much force. She was certain one of her upper crowns had come loose.

As soon as they were outside, all seated in the Subaru, Wee Gee lit into Nan. "That was a foolish thing you just did, sister."

"Don't care." Nan pouted.

"I think you do."

"Well, you'd be wrong."

Poppy broke in. "This is about your girl, isn't it?"

Nan burst into tears.

Wee Gee held her. "Now, honey, it'll be all right. Family gets to come at the end of the week. You'll see your girl then."

"I won't!" wailed Nan. "She won't even take my calls. She's left me. I know it."

"You know no such thing," scolded Wee Gee. "She's probably just taking a breather. Living with an alcoholic can be pretty crazy. Maybe she needed time to think. Get her head straight. Your getting sober would be a big change for her, for both of you."

Nan dried her tears on the back of one of Betty's horribly itchy mittens. "You think?"

"I know. Trust me, I've been through this sobriety thing a few times. Give your girl time. And stop jumping to conclusions. You don't know what she's thinking until she tells you."

Nan sniffled. "I suppose not."

"Damn right. Now let's go home. Tuck you into bed before Babe charges us all with grand theft auto."

Poppy jumped out of the Subaru and slid in the snow toward the Toyota. She wheeled it cautiously up beside the Subaru. As soon as Wee Gee gave Poppy an acknowledging wave, the two vehicles headed out of the parking lot back up the steep mountain road to rehab.

Safely belted into the passenger seat of the Subaru, Nan finished drying her tears as the blinking bar sign faded into the snowy distance. She really had wanted that drink. Badly. Somehow, over the years, she'd come to rely on alcohol to numb her feelings. Keep her sane.

"I am an alcoholic," she mumbled to herself as the Subaru chugged up the hill.

And for the first time in her life she believed it.

29.

Beyond Ecstasy

The next morning Babe slapped a new message on her white board. "It is forbidden to use my car." Then, under that: "Especially in the middle of the night." Under that: "Especially to go out and get drunk."

"Hell!" said Dylan, delighted with the news. "Who had the balls to do that?"

"Doesn't matter who did it," barked Babe. "My car's back, no worse for the wear. And for the record, the guy who runs the End of the Road bar and grill is a very dear friend of ours. We buy firewood from him. He was kind enough to call this morning and report an escapee sighting. He also told me no alcohol was consumed. So I'm letting this one ride, ladies. But trust me, if any of you ever do anything like that again, you will be given your walking papers. You want to drink, go right ahead. But don't do it under my nose while you're making me listen to you whine about the pain of getting sober."

The room grew still. Babe let it stay that way for several moments before moving on to the next topic: family weekend. Babe explained that at the end of the week everyone was expected to invite their families to visit, to actually join the therapy group for the weekend.

A good many groans went up.

"Why?" asked Candice. "Why on earth would we want to do that?"

"Because it's part of your treatment. You girls got messed up somewhere along the way. For most of you it started with your parents. Something went wrong that taught you the way to deal with life was to numb yourself with alcohol or drugs or sex or food. It's important you face those familial demons."

Candice raised her hand. "What if you have no family?"

"That condition doesn't apply to you, Dr. Antwerp. The medical association provided contacts for your next of kin. Your parents have been invited. And for the record they are coming."

Candice turned as white as Frosty the Snowman. "You can't do that," she croaked.

"Already did." Babe was in no mood for an argument. She was still pissed about her stolen car. "Besides," she continued, "I want to see how each of you functions around your loved ones. People can talk about their spouses and parents until the cows come in, but nothing paints a clearer picture than having everyone in the same room, yelling at each other."

Nan raised her hand. "Have you contacted my partner, Birge Hathaway?"

"Yes, she's coming. Also," Babe continued, "each of you will be expected to admit the exact nature of the wrongs you have committed toward your loved ones in the throes of your addiction. Now, given the depth and severity of some of your addictions, this last step could well take the rest of eternity. Start working on your lists now. And try to keep it brief."

Babe handed printed sheets to each woman and asked them to pair up to begin this new exercise. The sheet said: "List below the exact ways your addiction has harmed those you love. P.S. Feel free to ask for extra sheets."

An hour later Dylan was pacing Bunny's room, frantic. She kept running her hand through her hair and her hair kept flopping back into her eyes. "Shit — man, this is bad."

Bunny, who was sitting on her bed painting her toenails lemon yellow, looked up at Dylan. "You're actually sweating."

Dylan slapped a hand to her neck. "Big deal."

"Okay, so, like, what's up with you? It's just a silly exercise. No sweat."

Dylan plopped down on the bed. "I don't care about the exercise."

"What?"

"Family weekend. Freaking family weekend."

"Like you've never talked to your family before?"

"You don't understand."

"Try me."

Dylan, who was reclining next to Bunny, slapped her hands across her cheeks. "You really don't understand."

"Ah, duh, not unless you explain it to me. What? Is your family Mormon? Republicans? A bunch of serial killers?"

"No."

"Well, what?" yelled Bunny. "Just tell me."

Dylan sat up. "I have a husband."

"You're joking?"

Dylan's face tightened.

"Oh my God, you're telling the truth. You? Ms. Dykey Dyke? A husband? How in hell did that happen?"

"Ecstasy," Dylan groaned. "Last year. I tried this super-loaded stuff."

"And you didn't notice your new girlfriend had a dick?"

"I was stoned."

"I'd say so."

"We were in Las Vegas. When I woke up there was this guy in bed with me and this marriage certificate."

"Oh yucky-poo." Bunny bent and blew on her toes. "You woke up in bed with a guy? Hey, that might be that bottoming-out thing Babe keeps harping about."

"Ya *think?*"

Bunny grabbed the polish and began painting another coat on her toes. "What makes you think this guy will show up for family weekend?"

"Babe told me he's coming. His name is on the court papers as my legal next of kin. My parents are dead. I had to list someone, or the judge wouldn't grant me rehab instead of jail."

"He was okay with that?"

"Yeah, turns out he's in love with me."

"Really?"

"What?" complained Dylan. "Is that so hard to imagine?"

"Yeah, as a matter of fact, it is. I mean, it's not like you're all soft and lovable. You're kinda mean. Almost like a guy."

Dylan looked hurt. "Really?"

"Yes, really."

"Well, Roger thinks I'm sweet."

"Well, Roger can't be too smart. He's in love with, like, the world's biggest homo lezzy from hell. He knows you're gay. Right?"

"That doesn't matter to him. He's an artist. He loves my soul."

Bunny rolled her eyes.

"Don't roll your eyes about my husband like that."

"Fine," sighed Bunny. "Let's talk about something else, okay? We're supposed to start that stupid list. Get yours."

Dylan retrieved the crumpled list from her jeans jacket pocket.

"You write anything on your list yet?"

"No," sniped Dylan. "I think it's stupid. Taking drugs is my business. *My* business. It never hurt anyone."

"What about Roger? You got messed up. You slept with him. And now he's in love with you. That's tragic, if you ask me."

"God, I never thought of that."

"Of course not, because you're a drug addict. All you ever think about is yourself."

30.

Liar, Liar

Betty stared at a blank sheet of paper. She stabbed the sheet several times with the point of her pen before casting the paper aside. "I don't think my pot use has hurt anyone," she huffed toward Dirk. "I just use the stuff to relax. Makes me more pleasant. Helps everyone. Marijuana is only illegal because the Republicans don't own the pot fields of Mexico or Afghanistan. If the Bush family owned pot fields, the stuff would be sold at the candy counter at Walmart."

Dirk shrugged. "Why you here, then?"

Betty ground her teeth. "Never you mind. What do you have listed on *your* paper?"

Without waiting for a response, Betty grabbed Dirk's paper, which Dirk had rolled into a tube and been using like a paper kazoo to hum out the theme song to *The L Word* while waiting for Betty to finish her side of the assignment.

Betty was surprised to find Dirk's sheet neatly filled in.

Dirk spoke. "Well, first off, there's my mom, Sheila. My using 'roids has hurt her the most, I think."

"How?"

"Mostly because she trusted me. I told her we'd be okay, me and Thumper. I promised her I could handle the Olympic pressure. She never would have let us start using the 'roids. I really let her down."

"Touching," said Betty.

Dirk ran a hand across her hair. "Yeah … it kinda is." Dirk paced the room, stopping by the window. Below, in the side yard, she could see her sister, Thumper, practicing on her snowboard. "My sister. I really hurt her. I told her it was okay. I knew it wasn't. She begged me to stop a long time ago but I kept her going."

"Why?"

Dirk turned toward Betty, arms tight against her chest. She worked her jaw silently.

"Why?" Betty repeated.

Dirk rubbed her hands across her face. "I wanted to win. I needed to win."

"That simple?"

"Yeah, I'm not proud of it, but it's that simple."

"You realize you turned yourself and your sister into freaks."

"Don't see it that way."

"No?"

"No."

"Okay, so you know you both look like Arnold Schwarzenegger?"

"Give me a break." Dirk balled up her sheet of paper and tossed it over her shoulder into the trash can. "I'm a lot better-looking than him."

"But you are a freak."

"I dunno." Dirk stopped to study her profile in the mirror. Her jeans hung low, exposing the hollows of her hips. "I kinda like the way I look," she announced as she bent and peeled off her T-shirt in one swift jerk. She turned to face Betty, the afternoon sun glinting off her finely muscled chest. Her jeans rode low, exposing the top white band of tighty-whiteys, not some girly version but the real thing with a slit fly and a built-in double-reinforced pouch, known in the garment trade as "the trophy shelf."

Betty swallowed hard. "You look like a boy."

"Feel like a boy," Dirk sniffled. "Always have."

Betty was starting to feel uncomfortable now. "Put your clothes on, okay?"

"Why?" Dirk grinned. "You getting hot? Hey, how about I take my pants off?" She slid one hand along her zipper, peeling back just enough cloth to reveal …

"That's enough!" cried Betty. She covered her eyes with her hands. "I don't want to see it."

"See what?"

"It!" she shrieked. "Whatever you keep in your pants."

"Are you afraid of me?" Dirk advanced.

"Don't be silly."

"I'm not. Answer my question."

"I think it's wrong."

"What's wrong?"

"This transsexual stuff."

"Why?"

"You're a woman."

"Never said I wasn't. But who says a woman can only look one way? I mean, look at you. A lot of people would say you don't look like a woman."

Betty puffed up. "What do I look like?"

Dirk stepped back. "A dyke."

"A dyke is a woman."

Dirk shook her head. "Not according to a lot of people."

Betty raised one hand. "Stop right there. That's enough personal stuff. Do what you like. What do I care?"

"Okay," said Dirk with a shrug. "What do you want to talk about?"

"This assignment. This stupid thing about listing how our addiction has harmed the people we love."

"Okay. You read my sheet. My mom is coming this weekend. I intend to apologize to her, and to Thumper. Who are you apologizing to? You got a wife, right?"

"A partner, yes. Alice."

"Alice sent you here?"

Betty puffed up. "Alice and I reached a consensus. We decided it would be good if I took a little break from the pot. I came here to show her I am *not* an addict."

Dirk bent and sniffed Betty's wild tumble of hair. "You'd be lying, then," she whispered hoarsely into Betty's ear.

"I beg your pardon." Betty shoved Dirk aside.

"You haven't stopped smoking pot. You reek of the stuff."

Betty ruffled her hair. "Just sweating out the old stuff."

Dirk plopped down in a rocking chair. "That's just it. You hit the old nail on the head. The thing I hate the most about being an addict."

"What? What are you jabbering about now, freak-girl?"

"The lying. I hate the lying I've done to everyone these last few years. My mom. Thumper. My teammates. The Olympic Committee. Everyone. That's why I came here. To show them they can trust me again."

Dirk strolled out of the room, leaving Betty alone in the mounting darkness, the anemic winter sunlight retreating fast now. The yard outside the farmhouse was quiet, marred with the long flat swatches Dirk's twin had cut across the slopes that bled downward onto a frozen pasture.

Betty picked up her unmarked sheet of paper. She double clicked the cartridge on her pen and began to write furiously: "Dear Alice: My addiction to pot has hurt us. Mostly it has hurt you." Just as abruptly Betty stopped writing. She wadded the paper and threw it against the door just as Storm popped in.

"Hey!" cried Storm. "That meant for me?"

"Sorry," mumbled Betty, who was still irked by Dirk's unwelcome insight into her nature.

"Babe has called an emergency meeting," announced Storm. "Downstairs. Pronto."

31.

We Are Family

Babe stood in the center of the group and chugged a long drink from her bottle of vitamin water. Then another chug. Everyone was sitting on the edge of their cushions, eager to learn why Babe had called an emergency meeting. Each member of the group was wondering which one of them had fucked up.

Poppy was biting her fingernails, hoping it wasn't her.

Dylan slumped down, wishing she didn't have a baggie of E stuffed in the watch pocket of her jeans.

Betty was glad she'd stuffed her stash in the roll band on her oversized cotton granny panties rather than leave it in her room where any nosy person might easily find it. She was no fool. This place was filthy with addicts. No way she'd trust these women to keep their paws off her stash.

Babe cleared her throat.

The silence intensified.

"I suppose you're all wondering why I called this late-night meeting?"

Murmurs.

Bunny spoke up. It was lights-out time and she'd already slathered her face with pink nighttime rejuvenator cream. Her lips danced inside a tight pink mask. "I need my beauty sleep," she whined. "Can we get this over with? Pleeease!"

Babe strolled the interior of the circle. "As you all know, tomorrow is the day your family members will be arriving."

"Yeah," said Dylan with a smirk. "Thanks bunches for that."

Babe continued. "There are a few ground rules. First, you will each have a two-hour private session with your family members. Only you, your family, and myself will be present for these meetings."

"Jolly!" piped Poppy.

"Everyone *must* attend their family meeting," continued Babe. She stopped and glared at Dylan. "And I do mean *everyone*. If any of you go AWOL, you will be tossed from the program instantly. No second chances. No do-overs. And remember, for some of you this means I will have to inform the court of my professional decision to terminate treatment. Understood?" Babe stopped in front of Candice.

"Of course I understand," said Candice crisply.

"Good."

"Now, before you go to bed tonight, are there any questions?"

No one said anything for the longest time. Storm spoke at last. Her voice was uncharacteristically quiet. "What if you don't have family?"

"In your case," said Babe, "your agent will be coming."

"Why her?" moaned Storm.

"She's paying for your stay. Claims it's part of your contract. If you don't test sober, Storm, you won't be allowed to return to work. Your agent has a huge stake in seeing you sober."

"I realize that!" wailed Storm, "but you said family. She's *not* family. What am I supposed to work out in therapy with her?"

"Same as with family. You'll start by apologizing for all the ways your addiction has affected her life. You'll commit to getting sober and staying sober. Most of all you'll have to convince her why on earth she should trust you to get straight and stay that way."

"Yucka poodle!" cried Bunny. "Does that mean I have to do all that with Daddy?" Her face mask tightened.

"Yes," said Babe. "You'll have to do the same with your father."

"But Daddy doesn't care!" pouted Bunny.

"He must or he wouldn't have sent you here."

"Don't be naive," said Bunny as she tucked a stray lock of blonde hair into her blue satin night turban. "Daddy's a politician. He sent me here because rehab is in. Chic. Americans love fucked-up rich people in rehab. His election team did a poll. The poll results said it would make him look more approachable, more human, if they showed he had a family member who struggled with addiction."

"No shit?" whistled Dylan. "You're here merely as a political ploy?"

"What?" frowned Bunny, her face mask cracking. "You thought I had a real problem? You're joking, right?"

Babe raised her hand. "Bunny, I know you're scared. Everyone is scared."

"I'm not scared!" whined Bunny.

"Are too," said Dylan.

"Not!"

"Enough!" cried Babe. "Those are the ground rules. Everyone must participate in family weekend. It will be your chance to talk to your family members and try to make things right with them. And girls …" Every set of eyes were tacked to Babe's lips. "Try like hell not to fuck this up, okay?"

32.

The Petersons' Cat

Unable to sleep, Nan was up at dawn Saturday morning. She went straight to the tiny corner desk, turned on a desk lamp, and began to write furiously.

Dylan sat up in the twin bed across the way from Nan and rubbed her eyes. "What's up?" she mumbled.

"Making notes," said Nan.

"Notes? What? Are you kidding me? We have a test?" Dylan swept a mop of hair from her eyes. She stretched out on top of the down comforter but didn't attempt to get out of bed. She wasn't wearing pajamas, just the same white ribbed wife-beater and torn black jeans she'd had on for days now. "Got any fags?" she asked Nan.

Nan glanced up. "Yes, I do. But you can't smoke in here. You know that." Nan had watched as the dark circles under Dylan's eyes had grown deeper each day. In the dim light of morning, she looked like a skinny football player with a bad haircut, and black war paint smudged under her eyes. "Kid, I hate to tell you this, but you look like hell."

"Fuck off! You're not my mother."

"Thank God for that," muttered Nan.

Dylan swung out of bed. "Can I have a cigarette, Mommy? Pretty please? I promise I'll take it outside to smoke."

"Help yourself, girlfriend." Nan tossed Dylan an unopened pack of Dunhills from the pocket of her robe.

Dylan caught the pack midair. "Pay later. Okay?"

Nan stopped writing. "No money. All I want is for you to listen to this."

"Huh?" Dylan crossed the room to stand by Nan and squint at the paper she'd been writing on.

"It's my apology. To my partner, Birge. I want to get it right. Listen to it for me?"

"Sure," said Dylan as she plopped her ass down on the edge of the desk where Nan was working. "I'm awake. Go ahead and yak at me."

Nan cleared her throat twice before beginning. "My dearest, darling life partner, Birge —"

Dylan held up a hand. "Whoa!"

"What?" asked Nan. "What's wrong with that?"

"Kinda precious, don't you think?"

Nan bit a cheek. "You think it should sound more casual?"

"How long you been with this chick?"

"About thirty years."

"Yeah, I'm thinking more casual would probably be good." Dylan rolled her eyes. "I mean, that thing sounds like your will." Unable to light a cigarette, her lungs aching, Dylan plucked up a pencil and chewed the eraser tip. "Continue."

"Okay. Birge, darling?"

"Better." Dylan twirled the pencil in the air like a baton.

"Birge, darling. I am an alcoholic. You know that, though. You've probably known that for quite some time and had no way to tell me. Perhaps you were afraid to tell me. Maybe that thing I did to the Petersons' cat last Christmas worried you —"

"What the hell did you do to the Petersons' cat?"

"Never you mind. I was drunk."

"Do you kill that cat?"

"Worse."

"Torture?" croaked Dylan. "You, Ms. Clean and Squeaky of Wall Street?"

Nan narrowed her eyes. "I've done worse than kill a cat in my time."

"You hide it well."

"Everyone on Wall Street does the same. We're just a bunch of well-spoken thugs with great wardrobes. Never give your money to a professional broker or financial planner to handle. Especially if they are Ivy League educated."

"No worries there." Dylan smirked.

"Yes, I imagine what money you have you snort."

"That was mean."

"Sorry, but you started the insults, not me."

Dylan raked a hand through her hair. "I just wanted to know about the Petersons' damned cat."

"Forget about it." Nan continued reading aloud. "I am grateful you left me in this place. I am working at getting sober. And you know how hard I work. I will do this for me. For us. I love you, Birge. Please give me the chance to demonstrate this to you once again."

"Sounds decent."

"Not too dry?"

"For me, yes, but your girl, she's button-down, yes?"

"If by button-down you mean well-educated and success-ful, yes."

"She'll lap up that sorry shit, then."

Nan eyed Dylan as she tossed the pencil around as if it were a hot potato. "Have you ever had a relationship?"

"I have them all the time."

"Longer than a week?"

"Why are you picking on me?" Dylan looked hurt. "I'm, like, barely thirty. It's different these days, being a dyke. You old farts fondled each other's nipple once, then boom, you were mated for life!"

Nan leaned back in her chair. "Some of us old farts don't just fondle. We fuck. You think your generation invented fucking?"

Dylan found herself with no comeback.

Nan broke the awkward silence. "You want me to listen to your apology letter?"

"I'm not apologizing."

"Who's your family? Parents?"

"Dead and rotten. I got no one."

"You have to have someone. We all do. Girlfriend? Grandmother?"

Dylan sprang up and stalked across the room. "Trust me. It's like the Petersons' cat," she tossed over her shoulder on the way to the toilet. "You don't even want to know."

33.

Candy Unwrapped

Candice Antwerp stood at the window in her room and peered cautiously out the slit between the sheer white curtains. Daybreak had barely begun to spread across the frosty pasture yet the doctor had been staring out the window in the same position for over an hour. Her face seemed transfixed. Frozen.

"You've been standing there since, like, yesterday," complained Bunny, who was sitting at the vanity combing out her hair. "You in a trance, or what?"

Candice turned to face Bunny.

"God, you look awful!" squealed Bunny. She tossed the surgeon a tiny blue tube of French under-eye lightener.

Catching the tube, Candice squinted as she read the label. She made a face as she tossed the tube onto the bed. "This stuff is a temporary fix. You ought to come to my clinic. I could tighten your eyes. You'd look thirty again," promised the surgeon as she crossed the room to stand behind Bunny.

Bunny was in reality a very attractive woman. Amazing bone structure. She just needed everything yanked up a bit. A little nip. A lot of tuck. Clients like Bunny made Candice look good because no matter what operation the surgeon performed, nature had given her an almost perfect canvas.

Virtually no way she could mess it up. Even stoned out of her head on downers, Dr. Antwerp couldn't make a woman like Bunny look anything but breathtakingly beautiful.

Bunny turned to face Candice. "Why are you staring out that window?" she asked again as she slapped cream onto her cheeks, then wiped it off with an obscene amount of facial tissue.

Candice shrugged. "Nervous, I guess."

"Nervous? You? About what?"

Candice hesitated, then, remembering Poppy's advice that she open up more, decided to go ahead and take Bunny into her confidence. "My parents."

"They're coming?"

"Babe said they were."

"My dad's coming, too. No biggy." Bunny shrugged as she stepped into a silk-and-taffeta designer skirt. "I know what he'll say. It's all scripted. He hasn't said a word in decades that the spin doctors didn't write for him."

Leaning into the mirror, Bunny puckered as she applied lipstick. "He'll say his thing and I'll say mine. I'll promise never to drink or take drugs again. Yadda, yadda, yadda. Done deal." She snapped shut her lipstick tube and dropped it into her clutch.

Candice eyed Bunny. "You're not going to drink or do drugs again?"

"God no!" Bunny snorted.

"Why lie?"

"Because that is what he wants to hear. If I lie, I'll get to go home and everyone will be nice to me."

"Until you end up back here again."

"Whoa, what's this? I thought we were friends. Me and you."

"We are, but Bunny, I have to be honest with you: I think you have a problem with drugs. Sex, too."

"Me? Get real!"

"I am being real. Look, you're sleeping with Dylan, right?"

Bunny raised a hand defensively. "Not sleeping. Fucking."

"Okay, fucking. And when you sleep with her, are you ever sober?"

Bunny sighed, loudly. "Does it matter? I mean, honestly, does it *really* matter? Have we all turned into born-again Republicans or what?"

Candice wasn't sure she had an answer for that. She was surprised in fact that she seemed to care. It was no business of hers, really, what Bunny did or did not do. Candice sat in a chair by the window. She tried to relax, but her spine pulled her upright. Her arms locked across her chest. "I don't know."

"You don't know?"

"That's right."

Their conversation was interrupted by the sound of a car turning into the driveway. Ice cracked under the tires as the auto rolled toward the farmhouse. Leaning toward the window, Candice parted the curtain cautiously with the side of her hand. She held her breath until she saw the car was an antique silver-blue Mercedes: definitely not her parents.

A young man with flowing blond hair stepped out of the car. He was wearing a maroon velvet shirt, open to his navel, and black leather pants. He had the long gangling gait of a rock star. An ankle-length white fur coat gave him the odd appearance of a blond polar bear. A guitar hung casually upside down on his left shoulder, the strap studded with twinkling gemstones. He wore reflective aviator sunglasses, which he flipped up as he studied the sign above the front door.

"Who's that?" whispered Candice. "Guy in an expensive fur coat. Must be lost."

Bunny ran to the window. "My God, I bet that's Roger!" she gasped.

"Roger?"

"Dylan's husband."

"Husband? Hello!" Candice slid a hand to her throat. "Husband? Ms. Big Pink Pussy has a husband? You're kidding. Right?"

"I'd never joke about something torrid like that," assured Bunny, her face dour.

"I though Dylan was Ms. Super Dyke. All that in-your-face talk about her *Big Pink Pussy* and all."

"Oh, she's gay. But she's a terrible addict. She married him" — Bunny jerked a thumb toward the window — "while on a bender in Vegas."

Candice scrutinized the lean musician as he stumbled up the front steps, his guitar throwing him off balance. "Dylan married *that* … and she thinks drugs are not causing serious problems in her life?"

"Believe you me, I pointed that out to her. But you know how these addicts are."

Another car chugged up the hill, black smoke bellowing from its tailpipe. The car, an old Buick, slid to a stop beside Roger's Mercedes. The car, white with black trim, circa 1977, boasted an undercarriage riddled like rusty Swiss cheese. Its license plate read, "Indiana." Bumper stickers proclaimed, "Pro Life. God is My Co-Pilot. Hell Is Real: Prepare."

A thin, bald man wearing a cheap three-piece suit fell out of the driver's side. It took him several seconds to hoist himself up off the snow-trodden ground by grabbing at car door. By the time he was up, a woman had emerged from the passenger side and was trying to assist.

The woman had long, gray hair and thick, silver-rimmed, cat-eye glasses of the type that went out of style in the '60s. She was rail thin. A tattered black woolen coat hung on her frail frame. She had a firm grip on what appeared to be her husband. Despite her smaller size and frail appearance, she was clearly the stronger of the two.

"Hello!" squealed Bunny. "Get a load of Mom and Pop Bible Belt. These two are definitely lost." Bunny turned to see what Candice thought of the weird arrivals, but the good doctor had fled.

34.

Kinky Kincaid

Storm Waters hung at the edge of the living room, one combat boot tucked flat against the wall, which, from a distance, she appeared to be holding up. She fiddled nervously with the name tag on her scoop-neck T-shirt as people poured into the farmhouse. Babe was strolling around the lobby, handing out name tags and rule books and printed schedules. She swarmed each newcomer like a mother hen.

Storm felt uneasy about this family weekend thing. Sure, her biological family was long gone, but in their place Babe was excepting her to work things out with her agent, Hunter Kincaid. Storm didn't relish the thought of spending time with Hunter Kincaid (aka Kinky Kincaid) right now.

Rehab had been Hunter's idea, suggested after Storm had flunked the network's drug test three times running after each tour of duty in Baghdad. Yet Storm had not resisted rehab. As much as she loved her job, the idea of getting away from gunfire and guts for a while had, for the first time in Storm's life, seemed appealing, at least momentarily.

Her last tour, where she'd witnessed a school bus full of children blown in half for no good reason, had shaken her to the core. She wasn't sure she could return to a battlefield again.

A thought she'd been keeping to herself, but which Babe was pushing her to discuss outright with her agent.

Storm was sure now that she had a drug problem. What scared her was she wasn't sure she could kick it. Even now, two weeks away from the gunfire, she wasn't sleeping. Mostly she stayed up all night and read. And paced. Or ran the treadmill for miles. She'd thought about having sex with Poppy — more than once, truth be told — but that, too, seemed wrong.

She could talk to Poppy. Really talk to her. That had never happened to Storm before, at least not since grade school. Poppy was her friend. A true confidante. The only one other than Babe who knew how scared Storm was deep down.

Super-scary stuff.

Storm was deep in thought about Poppy when a warm kiss slid across her cheek.

"Hi there, stranger," said a sexy voice.

Storm looked up into scintillating turquoise eyes that could belong to only one woman: Hunter Kincaid. Hunter had a name tag stuck sideways on her cowl-neck cashmere sweater. The expensive sweater showcased a pair of petite bosoms that Storm had enjoyed on more than one occasion. (Hunter Kincaid was not known on the agent circuit as "Kinky" for no reason. She'd earned that moniker, with relish. Not just with Storm, but with her entire stable of high-powered lezzy celebs.)

Storm reluctantly returned the kiss to Hunter's smooth cheek.

Unsatisfied with the polite peck, Hunter leaned in until the two women landed in a lip lock. Tongues tangled.

"Mmm," hummed the agent. "You taste good."

Storm pulled away. She shook her head, upset with the liberties her agent had taken. "Why did you do that?" she spat out.

"Mmm, I seem to recall you like *that*."

"I *used* to like *that*."

Hunter looked puzzled. She tossed back her long ebony hair. "Used to? Are you straight now, or what? I thought this place was for rehab, not sexual reconditioning."

"Don't bait me, Hunter," warned Storm.

"Grumpy, aren't we?"

"This place isn't exactly fun."

Hunter cast an eye about the room. "Yes, I can see. Sorry, honey, but the execs wanted you clean and sober. What was I to do?" She shrugged.

The conversation was interrupted by Poppy, who'd suddenly popped up between them. "Hello, love. Introduce us?"

Hunter turned all smiles and congeniality. "My God, you're Poppy! Of Poppy and the Pop Tarts. That British girl band. Right?"

"Spot on. Last I checked, yes, that would be me. And you would be …" Poppy stood on tiptoe trying to read the sideways name tag. "Hummer?" she asked.

"Hunter. Hunter Kincaid." The agent offered her hand to Poppy.

"My agent," growled Storm. "She signed me in. I need her permission to get out."

Hunter rolled her eyes. "Ignore her," she advised Poppy. "I put her here for her own good. The little darling needed a little R&R."

"My own good!" wailed Storm. "What about your good? Don't think I don't know the execs offered you an extra twenty percent if you return me sober."

Hunter grunted. "Extra work. Extra pay. You *can* be a handful, dear."

Storm was about to protest when Lily rang the bell calling the room to attention. The room was so crowded no one could move. Lily waited until the noise settled before speaking.

"Welcome, everyone. You should all have picked up a schedule when you selected your name tags. We'll begin by taking one group of you aside, for private therapy. You others are free to wonder around the farmhouse. Catch up with each other. You'll be called when your time comes. That room in the corner" — Lily pointed to Babe's office — "is where you'll convene for private family sessions. Check the schedule to see your appointed time. And please, everyone, be on time!"

Hunter checked her yellow schedule sheet. "Looks like we're up first, darling." She beamed at Storm as she grabbed the newscaster's hand and tugged her across the crowded room toward the promise of a more private space.

As Storm bounced through the sea of people, she caught sight of Poppy fading into a corner. Poppy, she thought, looked sad. An elderly woman sat in the corner. The woman wore a tall green hat which reminded Storm of something the Queen of England might wear.

Poppy's mother, no doubt. She looked quite the battle-ax.

"Good luck!" Poppy mouthed across the room to Storm as the pop star slid uncomfortably onto the settee beside her mother.

Storm was about to return the wish when Hunter grabbed her by the waist and shoved her into the therapy room.

Babe wasn't in the room yet, a fact that didn't seem to bother Hunter. She lit into Storm as soon as the door was shut. "You're sleeping with that English slut puppy!" raged Hunter. "How could you?"

Storm crossed her arms. *Oh boy, here it is. Dyke drama.* She hadn't missed this part of the real world at all. "I am not," declared Storm.

"Fuck it, don't lie to me. Of course you are. I can see it in your eyes. The way you two look googoo-eyed at each other."

"We're just friends."

"Friends? Is that what they're calling it nowadays? Is that bitch even legal?"

"She's in her twenties."

"She looks like a twig with lips. Good lord, if you're going to cheat on me, you could do better. Much better. Go fuck Rosie or something. At least that woman has an ass on her."

Storm puffed up. "Don't accuse me of cheating. You and I are *not* an item."

"We're not?"

"No, we are *not*. We slept together a couple of times. Don't go all lesbo on me and send out the wedding invitations. Besides, that was months ago. And, in my defense, I was stoned. Fucko on pain meds. Meds which *you* gave me, by the way. Meds which you have always given me in an effort to keep me upright and working so you can keep collecting commission checks."

Hunter rolled her eyes as she threw herself onto the sofa. "You were stoned. How convenient. Is that what they teach you in here? If you do it when you're stoned, it doesn't count?"

Babe quietly entered the room. "Actually it kinda doesn't."

Hunter shot dagger eyes at Babe. "Who are you?"

"Therapist. Mind if I come in? Sounds like you two could use a referee."

Hunter shrugged. "Suit yourself. So, since I'm paying for this rehab thing, how is our girl wonder doing? She clean?" Suddenly Hunter was all business. All agent. Clear eyed and hard jawed.

Babe raised her eyebrows. "You two have a personal relationship?"

"Had!" shouted Storm.

"Because if you have a personal relationship, this seriously changes the nature of what we'll discuss in here today."

"Save your breath," hissed Hunter. She sat stiffly erect on the couch, her legs crossed at the ankles. "This will be strictly professional."

<h1 style="text-align:center">35.</h1>

All Hail the Queen

Poppy shifted uncomfortably on the settee. Her mother hadn't exchanged a dozen words with her since arriving. She turned to face her mother, her throat dry, her heart racing. "That's quite a nice hat, Mum."

"Yes, it rather is." Dame Diane, Poppy's mother, folded her leather gloves into a neat square and pocketed them in her purse. "This place seems quite nice," she offered as she straightened her hat and studied the high tin-clad ceilings.

"It is."

"The other girls Yanks?"

"Except me."

Poppy clasped her hands in her lap. She was finding it difficult to focus on her mother. It was difficult enough to admit to her mother that she'd been right in locking her up in rehab. Yes, that was going to be hard to admit. But what gnawed at Poppy more at the moment was an even sharper pain.

That woman: the one Storm claimed was her agent. Poppy had arrived in the living room just in time to see Hunter tonsil-probe Storm. And Hunter was a looker. Babelicious, to say the least. Tall and willowy with petite pert bosoms and a nice pert bum. Long dark hair that flowed down her perfectly arched back like a river of silk. Worse still, she'd seemed oddly comfortable sucking on Storm's face.

Storm had never mentioned a steady girl. Then again, Poppy had never asked …

Dame Zigfield took her daughter's hand, drawing her out of her obsessive wondering about Hunter Kincaid. "I didn't want this for you," Dame Zigfield said, her voice soft. "I didn't know what else to do. I just didn't know."

Poppy sighed as she squeezed her mother's warm, soft hand. "I know, Mum."

"You forgive me?"

"Forgive you!" Poppy squealed. "Mum, you did me a bloody favor. Forgive you? I ought to give you a royal medal."

"What? You're not mad?" The dame's eyes widened.

"I was mad. Steaming like a pot. But this place has me thinking. I need to open my heart to the world again. You were dead right. You saw it. The drugs were starting to get the best of me."

"Oh, honey, what I saw was that I was losing you. You used to be so sweet. My little Prudence." The dame proffered a hug.

"Mum, please," begged Poppy, whose face reddened at the mention of her true legal name. "Don't use that name out loud."

"But honey, it's your name. I gave it to you when you were born. It's your grandmum's name, and her mum before her."

"Mum, please," Poppy pleaded. "I don't want the tabloids, or these women, to know that."

Her mother sighed deeply. "I suppose you don't want them to know you're truly a kind, sweet girl, either."

Poppy fingered a broken rosary that hung from her neck. "Doesn't go with the image," she muttered. "I need to keep up my image."

Dame Diane straightened. "Need that image be so sexually filthy?"

"Afraid so, Mum. That's what sells these days."

"I see."

Poppy struggled to find some way to reach her mother. She knew her mother loved her. And she loved her in turn. But they had such problems communicating. Everything about Poppy seemed to repel her mother. Poppy didn't know anymore how to be herself and still be her mother's daughter. Her mother disapproved of everything: her clothes, her lyrics, her concerts - most of all her lesbianism. Every conversation in the last year had ended with Poppy screaming, her mother snapping shut door after door, both physically and mentally. Drugs, for Poppy, had become large earmuffs. The more she took, the less she heard her mother's silent screams of disapproval. If Poppy hoped to stay sober and regain her life, she realized she needed to find a way to communicate with her mother. They didn't have to be huggy-huggy-kissy-face, but they had to call a truce.

Poppy studied her mother. "Want to take a walk?"

"Oh dear, I suppose we could. I'd need rubbers, though." She stuck out her feet, which were clad in sturdy seasonable low-heeled shoes. "It seems mucky out there."

"I have just the thing," Poppy assured her mother as she led her to the kitchen.

Dame Diane sat on the kitchen bench by the door patiently waiting as her daughter switched her old-lady shoes for snow boots, then laced those into a pair of snowshoes.

"My!" exclaimed the dame as she admired her huge feet. "Never walked about in anything quite like this before."

"Trust me, Mum. I'll show you how."

After putting on her own snowshoes, Poppy helped her mother clang across the wooden floor of the kitchen toward the back door. Holding hands, they jumped into the snow together.

"Oh my!" called her mother who struggled to stay erect. "These Yanks do know how to have fun."

36.

Mama McGraw

Dirk and Thumper slouched on the couch in the therapy room. Their mother, Sheila McGraw, sat sandwiched between them. The trio hadn't said a word since entering the room. Babe, for her part, was letting them bask in a soup of their own awkward silence.

Sheila looked uncomfortable. She, unlike her daughters, was not a tall woman. In fact, she wasn't even five feet tall with her snow boots on. She did, however, boast a fair complexion and a Germanic jaw, features that echoed in her athletic daughters. Her cropped strawberry-blonde hair had begun to gray at the temples. She wore what appeared to be a new pair of men's blue jeans, cuffed at the bottom. Her jeans were complemented by a black knit turtleneck sweater, also from the men's department. Her eyebrows had never been plucked. In the dim light of the therapy room they resembled a pair of red geese spanning her forehead. She looked like a farm wife, or a middle-aged country dyke; Babe couldn't decide which.

After several minutes of silence, Babe began. "Hello, Mrs. McGraw. Thank you for coming."

"Please, call me Sheila."

"All right, Sheila. You know why you're here today?"

She nodded. "My daughters need me."

Babe was taken aback by the unadulterated honesty of Sheila's answer. Most people when asked that question responded evasively, trying to deny or normalize the situation. "You know why they are here?" She nodded at the twins.

"Because I failed them."

"Mom!" wailed Thumper.

Babe raised a hand. "Let your mom speak. You'll get a turn."

Sheila bit her lip. "Yes, as I was saying, I failed them. They needed guidance and I didn't understand that. I was busy trying to keep the farm together after their father left. They were always good girls. I thought they were raising themselves fairly well."

"And now?" asked Babe.

"Like I said, I failed them." Sheila turned to each of her daughters. "I'm sorry." Tears choked her words. "I shouldn't have let you travel without me. I should have kept you home. Raised you right."

Dirk's right hand shot up in the air.

"Yes," said Babe.

"Can I say something about all this stuff?"

"Go ahead."

"Mom, this isn't your fault. Lots of parents let their daughters tour for athletic events. You didn't know."

"I suspected."

"How could you?" doubted Thumper.

"Well … the mustaches, for one. Those weren't normal for fifteen-year-old girls."

Dirk objected. "But we're dykes."

"I realize that, and that may have confused me a bit, I admit. But I still *should* have known. Dirk, you have run wild for years now, and I just let you. You make all the money in the family. I figured that entitled you to some leeway. I treated you like the head of the family, like a boy, and that's not right because you're a girl and you needed me to give you more guidance. I see that now."

Babe sensed Sheila was holding back. "But?" she asked, hoping to encourage her.

"But—" Sheila took a deep breath. "You can't do those steroids no more. I won't allow it. Not in my house. Not ever again. I agree with the Olympic Committee. I'm glad they sent you here. I was reading about those steroids on the Internet and they can kill you. Kill you! You girls understand that?"

"Yes, ma'am," mumbled Dirk.

Sheila turned to face Thumper. "You understand that also?"

Thumper's head bobbed.

The silence was so thick it seemed an icy fog had settled across the room.

Babe let it linger.

It was a long time before Dirk cleared her throat. "I'm sorry, Mom."

"I'm sorry, too," joined Thumper.

"I know," said their mother, tears in her eyes. "We were all trying. We all did our best."

"Yes," confirmed Babe. "You have been trying. All of you."

"What now?" asked Sheila, her eyes clouded.

Babe: "Let's ask your daughters."

Dirk bit her lower lip. "We've stopped the steroids."

Sheila eyed each daughter. "Both of you?"

"Yes," confirmed Thumper.

Sheila's eyes narrowed. "Why should I believe you?"

No answer.

Babe tried: "Your mother asks a good question. How does she know you'll stay off the steroids? Why should she trust you?"

Dirk sulked. "Dunno."

Thumper volunteered an answer. "Because we get it, Mom. We see how we've hurt you. Our bodies." Tears welled in her eyes. "And we care about that."

"Why did you do it?" asked Sheila. "You were good, both of you. Amazing on those little boards of yours. You flew like penguins on those boards. Both of you. Day one. Sliding all over the back pasture, never afraid of falling. Why the steroids?"

Dirk chewed her lip before answering. "I wanted to win. All the time. Thumper went along with me."

"Mom, we said we're sorry. Really, we are. We won't do it again."

Sheila looked to Dirk for confirmation. "Can't promise that," she mumbled.

"What was that?" asked Babe.

Dirk paced the length of the couch. She stared out the window at the vastness of freshly fallen snow. "I said I can't promise. Can't promise I won't do steroids."

Thumper jumped to her feet. "Of course you can! You went cold turkey first. You're the one who turned us in. You blew the whistle. This has all been your doing. You made me throw my stuff away. This was all your idea."

"I know, but for me it's different. Different. Different than you. Understand?" Dirk stared at her twin pleadingly.

"Different? Get real. We're twins. We took the same drugs. How can it be *different?*"

"Maybe I want to keep taking them, that's how."

"Dirk!" Sheila was on her feet, at her daughter's side. Dirk was weeping now, her body racked with emotion as she tried to hide her face in the curtain by the window.

"Dirk, honey?" Her mother had an arm around her. "Talk to me, Dirk. Tell me what has you so upset. Honey, please. I'm your mother. Spit it out."

"Mom!" wailed Dirk.

"What, honey, what is it?"

"I think I want that operation."

"What operation, honey? What are you talking about? Your knee? Did you hurt your knee again?"

"No! The other operation. You know!"

Babe suddenly understood.

Thumper, too.

Sheila cradled her tall, gangly daughter close to her as best she could. "I see," she said. "Okay, honey. If that's what you want. I mean, if you're sure."

"I am, Mom. I really am sure."

Sheila looked at Babe, her eyes pleading.

Babe nodded. "If that's what she wants, she'll have to take the steroids again. But it will be with a doctor's guidance this time. And she'll need therapy to make sure she understands all the things that will happen to her if she continues with the steroid treatments."

Sheila cradled her daughter's head. "Okay, honey," she said. "We can help you. We *will* help you."

Sheila glanced at Thumper as if to ask, *You want this surgery, too?*

Thumper shook her head. *Absolutely not.* And for the first time in her life she felt alone. Dirk had always been her twin. The stronger of the two. Thumper had always looked up to Dirk as who she might become, if only she were braver and pushed the envelope.

But this was something Thumper did not share with her twin. One envelope she didn't want to push. Something which would physically and emotionally separate them forever. Thumper wanted to cry, but instead she joined her mother and sister in an emotional huddle.

37.

Trust Me, Dear

Nan Goldberg wanted a cigarette. Badly. But they were sitting at the kitchen table in the farmhouse, and smoking was forbidden in the house. A fact she regrettably had to enforce when her partner, Birge, retracted a silver cigarette case from her jacket pocket and plucked out a Dunhill.

"Can't smoke in here, dear," said Nan, her hand atop her partner's.

"You? Forbidding me to smoke? That's a switch," scoffed Birge.

Though Nan and Birge had been together for almost thirty years, they were finding it difficult now to sustain a conversation. In Nan's opinion, much of the strain came in the form of Nan's leggy new brunette assistant, Mirabelle.

Mirabelle, who sat across the table from Nan looking bored beyond belief, was not yet thirty years old. She had a bosom like Marilyn Monroe and legs that would not quit, which she had dressed in two hundred dollars' worth of designer silk stockings.

Birge loved women in stockings: the real thing, with elaborate silver garters, not pantyhose. Nan was keenly aware of this. She was also aware that Mirabelle — whom she'd already dubbed Tinker Bell, just for spite — had a raspy Lauren Bacall voice that made everything she said sound impossibly sexy.

Nan hated Mirabelle to the ends of the earth.

"So," said Nan, turning to address Mirabelle, "you came from the Jamison Agency?" The Jamison Agency was the most exclusive executive talent agency in Manhattan. They recruited young women with Seven Sisters pedigrees to serve as assistants at Wall Street's most prestigious financial houses. Jamison girls were known for their brains as well as their knock-'em-dead good looks. (The term "gold-digging whore" also often accompanied their professional efforts.)

Nan found it suspicious that as soon as she left home, Birge signed on a ta-ta girl to wait on her hand and foot. Birge's last two executive assistants had been old English fags, sticklers for details, very good at pomp, which Birge's position as head of Wall Street's smartest accountancy firm called for in no small dose.

Mirabelle smiled at Nan, a very expensive smile, which, if Nan was correct, had been brightened and whitened and veneered to the tune of about seven thousand dollars: a smile that reminded Nan how old and imperfect her own teeth appeared these days.

Nan chewed the inside of her cheek.

"I signed with Jamison right out of Vassar," confirmed Mirabelle. "I intend to go back to graduate school at Harvard for my MBA next year. I was delighted when Birge here snapped me up."

"Yes, I imagine you were. Birge is quite the catch."

Birge changed the subject. "So, how is this place? A little rustic, yes?"

"I'm not here for the decor, as you recall."

"Yes, well, let's not get nasty, dear."

"Nasty?" fumed Nan.

Sensing an imminent catfight, Mirabelle excused herself. "I'll be in the limo, making calls, if you need me," she assured Birge as she departed.

Silence fell between the two women.

"You want to tell me about Tinker Bell?" Nan grunted at last.

"Mirabelle," corrected Birge.

"You know who I mean." Nan was standing, arms crossed, back to the refrigerator.

"She's my new assistant."

"You couldn't find an ugly one?"

"I suppose I could, but why on earth does it matter?"

"Because I don't like the way she looks at you."

"How is that?"

"All adoring." Nan molded her face into a mask of adoration. She batted her eyelashes.

"I'm her mentor, dear. She damn well ought to adore me."

"She wants to sit on your face."

Birge was quiet for a second. "What if she does? I needed a new assistant. She's who the agency sent. You want me to send her back? Fine, I'll send her back. But you have to tell me what's eating you. You seem jealous. You've never been like this before. If this is what you're going to be like sober, we might well reconsider this whole sobriety thing."

Nan sat down at the table. She batted a salt shaker between her hands. "Tinker Bell is gorgeous. Any woman would be jealous."

"I suppose. But it's not like you. Hey, this is me. Birge. We've been together since the dawn of civilization. I've never cheated on you." Birge took her partner's hand and patted it assuredly.

"Never?" whined Nan, hating how insecure she felt. She felt twelve years old. Out of control. Feelings raged inside her searching for an outlet. She'd numbed herself with alcohol for so long she no longer knew how to talk about her own inner turmoil.

"Of course not."

Nan decided to accept Birge's declaration of lifelong love and change the subject. "We have to talk about this addiction thing. Babe will make us talk about it so we might as well warm up before she lights the fires of hell under us." Nan sighed, wishing she could avoid talking about her addiction and how it had, for the last year, embarrassed and fatigued them both.

Several hours later, Birge left the farmhouse for the night, emotionally exhausted. Too much talk. Too many feelings. Way too many feelings. Nan had poured her heart out. Apologized in so many ways. In many ways today's Nan reminded Birge of the emotionally driven girl she'd fallen in love with in grad school.

This did not, however, make Birge happy. Instead, it filled Birge with heavy guilt. By the time the limo dropped Birge off at her hotel for the night, she was in a foul mood.

Mirabelle had booked them at a ski resort in Stowe, an A-grade spa with heated whirlpools in each room and personal chefs for every guest. Birge wasn't surprised to find Mirabelle sprawled on the triple-wide, down-ensconced bed typing financial reports on a laptop when she keyed open the door.

Mirabelle sprang up from the bed, and, after helping Birge off with her coat, handed her a cut-crystal glass brimming with Scotch.

"When are you going to tell her?" asked Mirabelle as she filled another Scotch glass, this one for herself.

"Oh, honey, I can't now. You saw her. She's fragile." Birge lay down the bed and tried to ignore the headache that pounded behind her eyes.

"I'm fragile, too," whined Mirabelle as she suggestively parted her hotel robe. Underneath, Mirabelle wore intricately laced black stockings and a matching bustier that held her ample breasts barely together with the aid of a delicate, red, silk string. "Really delicate," she purred as her long legs expertly straddled Birge's lap.

38.

Homo-sex-u-all

Babe eyed the wall clock. It was time for Candice's family therapy session; ten minutes past time, in fact. Candice's parents were in the room, but the good doctor herself was nowhere in sight.

"Maybe she got called to a medical emergency," suggested Ellie, Candice's mother. "She's a doctor, you know."

"Probably thinks we're not important enough," snorted Daniel, her father. "She doesn't like us, you know. Never has. Born with her nose out of joint."

"Don't say that, Daniel! Please don't start with that!" Ellie cried.

"Why not?" objected the old man as he straightened the vest on his suit, which was creeping up his belly. "It's the truth. You're always making excuses for that girl. Since the day she was born. She don't fool me, though. I see who she is. *What* she is."

Babe watched as the hands on the wall clock advanced. It was becoming clear to her that Candice did not intend to show for her family session. It was also starting to dawn on her why Candice might choose avoidance to time alone with her parents. "Mr. and Mrs. Antwerp?" she said with a sigh.

"Yes?" they answered in practiced unison.

"I'm going to find your daughter." Babe scraped back the chair and stood.

"Don't bother yourself," declared Daniel. He rose with the help of his cane. "We can take a hint. She hates us that much. Always has. We'll be on our way."

"Sit down, Daniel!" It was Ellie speaking. For a small-framed woman, well into her seventies, she had a commanding voice.

Daniel fell back onto the sofa.

Ellie faced Babe. "You go and find our daughter. We want to speak to her. Tell her we'll not leave until she talks to us. She wants us to leave, she needs to tell us that to our face."

It didn't take Babe long to locate the doctor. She was in the cellar exercise room climbing the StairMaster, sweat running off her face, down the hollows of her back. The green silk headband she'd tied through her red hair was soaked through. Ignoring Babe's many shouts, she refused to shut off StairMaster. If anything, she quickened her pace.

Babe, not one to be put off, yanked the power cord on the machine.

Candice fell forward, off the machine, onto the floor. She yowled as she clutched her right ankle. "You could have hurt me!" she spat at Babe.

"Yeah, well, you're late for your therapy session. Get those tight-assed buns of yours upstairs. Pronto."

"No." Candice sat cross-legged on the floor, nursing her injured ankle. "I don't want to see my parents."

"Why not?"

"They don't like me."

"They seem to think it's you who doesn't like them."

"They said that?"

"Your father did."

"You mean the great and mighty Reverend Antwerp?"

"He did mention he headed a church."

"They don't like me. Especially him. I haven't seen them in twenty years. They are not my family."

"Well, the medical association says they are. And for purposes of your stay here, they are your only legal family. You have to see them. Either that or you have to leave treatment. Now. Today. This very hour."

"I can't leave treatment." Dr. Antwerp glared at Babe.

"You can leave anytime you'd like."

"I'll lose my medical license if I leave."

"It's your choice."

"I really hate you," said Candice, her eyes alive with malice. "Really. I hate your stinking lesbo guts."

"I'd say that means we're making progress," said Babe. "Now, get up. I'll get some ice for that ankle and we'll walk into that therapy session together. You can face this. Whatever has you so scared, you can face it. You have to face it."

Dr. Antwerp got up and hobbled toward the door. When Babe offered her a shoulder, she refused. Though the pain in her ankle felt like razor blades shooting up her calf, the doctor walked, unaided, up the stairs, into the therapy room.

"I'm here. What do you want?" she roared at her parents. She did not sit down. She stood instead, facing the large window that looked out over the pasture.

Daniel turned his gaze away from his daughter.

Ellie slid a hand over her mouth. "My God, Candice. Is that you?"

"Of course it's me." Dr. Antwerp turned to face her parents.

Daniel narrowed his eyes. "You look different."

"Very different!" gasped Ellie.

"I've undergone plastic surgery. That's what I do, Mom. I'm a plastic surgeon."

"We know that," griped Daniel.

"Yes, we saw an article on you last Christmas. In *People* magazine. The photo in that article didn't look like you, either."

"I told you, I had some work done."

Her father cocked his head. "Whose face is that you're wearing?"

"Mine, Dad. It's mine. I created it. It's all mine."

"What happened to the face God gave you? The one we gave you?"

"I didn't care for it. I thought I could improve on it."

"Improve on the work of God? That's blasphemous. Disgusting," he growled.

"It's not disgusting. It's what I do for a living. I make people feel better about themselves." Candice turned toward Babe. "You see now why I don't speak to them? It's useless. They hate me. Always have."

"That's not true, Candice!" objected her mother.

"Speak for yourself, Ellie. She's a demon as far as I'm concerned."

Babe decided to intervene. "Why is that, Mr. Antwerp? Why is Candice a demon?"

"You know what I'm talking about. You and your kind can 'mister' me and smile at me all you want. I'm no idiot. I know full well what kind of place this is. What you all are."

"Excuse me?" asked Babe.

"Daniel!" cautioned Ellie, but it was too late.

"Homo-sex-u-alls!" raged Daniel. "That's what this place is. A place for sick homo-sex-u-alls. Our daughter there" — he raised his cane — "is a homo-sex-u-all. We caught her in our own house. In bed with her college roommate. Big bull dyke from Tennessee by the name of Harley. Disgusting."

Babe turned to Candice. "Is this true?"

"Of course it's true. I tried to talk to them about it, but he" — she pointed at her father — "locked me up. Sent me to one of those Christian clinics in Arizona that is supposed to cure homo-sex-u-alls."

"You told us you were cured." Daniel was foaming at the mouth now.

"I was a teenager," Candice spat out. "I lied. Teenagers do that, Dad. I didn't want to lose your love. I lied."

Ellie raised both hands. "Candice, we're not here to hurt you."

"You're not?"

"No. We're here to apologize. To help. You have to let us."

"Mom, the last time you helped me, you put me in that awful place. Do you know what they did to me? Do you have any idea?" Candice was sobbing now.

Her mother stood and draped her arms around her. "Honey, that was a long time ago. I didn't know. None of us did. I thought it was a sickness. I realize now we were wrong."

"We were not wrong!" boomed Daniel. "It is a sickness."

"Actually," interjected Babe, "it is definitely *not* a sickness. The American Psychological Association decided that it definitely was not a sickness of any kind back in the '70s."

Daniel narrowed his eyes. "You're one of them, aren't you?"

"You mean gay?"

"No. I mean homo-sex-u-all. Nothing gay about it."

"Yes, I am a lesbian, Mr. Antwerp. And this is a treatment center for lesbians who have addiction problems."

"A drug addict, too, is she?" The Reverend raised his chin in defiance. "Doesn't surprise me one bit. How else could she live with herself?"

39.

Tele-Daddy

Babe took a long break between the Antwerps' family session and Bunny Van Randolph's family session. During her break, she burned a pot of sage in her office in an effort to cleanse the hatred Candice's father had spewed. Raging familial homophobia was not new to Babe. But it was unpleasant. And it always left a stink.

Still, Babe had a feeling that Candice's confrontation with her parents after all these years might help the surgeon stop running from her own sexuality. Queer was queer. Any attempt to make a compromise on that issue could easily lead to erasure. The world was very straight. Give it an inch and it would happily assume the same of everyone.

In Babe's opinion, at some time or another every self-respecting lesbian had to look her parents in the eye and say, "I'm queer." If that confrontation never happened, a woman risked spending her life being gay, but only behind closed doors. Straight in the streets; gay in the sheets. Candice, in her estimation, was that kind of lesbian.

Babe could see why Candice was reluctant to call herself gay. Her upbringing had clearly not been conducive to self-acceptance as a sexual person, let alone as a gay person. Babe wondered if the effort the surgeon had thrown into perfecting her external appearance was a cosmetic cover for the ways in which her parents had made her feel imperfect, loathsome even.

Babe's skin crawled at the thought of a young Candice sentenced to a queer deconditioning camp. Only God knew what tortures Candice had endured in that camp two decades ago. No wonder the woman exhausted herself trying to achieve perfection; and no wonder she'd turned to prescription drugs for release. She wondered what lasting effect today's open confrontation might have on Candice. In session, Candice had come out of her closet of denial. In fact, she'd embraced a gay identity fervently. That, decided Babe, was a good omen.

Candice's mother, Ellie, seemed truly sorry for her past behavior, eager to try and understand her daughter going forward. The father, Daniel, on the other hand, was not budging an inch. Babe was eager to know what Candice would do with her mother's attempt at reconciliation and her father's continuing scorn.

By the time Babe's office was cleansed, she was ready to face her next session. It was dark now. Most of the residents were saying good-bye to their guests for the night. They'd all return in the morning for more therapy as well as free time with their family members.

Bunny Van Randolph was sitting, legs crossed at the ankles, on the couch in the therapy room as they clock struck seven, time for her therapy session. Problem was, Bunny's family was nowhere to be seen. Justin, Bunny's personal valet, sat stiffly upright in a ladder-back chair across from Bunny. He nodded as Babe took her seat behind the desk.

"What's this?" asked Babe. "Where is Senator Van Randolph?"

"D.C.," said Justin. "He sent me."

"Sent you?" Babe could not hide the incredulity in her voice. "He can't send you. You're not family."

"He sent me," Justin said, determined to carry out his duty.

"Justin, no disrespect, but you can't have a therapy session with Bunny. You're an employee. Not family."

"Can't you just give me a report?"

"A report?"

"Yes, on Bunny's progress." He faced Bunny. "You are progressing, aren't you, dear?"

Bunny smiled as she recrossed her legs. "Of course."

"No more drugs?"

"Not even an aspirin."

"Hold on here!" cried Babe. "I need to talk to the senator."

"I told you, he's in D.C. Meeting of the foreign affairs committee. About Syria. He could not come."

"Get him on the phone."

"Excuse me?"

"The phone." Babe made a dialing motion with the fingers on her right hand. "We'll have the therapy session on speakerphone."

Uncertain what to do, Justin flipped open his cell and dialed the senator. "Sir," he said, "I'm here at the rehab center, and this woman wants to talk to you. Bunny's therapist. She insists she has to report to you."

"Not report," corrected Babe. "His daughter needs him. She has some things to say to him. We need him to *participate* in this rehab."

Shrugging, Justin handed the phone to Babe. In less than a minute the senator had agreed to call back on Babe's speakerphone so they could conduct a family session.

Babe nodded toward the door. "You can leave," she said to Justin. "We'll call when it's over."

Before the senator had dialed in, Bunny tried to dissuade Babe from continuing with the session. "I'm fine. I'm cured. I'll tell Daddy that, then we're done."

"You're cured?"

"Totally."

"You are such a liar," said Babe, as she pushed the speaker bar on the phone and welcomed the senator.

"Hello, Senator."

"Hello, Ms. Swenderson. Happy we could meet today."

"Me too, and call me Babe, please."

"Fine. Where do we start, Babe? How's my daughter?"

"I'm fine, Daddy," Bunny shouted from across the room.

Babe motioned for Bunny to pull a chair up to the desk so she'd not have to shout.

Sulking, Bunny complied.

Babe stepped into the silence. "Senator, your daughter has some things to say to you."

"What is it, Bunny?"

"Hi Daddy," Bunny repeated to the phone.

"Bunny, are you okay?"

"Yes."

"You sound funny."

"I'm fine."

"What did you want to tell me, honey?"

"I'm cured, Daddy."

"Already?"

Silence.

Babe stepped in. "Your daughter would like to apologize."

"Apologize? For what?"

Bunny also looked puzzled.

Babe began. "For her behavior. How she has disappointed you and the family."

"Oh, not disappointed. Bunny could never disappoint us."

Babe tried again. "It's all right, Senator. You can tell the truth here. No press is listening."

Babe and Bunny listened as the senator shuffled papers on his end. An aide come into the room and asked some muffled questions. "Sorry," said the senator at long last. "Now, where were we?"

Bunny jumped in. "I'm cured, Daddy. No more drugs. I promise."

"Bunny, that's wonderful!"

"Thank you, Daddy."

Babe raked her hands across her face, exasperated. To achieve therapy someone in the room had to have true feelings. This father-daughter team seemed expert at sticking to the script. They'd talk in meaningless circles unless Babe could find a way to crack their compact of meaningless chitchat.

And that would not happen tonight. Babe was simply too tired.

40.

Queen of the Carpet Munchers

Roger Winthrop was ecstatic to see Dylan Redford. Casting aside his guitar, in the TV room, where he'd been waiting for hours for Dylan to arrive, he opened his arms and scooped her up. A tall man, he pulled her off the floor. He kissed her first on one cheek, then the other. He aimed for her lips, hoping for a grand finale, but missed.

For her part, Dylan struggled to get loose from his grip. His white fur coat made hugging him feel like gripping a bear, and Dylan had never been a hugger (of men or bears). Free at last, she jammed her hands into her back jean pockets and mumbled a weak hello.

Stripping his coat off and tossing it aside, Roger continued. "Glad to get the call, baby. Like, happy you want me." He beamed. His open velvet shirt revealed a smooth chest that had been waxed and bronzed to star perfection. Roger wasn't yet a star, but he was a contender, the hottest new male musical talent in Hollywood, a real catch.

"Calling you was not my idea," grumbled Dylan. "*Definitely* not my idea."

"Hmm, guess not. Still, I was hoping you'd be happy to see me." Roger ran a hand through his long, silky blond hair.

Up close he was very pretty. His nose was fine and delicate and he wore eyeliner as well as a light mauve eye shadow. Seeing him again up close relieved Dylan. Mistaking him for a woman wouldn't have been *that* difficult. Not in the dim light of a concert hall.

Maybe she wasn't such a hopeless drug addict after all.

"Happy to see you, too," Dylan lied.

Betty Frump erupted into the TV room, dragging along Alice Everwright, her partner. The tall, thin woman had long gray hair and wore a simple tie-dye cotton shift. Eyeglasses slid heavily from her hawkish nose. She did not look happy, but that might have been because of all the children she had in tow, thirteen of them to be exact. Several of them screaming.

"Whoa! What's that about?" Roger asked Dylan, with a shoulder throw in Betty's direction. "Looks like some sort of third-world PBS parade." None of the children were Caucasian. Few spoke English. The TV room was immediately flooded with multi-lingual chatter and confusion.

"God, don't ask!" groaned Dylan. Taking Roger by the hand, she led him out of the TV room, upstairs to her room. At least it would be quiet there. She didn't have any idea what to do with Roger. Their "family" session wasn't until tomorrow but here he was, eager to be of assistance. His presence made Dylan nervous. She wasn't sure why. Maybe because he was a graphic reminder that no matter how loud she protested, drugs had begun to get the better of her.

Roger strolled around the bedroom. "Cool. Like a nun's place or something. Very spiritual, babe."

"I think it's supposed to be simple. There's a saying here: Keep It Simple, Stupid. K.I.S.S."

"What's that mean?" Roger slid his guitar down onto his chest and plucked out a tune.

"Not sure, really," Dylan lied again.

"My agent has me booked on an Asian tour."

"Cool, I guess."

"Yeah, it is."

Dylan was starting to sweat. She wished Roger gone. Whoever he was, he was not family.

Roger strummed another few lines then put aside the guitar. "I was hoping … well, I was hoping that your calling me here meant something. That maybe you had decided to give us a go."

"Give us a go?"

"The marriage. *Us.* You know." Roger grinned in a way that made Dylan feel bad for what she knew she had to do.

She sat on the bed next to him. But not too close.

He took that as an invitation and slid his hand suggestively across her thigh.

She removed his hand. "Roger, I'm gay. Big old lezzy girl. Queen of the Carpet Munchers."

"That's cool."

"Stop effing saying that. It isn't cool. It's who I am. I like girls. Not boys."

"You like me." He grinned again.

"I thought you were a girl."

"Oh, come on!"

"No, really. Roger, the night we met I was wasted. Fucked in the head big time. I'd smoked, like, three fry sticks and dropped a double load of E and drank a pint of tequila. And that's just what I *remember* doing. I had no idea you were a guy."

"What about my penis?"

"I thought it was strap-on, dude."

"For real?"

"Yeah, for real."

They sat in the growing darkness together. For the first time, Dylan was starting to understand everything Babe had screamed at her about her life being unmanageable because of drugs. It was absurd, this whole scene with Roger. And he was a nice guy. Genuinely in love with her, it seemed. The guilt was starting to eat at her.

Dylan turned to face her husband. "Roger?"

"Yes?"

"I am an addict. Sleeping with you is something I never would have done if I'd been sober."

Roger's eyes grew dewy. "What about our marriage?"

"Definitely a result of drugs. I told you, I'm an addict. I need help."

Roger considered that statement for a moment. "Maybe we should try again. Now that you're sober."

"Try what?"

"Sex."

Dylan recoiled. "Not on your life."

"Why?"

"Because I'm sober now. Sane. This is me. And I don't do guys." As if to punctuate her comments, Dylan trounced to the bathroom. With Roger watching, she fished the remaining Ecstasy tablets out of her watch pocket and flushed them down the toilet. As a precaution, she flushed twice more before leaving the bathroom.

<h1 style="text-align:center">41.</h1>

Jelly Doughnut, I Love You

Wee Gee was awake at sunup on Sunday. Not unusual for her, as she often wrote reams before sunlight spilled over the horizon. As a young mother, the only time she'd been able to write were the wee hours while her children slept. A grandmother now, and rich enough to afford several nannies, she still enjoyed pounding the keyboard while others slept.

This morning she was sitting at her desk dressed in a flannel robe, staring at the blinking blue cursor. She couldn't think of one word to write. She tried several sentences but they all read like pale rewrites of her previous dialogue. With more than fifty romance novels under her belt, Wee Gee Judd, known the world over as Foxy Hot Pants, was going stale.

Frustration with her work was a large part of what fueled her overeating. Most people glamorized a novelist's life. They imagined writers as a clever, attractive, rich lot who did smart things like pilot airplanes and speak French and engage in duels. Born dirt poor, Foxy Hot Pants knew little of these things, other than what she had imagined.

The problem, as near as Wee Gee could figure, was that she wasn't very confident romance existed these days. Or ever had. The older she got, the more love seemed like a marketing ploy. An irrational, mercurial outburst: the least reliable thing in the world to build a relationship upon.

Or is that sex?

Pushing back from her desk, Wee Gee heaved a sigh. She needed to concentrate on her new romance trilogy, for which she'd already been advanced half a million, but all her mind could conjure were visions of jelly doughnuts. Writing was the most boring, tedious, damn hard work in the world. Jelly doughnuts understood this. People did not.

Poppy stirred in the bed across the way. Wee Gee watched as Poppy's head emerged from under the covers, like a wee turtle reluctant to come out.

"Girl, you look whipped!" Wee Gee greeted.

Poppy groaned as she threw aside the covers. "It's my mum."

"Hmmm."

"Did you see her?"

"I think. After lunch. Either her or Mary, Queen of Scots. In the kitchen."

Poppy snickered. "That would have been my mum."

"She giving you a hard time?"

Poppy kicked off her flannel sleeping pants and slid into a stretch micro-mini. She pulled on a matching spangle top. "Just being herself." Poppy strolled over to the window and cast a glance at Wee Gee's blinking blue cursor. "Blocked?" she asked as she rubbed her nose to ward off the cold.

"Maybe. But maybe I'm just all out of stuff to say."

"You? Struck dumb?" Poppy rolled her eyes. "I doubt that."

When the laughter faded, Poppy grew serious. "Does it ever bother you?" she asked as she sat down at the vanity to apply her makeup — a task that could take her an hour or two.

"What?" asked Wee Gee. "Does what bother me?"

"The pressure. All the people watching. Waiting. Everyone wanting you to produce so they can get a piece of the pie."

Wee Gee grunted. "It's the American way, honey."

"I'm British," complained the pop star.

"A dollar's a dollar, even if it's a pound," laughed Wee Gee. "That why you perform? The money?"

Poppy waited until she'd whisked on a third coat of mascara before shaking her head in a virulent no.

"Didn't think so. Not why I write, either. Not originally, anyway."

Poppy flicked rouge across her cheeks. "Why do you write?"

"I'm naturally mouthy. Always thought I had something to say."

"That computer screen doesn't look very mouthy to me."

Wee Gee sighed. "I'm supposed to write romance."

"And?"

"Not sure it exists anymore."

"Come on, love!" protested Poppy. "How can you say such a wicked thing?"

"I'm a lot older than you, that's how."

"Well, if you'd like my opinion, I believe it exists."

"Which? Love or romance?"

"Both. *Definitely both.*"

"Hmmm. This opinion have anything to do with that little war correspondent with the ice-blue eyes you've been mooning over?"

"Oh, stop it!" cried Poppy. "I have not been mooning."

"Yes, you have. She's a doll, that one."

"You think so?"

"I said I was old, not blind. I like strong women. That one is a tank. Very sexy, in my book: strength."

Poppy twisted her lips.

"What? What's wrong now?"

"I do fancy her, but she's not even tried to wank me. At least not since that first day, in the vegetable closet. She was all over me then, but since she's been hands off, like I've got the bloody plague. All we do is talk. Yakety, yakety, yak."

"No kidding?"

"No kidding."

"Why you think she's acting like that?"

Poppy shrugged. "I guess she sees us as friends, sisters, or something weird like that."

Wee Gee grunted.

"What? What was that for?"

"More likely it's because she really likes you. A lot."

"Huh?"

But the two had to stop their conversation. Babe was shouting for them from the hallway. It was time for them to start breakfast, and this morning they'd have more people to feed, as several visiting family members had decided to begin the day with breakfast at the farm.

42.

Bad-Mouthing Baby Jesus

After breakfast, Wee Gee was first up in the family therapy room. Unlike most of the others, she'd checked into rehab voluntarily. She didn't have to work things out with a legal guardian, the courts, or an insurance company. She didn't have to please anyone, other than herself. She had no life partner: a true gift at times like this, she reasoned.

No fool, Wee Gee realized full well how much emotional work partnership required. With two ex-husbands, seven grown kids, and a stable of ex-girlfriends, Wee Gee had apologized for almost every imaginable bad act of addiction over the last forty years.

She was damned tired of making amends.

For this stint in rehab, she'd chosen her oldest daughter, Shawnee, to work with her in family therapy. Shawnee had been reluctant at first. She'd not always approved of her mother's actions: Of all Wee Gee's children, she approved the least of her lesbianism. Shawnee was the one family member that Wee Gee felt she had truly failed. Both women weighed over two hundred pounds. Both were twice divorced, currently alone in life. Whatever issues Wee Gee had about weight and food and relationships, Shawnee certainly shared. Wee Gee figured she owed it to her daughter to discuss this possibility out loud.

Shawnee sat on the couch, her hands clutched in her lap. (Babe had never met this particular daughter and was startled to see how much the two woman looked alike: mirror images staring at each other across a twenty-year gap in time.) "Mom, I don't want to be here," mewed Shawnee.

"I know, honey."

"Why is she here?" asked Babe.

"Because I think I've failed her. I need to make amends."

"Mother, you know I don't like that kind of talk."

Babe looked puzzled. "What kind of talk?"

"Making amends. All that AA stuff. It's like a cult." She fingered a string of pearls around her neck.

"You go to church," Wee Gee reminded her daughter.

"Mother, the Christian church is not a cult."

"Honey, it's a bunch of people who believe a dead guy will rise up and save them. You all sit around on Sunday morning and drink his blood and eat his body. Christianity, baby girl, is definitely a cult."

Shawnee clutched her hands together more tightly. "Mom, if you're going to bad-mouth the Lord Jesus, I'll have to leave."

Babe intervened. "Let's not talk about religion right now. I think what your mother means to say is she believes she may have set bad examples for you. She wants to talk about that."

Shawnee's eyes widened. "You mean the lesbianism?"

"No," bellowed Wee Gee. "I mean the overeating."

"I don't overeat."

"You're overweight."

"I'm not so sure of that."

Wee Gee stared at her daughter in disbelief. "Honey, you've got the sugar, just like me."

"Mom, no one calls it 'the sugar' anymore."

"I do."

"You do a lot of things in odd ways."

"True."

Sensing a dead end, Babe interjected. "Shawnee, I think what your mother means is that she's concerned about your health. The diabetes, and all. Is it okay if we call it diabetes?"

"Yes," agreed Shawnee, through tightly held lips.

"Okay," said Wee Gee. "Babe is right. I worry about you, baby girl. You've got" — here Wee Gee hesitated — "the diabetes, and like me you're alone in this world. It's like you're trying to please me by being me."

"That's ridiculous, Mother!" Shawnee jumped to her feet.

"Sit back down!" bellowed Wee Gee. "Let me have my say!"

Shawnee wilted onto the couch.

Wee Gee stood this time. "Honey, when you were little, I fed you all sorts of things just to shut you up."

"That's love, Mom. Mothers do that."

"No, all mothers do not do that. I taught you food was love. I gave you more food than I ever gave you love."

"You were busy writing, Mother. That always came first for you."

"That what you think?"

"What?"

"That I love writing more than you?"

"You always said so. You never really wanted us children. You said that more than once. It was the topic of an entire speech you made Christmas 1975, as I recall, at Grandma Greeley's. That time you set the Christmas tree on fire."

Wee Gee fell silent.

"That true?" asked Babe.

"Yes, that is true." Wee Gee's face was lined with remorse. "I'm sorry to say I remember the Christmas she is talking about. I was still married to her father. We were about to divorce. We'd lost the house to bad debt, his gambling. I had a trunk chock-full of slutty novels no one would buy. At the time, me and Jack Daniel's were mighty tight."

"She was a sloppy drunk," said Shawnee, with acrimony in her voice. "Mean and nasty."

"I was unhappy most of my life, honey." Wee Gee looked at her daughter with pleading eyes. "I wrongly took it out on you kids."

"Got that right," her daughter sniveled.

Wee Gee sat on the couch next to her daughter. She took Shawnee's chin in her hand and forced her face up until their eyes met. "That is what I am trying to make amends to you for. I was young when you were born. And stupid. And headstrong. I wish to God I could live my life backward and clean up all the mistakes, but nobody gets to do that. This here is the best I can do. And whether you realize it or not, you are the spitting image of me, in many ways. All I'm asking is a chance to make us right. Here. Now. In the present. When I get out of this place, I want you to come to Louisville and stay with me for a month or so. I'm checking us into one of those swanky new health spas where we can have fun learning to cook like gourmets and learn new ways to deal with our diet. You with me or not, baby girl?"

"Oh, Mama!" cried Shawnee, who'd collapsed into her mother's open arms. "Of course I'm with you. I'm scared to death of this diabetes thing."

Wee Gee hugged her girl and kissed her forehead gently. She used the edge of her hand to squeegee away the tears on her daughter's round cheeks.

Shawnee swallowed hard. "Just one thing, Mama? One thing, okay?"

"What? Anything, baby girl. Just ask."

"Promise me you'll stop making fun of Jesus."

"I'll do my best," she vowed.

43.

Love Yurt

Right before lunch, Betty Frump and Alice Everwright arrived in the therapy room exactly on time, holding each other's hands as if united in a march on Washington for righteous marital recognition. Alice was wearing a thin cotton shift and brightly colored, hand-knitted woolen Peruvian socks on her narrow feet. Despite the minus twenty degrees temperature outside, her feet were stuffed inside a pair of Birkenstock sandals so ancient her blackened footprints were imbedded inside.

Babe found herself curious about this couple and how they'd deal with the topic of addiction. Clearly, Betty was in charge. Of all the women in treatment, Betty, next to Bunny, had been the least forthcoming about her addiction. Betty was a slippery fish, very political, which meant very used to working the room, and everyone in it.

Betty began the session by facing her partner and offering an apology. "I'm sorry. I was overworked. I guess I got used to using the pipe to wind down. I've got my head screwed right again. No more dope."

Alice said nothing.

"Well," continued Betty. "Do you forgive me or not?"

Alice remained mute.

"Alice?"

"I heard you, Betty," said Alice softly as she adjusted the glasses on her nose.

"Okay. So? Are we square or not?"

"Not." Alice moved a few inches down the sofa away from Betty. "Definitely not."

Babe leaned forward, curious about the quiet tone of dissent in Alice's voice. "Why not? Can you explain to Betty what you mean, Alice?"

"Yes, but first I have to say I think it's really *none* of your business. I don't even know you." She scowled at Babe.

"Fair enough," said Babe. "You don't know me. Try thinking of me as a mediator. I'm here to make sure everyone gets heard. That everyone gets equal time on the floor, so to speak."

Alice's face brightened. She crossed her legs at her knees and yanked up each sock before continuing. "I want a divorce." She pulled a roll of papers out of her canvas co-op tote bag. "Sign these, please."

"What the fuck are those?" Betty grabbed at the papers and began to paw through them, answering her own question. "You can't divorce me!"

"I most certainly can. We were married in Massachusetts. I'll file the divorce papers there Monday morning."

"You can't divorce me!" Betty repeated, as if she'd heard none of the last few snatches of conversation.

"I can. And *I will.*"

Babe had to gather her wits, fast. She too had been struck dumb by the announcement. "Can I ask why you want a divorce?"

"You can."

"Why do you want a divorce?"

"You've met her?" Alice threw a shoulder toward Betty. "Don't pretend you have to ask why."

"Divorce?" Betty cried. Her face was pale now. Her arms crossed. Sweat beaded her forehead. "Divorce!" she screamed. "We can't get a fucking divorce. What about the Family Foundation? We'll look like fools. People count on us to show the world that lesbian families are viable."

"Lesbian families are viable, just not this one," said Alice quietly.

No one said anything for quite a long time. The clock ticked loudly on the wall.

Babe tried to open dialogue again. "Is this something you are certain about, Alice?"

"Yes. I've known for a while now. Since Easter, in fact."

"Easter!" Betty raged. "And you're just telling me now?"

"I tried to tell you before. Frankly, you're not an easy person to talk to. You use your anger to shut down communication."

"What the fuck are you talking about?" raged Betty.

"*That.* That is precisely what I am talking about. Could you lower your voice, please? Your very tone is meant to intimidate, and I'm not falling for it anymore. You can go be a big bad bull dyke all by yourself for all I care."

Babe cleared her throat. "Is there anything Betty can do to change your mind?"

"Stop right there!" cried Betty. "Who said I want to change this woman's mind?"

"I thought maybe —"

"Thanks, but it's my life. Frankly, I think this divorce could be the right move."

Alice leaned forward.

"Sure," said Betty. "It'll be a test case for the Massachusetts supreme court. That means big-time press. I intend to sue for custody, of course."

"You wouldn't dare." Alice narrowed her lips and her eyes simultaneously.

"Try me."

"Frances warned me you'd be vindictive."

"Who the hell is Frances?"

"My lover."

"*You* have a lover?"

"Since Easter. Remember that Vernal Equinox party at the farm outside Northampton?"

"Yes."

"That was hosted by Frances. Frances Green. She wore that horned-bull, wood-spirit androgyny hat and led the fertility dance?"

"I vaguely remember. That awful dance, not her." Betty was picking at lint on the hem of her caftan, feigning a lack of interest now.

"While you were busy getting stoned, Frances invited me back to her yurt."

"Her yurt?"

"Yes."

"Go ahead," sneered Betty. "I can tell you want me to suffer the dirty details. Please, be my guest. It'll make me look good in the divorce suit. Tell me more, please."

"I like dildos," Alice blurted out. "Adore them, in fact. Love 'em as much as Raisinets. Can't get enough."

Betty squared her shoulders. "I get the picture."

"Frances owns one. Several, in fact. And the children adore her." Alice rose as she finished talking.

"Wait! You can't leave yet," admonished Babe. "We have twenty minutes left in this session."

"Fuck off!" said Alice, who was gone in the wink of an eye.

Part III

Bush Whacked:
Backsliding and Betrayal

Interlude

At the beginning of the final week of treatment, a foot of snow, and an equal amount of icy silence, slid over Sugarbush. Families had said their piece and vanished. The women, still locked in treatment, hung at the ice-flecked windows of the farmhouse watching the world vanish under rolling blankets of white.

The chill of sobriety trickled deep inside each woman.

Candice could not escape the image of her father shaking his cane. He was right: She was a homo-sex-u-all. Queer, lezzy, bull dyke. Her question now: So what? Why, oh why, had she ever let that man scare her? Wasn't it about time she flung open the door on her closet of fear and stomped honestly into the world? That idea frightened and thrilled her at the same time.

Storm had never felt more fragile. Her agent, Kinky Kincaid, had not reacted well to the new sober, sleepless, defiant Storm. Storm feared she was about to lose both her career and her income. If she couldn't get her act together, she'd never make it back to the war zone. What would happen to her then? She imagined herself on TV in a job like Jerry Springer, goading housewives to act like feral animals. "Fuck," was all she could whisper to herself as she lay awake nights staring at the stamped-tin ceiling.

Wee Gee continued to write, and to promptly rip apart every word. She dreamed constantly of jelly doughnuts. Big, plump, doughy rolls oozing raspberry jam. Of all the addictions she'd suffered, this one with food was the worst. With the other addictions — alcohol, for instance — she'd conquered her demons by walking away. She'd never allowed a bottle into her home again. But she could not walk away from food. She had to eat: Three times a day, demon food breathed foul, hot temptation into her face.

"Moderation," Babe kept whispering to her.

Yeah, right, easy for that skinny-assed cracker to say. Wee Gee Judd was not a woman of moderation. She loved to indulge. Loved it. Loved it. *Loved it.*

Thumper was spending endless hours snowboarding. Snowboarding was a real challenge now. The snow was deep. Drifts turned into mountains of powder. Dirk tried to help, but Thumper shook away her assistance. Dirk could not compete in the Olympics, or on any other women's athletic event, as long as she continued steroids. Thumper was alone. She doubted she could compete without Dirk at her side, setting the pace. What she refused to see was that while Dirk might be retiring from competition, she had no intention of retiring from her role as a caring sister. "Let me help you train," Dirk pleaded constantly to her twin's deaf ears.

Nan had experienced the most promising family session of all the women. Contrary to what she had feared, Birge had come to her with open arms. Birge had insisted all weekend that she was committed to starting over again. None of this was keeping Nan from chewing the eraser tips off her mechanical pencils. Nan lived by her instincts, always had. Something wasn't right with Birge. With them. She'd tried to kiss Birge when they'd been alone, but Birge had dodged her advance. Not like Birge. Birge was always ready. Every damned second of every blessed minute. One touch and that woman was primed for action. For Birge to dodge a sexual advance — that told Nan what she feared most. Birge was lying when she said everything was fine with their relationship. Nan paced, unhappy that she was locked up, unable to confront Birge and force the truth out into the open.

Dylan, off Ecstasy, indeed off drugs of all kinds for the first time in her adult life, had taken to strapping on snowshoes and forming backyard art by stomping frozen messages in the snow. Her work was frenzied, but not very imaginative. Today she'd spent three hours mashing "SOS" in frozen ten-foot letters in the far pasture. No one had responded to her desperate plea except that old moose, Winkle, who'd chased Dylan up a wide-armed oak tree where she'd sat shivering for an hour before Poppy had rescued her by snowballing the moose back to the barn.

Bunny was about to rip her blonde locks out of her head. She'd discovered on Monday morning that Dylan had done the unthinkable: flushed the drugs. Worse yet, Dylan was off sex, slinking around the farmhouse like a depressed teenager, grinding her teeth whenever Bunny tried to engage her in meaningful conversation.

Only Betty seemed to be holding on to some vestige of her former defiant self. Bunny found that odd, especially since everyone knew that Betty's partner, Alice, had dumped her and taken the children to start anew with some other old dyke who lived in a yurt (whatever that was). Betty seemed to hold some secret to staying sane in an otherwise insane place. Bunny soon found out it wasn't what Betty knew, but what she had: a stash of marijuana. Really great stuff laced with angel dust hallucinogen.

44.

Trip to Jamaica
(And Then Some)

Betty was suspicious the moment she opened the door to her bedroom and saw Bunny standing there draped in a lavender chiffon robe with her hair done up in a white silk turban. "What do you want?" Betty grumped.

"You?" Bunny flashed a coy smile.

"Get real," grunted Betty as she ushered Bunny into her room. Fearing a narc bust, Betty checked the hallway twice before slamming shut the door.

"What do you want?" she repeated as she watched Bunny sashay around the room.

They were alone. Betty's roommate, Storm, was in the exercise room, running the treadmill to hell and back again.

"What do you want?" Betty repeated.

Bunny bounced onto Betty's bed. "You have stuff?"

"Stuff?" Betty narrowed her eyes.

"Marijuana," said Bunny as she smoothed the robe over her thighs. "I want to buy some from you."

"Really?"

"Yes." Bunny pulled a hundred-dollar bill out of her pocket. "Here." She held the money out.

Betty eyed the money. "I don't have any drugs. This is rehab, you know. No drugs allowed."

"Oh please!" Bunny snorted. "Don't play coy with me, you old lezzy goat. Just get the dope, okay?"

"Would like to help you, darling, but I can't. No drugs." Betty held both her hands out, palms open.

Bunny fidgeted on the bed. She grabbed a pillow and hugged it. "Come on!" she whined. "What is it with you? You want more money? Fine. How much? Name your price." Bunny's bad eye had begun to twitch.

"I told you, no drugs." Betty crossed her arms and stood her ground.

"What's up with you? Would it hurt you to share? I hear you've got, like, a ton of the stuff. Give me a joint. One lousy fatty, I'm on my way."

Betty's face softened as she rounded the bed. "Okay. Maybe I can help."

"Goody!" Bunny squealed. "Here, take, like, a hundred. I'll give you, like, four more as soon as we're out of this hellhole."

Betty brushed away Bunny's hand. "Don't want money."

"What then?"

Betty went to her chest of drawers and slid out a bottom drawer. She reached into the back where she'd taped her mini bong and stash to the underside of the bureau. She drew out the drugs and the apparatus. "You'll have to smoke it here. Don't have any rolling papers."

"Fine," sighed Bunny as she patted the side of her turban. "Anything. I just need a little help getting to sleep."

"Before I give you this" — Betty waved the fragrant bag under Bunny's twitching nose — "I want you to promise as soon as we get out of here you'll set me up in a meeting with your father."

"Daddy?"

"Yes." Betty packed the bowl of the pipe and journeyed to the bathroom to draw water. She came back with the pipe ready, a book of paper matches tweezed in her left hand. She strolled to the door and kicked a damp towel into the crack. "Don't want to invite the world to our little party, do we?" she chuckled.

"Why do you want to see Daddy?" Bunny clutched at her robe.

"Need help with my divorce. With Alice. Your father is the senator in Massachusetts. I figure he can set me up with the attorney general, anyone else I want to see."

"Sure," said Bunny with a shrug. She cared little for politics and never saw why people made such a big fuss about it all to begin with. "He'll see you anytime I say."

On that note, Betty struck a match and lit the bowl. She puffed several times, not handing the pipe to Bunny until the marijuana glowed a bright orange in the darkening room.

"Here," Betty exhaled with a cough. "Good stuff. Angel Wings: special blend from Jamaica."

Bunny grabbed the pipe and inhaled deeply. As a veteran chain-smoker, she had an amazing capacity to toke and hold. She held the smoke for almost thirty seconds before exhaling smoothly. She felt her body begin to relax. Two more deep tokes and she felt her chest melting. Her toes began to glow.

"Yummy!" she murmured.

"I don't buy shit," said Betty, who took two deep hits in an effort to catch up with Bunny.

It took about ten minutes and as many tokes for the two women to reach that special place where they were floating above the ordinary world, feeling warm and content like sister angels. They glowed with love and goodwill.

Bunny began to laugh. Before long she was rolling on Betty's bed, her robe open, revealing an impressive amount of lingerie: high-cut, plum-colored Brazilian bikini bottoms complemented by a soft demi-cup bra embroidered with flowers. The bra straps cut into Bunny's soft, white skin like twisted vines.

"What's so funny?" asked Betty, who lay on the bed next to Bunny. From Betty's vantage point, Bunny's cleavage looked massive, like a pair of silk-ensconced Matterhorns.

Bunny rolled over to face Betty. "You mean this!"

Now Bunny's breasts were smashed hotly against Betty's face. Betty giggled in response. "Fuck, I'm hungry."

"Me too," sighed Bunny.

The two women got up and, without turning on the lights, sneaked hand in hand down the stairs, into the kitchen.

"The cupboard!" squealed Bunny. "I swear I saw Babe lock Twinkies in there this morning."

"Twinkies? Fuck, no!" exclaimed Betty.

"Fuck, yes!" squealed Bunny.

The two women slid into the dark cupboard together. Betty was fumbling around in the dark looking for a light switch when she found, by accident, Bunny's right breast.

Bunny giggled.

"You like that?" purred Betty.

"Maybe," teased Bunny. "Do it again. Let's see."

Neither of the women could stop giggling.

45.

Please Don't Eat the Cucumbers

Wee Gee slammed shut her laptop.

Poppy, who was sitting in bed, reading, glanced at her roommate. "You look awful, love."

"Starving!" Wee Gee rolled her eyes.

Poppy studied her wristwatch. "We ate not two hours ago."

"Not enough."

Poppy rubbed her belly. "I'm stuffed." Poppy, under Wee Gee's kitchen tutelage, had gained almost ten pounds since coming to Sugarbush. Free of the pressures of performance anxiety, and stripped of her laxative packs, the rock star had begun eating like a normal twenty-three-year-old. She was looking healthier than she had in years.

"Don't take this wrong, honey, but you're the size of a mosquito," said Wee Gee. "Swallowing your own spit probably fills you up."

"Food really bothers you?"

"And then some," sighed Wee Gee.

"Well, let's get you a snack. You can eat, right?"

Wee Gee checked her food diary. "Got two hundred calories left for the day." Her mood brightened on learning this.

"That's like a bloody food orgy!"

"Maybe to you, baby girl, but to old Wee Gee that's like rabbit food." Wee Gee made a dour face.

"Come on," urged Poppy. The rock star took Wee Gee by the hand and tugged her forcibly out of her chair. "Kitchen raid!"

Poppy and Wee Gee were at the threshold of the kitchen door when they heard giggling. Wee Gee stuck out her arm, warning Poppy to stop, be quiet. The rock star obeyed.

Wee Gee leaned over and whispered to Poppy, "You hear that?"

"Who is it?" Poppy whispered back.

"Don't know."

The two stood still stood, straining to hear in the darkness. Wee Gee didn't want to spook anyone by turning on a light.

The giggling in the pantry grew louder. Then it turned into moaning. And huffing. And groaning. Finally Poppy and Wee Gee heard a yodeling coming from under the closed pantry door.

"That's Bunny!" cried Poppy, recognizing the distinctive yodel from Bunny's first night getting finger-banged by Dirk.

Before Wee Gee could reply, light flooded the kitchen. Both women turned to see Babe standing behind them in her robe. Her hair was loose on her shoulders. Purple moons floated under her eyes. She looked tired. "Who the hell is in that pantry?" she groused at Poppy.

"Dunno," the rock star muttered.

"Stand aside!" ordered Babe.

Wee Gee and Poppy scurried away from the pantry door, but they stayed close enough to see inside the pantry when Babe sprang open the door and flicked on the light.

The first thing everyone saw was Betty's ass. Very bare. Large. White. Like a quivering vat of cottage cheese. Quite impressive, really. Her purple caftan was hiked up to her waist. Her white cotton granny panties were shoved down to her ankles. She was pressed tightly between Bunny's thighs.

Bunny was on her back on the floor. She still had her bra on, but her Brazilian-cut bikini panties were hanging on a hook next to some aprons.

"This is going to get ugly," Wee Gee murmured to Poppy.

"What do you mean *going to?*" Poppy whispered back.

Babe took a deep breath. "Get up! Both of you!" she bellowed at Betty and Bunny. "As soon as you're decent, I want you both in my office. Understand?"

Betty and Bunny struggled to stuff themselves into their clothes as Poppy and Wee Gee shuffled into the kitchen and tried to act nonchalant. Poppy drew a bag of carrots out of the crisper and threw them on the table along with some McIntosh apples. She knew these foods were on Wee Gee's list of stuff she could eat to her heart's content. Poppy busied herself slicing two apples into bite-sized bits and cleaning a fistful of carrot sticks.

Neither woman spoke as Bunny and Betty emerged from the pantry and slid across the hallway to the therapy room, where Babe had disappeared to after making herself a cup of green tea in the kitchen.

Poppy waited for the door to the therapy room to shut before leaning over to Wee Gee. "You haven't eaten any of your apple, love."

"Can't," confessed Wee Gee.

"Lost your appetite, have you?" snickered Poppy.

Wee Gee giggled.

Poppy followed suit, her hand her over mouth in an attempt to suppress what threatened to be a storm of laughter.

"Don't know about you, but I could have gone to my grave without seeing *that*."

"That was certainly something."

"Yes, but what?"

"I dunno," wept Wee Gee, "but it fixed my appetite."

"You like cucumbers, don't you?" teased Poppy with a roll of her eyes.

"No, ma'am, not anymore!" roared Wee Gee.

"You saw that cucumber? Where they had it?"

"Oh yes!" exclaimed Wee Gee, who was doubled over in laughter. "And I ain't never eating cucumbers again!"

46.

Queermobile

During group the next morning, Babe wasted no time announcing that Bunny and Betty were no longer with them.

"Huh?" cried Dylan. "What does that mean?"

"It means," said Babe, her arms crossed, "they broke the rules. Betty brought drugs into the house. Bunny used them with her. I kicked them both out last night."

"Just like that?" wailed Dylan.

"Have you not been listening these last three weeks?" squawked Babe.

"I've been listening!" objected Dylan.

"The rules are clear. You can't do drugs in rehab. Does that make sense to you? Do you ladies all understand this rule?"

"Yes," they murmured in slurred unison. "We understand."

"If any of the rest of you have drugs, I want them. Now!" Babe held out her hand as she circled the group. She stopped in front of Dylan and waited.

"I got shit," Dylan ground out. "Triple shit, in fact."

"Good," said Babe. Satisfied no one else in the house was holding, Babe moved swiftly to the next topic. "I think it's time for you all to go back into the real world. See what it feels like out there. A bus will be here before lunch. It will take you to Stowe, a ski village about half an hour from here. You can have lunch in town. Go Christmas shopping. Take in a movie. In short, act like normal grown women for the day."

Dylan eyed Babe. "You trust us out there? On our own?"

Babe shrugged. "Question is: Do you trust yourselves?"

No one said anything.

An hour later they were all bundled in their coats, huddled in the lobby, eagerly awaiting their ride into town. They were chattering like children, excited about their trip, very curious about what Bunny and Betty had actually done to win the express lottery out of rehab.

"Bunny and Betty," whispered Nan. "I heard they got stoned and did each other."

"Yuck!" said Dylan. "Thanks a bunch for that image!"

Poppy giggled and poked Wee Gee in the ribs. An action Wee Gee returned with glee. They'd made a pledge not to reveal the sordid details they had observed the night before.

Before long a purple VW minibus with rainbow-colored bumpers pulled up to the front door. A short, plump young dyke with a flattop haircut, a faint mustache, pierced lips, and a lumberjack plaid coat jumped out. She slid open the door to the passenger cavity of the van, beckoning the women to jump in, make themselves at home.

Candice groaned as, holding up the tail of her Burberry coat, she took a seat in the rear, as far away from the driver as possible. "What is this thing?" she complained as she studied the interior, which was plastered in political stickers. "A queermobile?"

"Don't worry, darling," said the driver with a wink as she took Candice's hand and helped her up. "No one will guess you're gay, long as you stick close to me."

"Oh please!" pleaded Candice. "You might as well have 'I Lick Chicks' tattooed on your bleeding forehead."

Dirk slid into a seat next to Candice. The minibus was small, so the two ended up squeezed together. Candice could feel the muscles in Dirk's thighs hard against the thin wool of her dress coat. "Heard about your decision," she whispered to Dirk.

Dirk nodded. "Been thinking about it a long time."

"I understand," said Candice as the bus lurched in the wrong gear down the driveway.

"You do?" Dirk turned to face her.

Up close Candice could see that Dirk had amazingly long eyelashes. Very sexy chocolate-colored eyes. Candice swallowed hard. "Think so. I never felt right in my body, either."

"Get out of here!" cried Dirk. "You're a knockout!"

"You think so?"

"Ah, like definitely. Triple-hot babe. Pant. Pant."

Candice blushed. "Here, let me show you something. Okay?"

"Sure." Dirk waited, curious to see what Candice was fumbling for in her purse.

Candice pulled out a dog-eared snapshot and offered it to Dirk.

Dirk squinted at the photo. It was of a teenage girl. A head shot. The girl had buck teeth and a tiny chipmunk chin. Her cheeks were hollow. Not much of a looker. "So?" asked Dirk as she handed back the photo.

"So," said Candice with a deep breath. "That was me."

"*You?* You're shitting me, yeah?" Dirk's eyes widened.

"No. That was me, in high school. I had work done on my face when I got out of med school."

"Wow!" said Dirk as she studied the doctor in profile then full ahead. "That's very cool. You're like a walking work of art."

"You think so? You don't think I'm a freak?"

"Baby, I think you're beautiful."

Candice blushed again.

47.

Girl in a Short-Bed Ford

Thumper could barely stay seated in the queermobile. As soon as the van arrived in Stowe, she found herself on the edge of her seat scanning the narrow streets for some sign of her girlfriend, Mary Lou. The village was crowded with people, ski vacationers. A group of teenage girls bumped up the sidewalk together, snowboards clutched to their chests. Thumper strained to see above the crowd, down the side alleys.

Mary Lou, who lived up the road in East Hardwick, had promised Thumper she'd meet her in Stowe; that they'd have lunch together at the Ski Kitty diner. Thumper yelped when she saw Mary Lou's cherry-red, short-bed Ford pickup tucked into a tight space in the parking lot adjacent to the diner.

The purple queermobile was rolling into that same parking lot when Thumper popped open the door and bolted full steam for the diner.

Wee Gee looked after Thumper. "Where the hell is rocket girl going?"

Seeing the truck, Dirk offered an answer. "Her girl, Mary Lou. That's her truck over there."

As Wee Gee studied the truck, the door on the driver's side shot open. A short, stacked blonde with long, curly hair bounced out of the truck into Thumper's outstretched arms.

"Looks like love!" gasped Wee Gee, happy to have stumbled onto a possible new plot line.

"I guess," grumbled Dirk, who was still mad at her sister for shutting her out of her life.

Candice squeezed Dirk's arm. "Have lunch with me?"

"Me and you?" Dirk offered a lopsided grin.

"Don't get your hopes up, you big stud bunny," Candice countered, catching the gleam in Dirk's eye. "I said lunch. I meant lunch. None of that hanky-panky you do with the young girls. I'm not like that. I'm respectable. Mature. A professional lezzy. Understand?"

"Not really," said Dirk with a shrug. "But, uh, I'll take you up on that lunch thing 'cause it looks like Thumper is gonna be busy."

As the other women tumbled out of the van and parted into pairs to explore the village of Stowe, Thumper and Mary Lou untangled from their hug and climbed into Mary Lou's truck seeking privacy.

"You look awesome!" said Thumper, who was happier than she could have imagined to see Mary Lou again.

"Thanks, honey," said Mary Lou. "You too! Your mom said you're okay? Off the steroids?"

"Yeah, but Dirk —" Thumper hesitated.

"Your mom told me. No biggy." Mary Lou adjusted the rearview mirror inside the truck before flicking out a tube of Pink Passion lipstick and freshening up her lips.

"Really?"

"Yeah, sure. I'm cool with it, if it's what Dirk wants. Aren't you?"

"I guess." Thumper slumped in the seat of the truck and shut her eyes. The sun was bright outside on the freshly fallen snow and Thumper's head hurt. She wanted to love her sister again, but she felt so betrayed. Why hadn't her sister ever told her she wanted to be a boy? They shared everything.

Mary Lou scooted over and pressed herself close to Thumper's lanky body. "Hey, it didn't surprise you, did it?" She found Thumper's hand and squeezed it tightly.

"What?"

"Your sister. I mean that Dirk wants to have that operation."

"Kinda." Thumper slid upright in the seat. "To tell the truth, it sorta freaks me out."

"Oh come on! Didn't you see it?"

"See what?"

"Your sister? How much she wanted to be a boy?"

"You saw that?"

"Uh, like, yeah! Since second grade when she made everyone call her Dirk instead of Dorothy."

Thumper sniffled. "I thought it was, like, a nickname."

"It's a boy's name. Dirk is a boy's name. Didn't you ever get that?"

Silence engulfed the truck cabin. Mary Lou keyed the ignition, turning the heat and radio back on. She fidgeted with the knob on the radio until she had a country and western station. The woman singer was belting out a song about soft kisses and hard hearts. "Miss me?" Mary Lou asked shyly.

Thumper opened her eyes and looked at Mary Lou. "Yeah, like, a lot."

"You're not acting like it," said Mary Lou. "I mean, you're way over there, like I have cooties or something." Mary Lou pointed to the vast two inches of space between them on the perfectly restored, red leather seat. (Mary Lou was training to be an auto mechanic at the vo-tech school.)

Thumper took Mary Lou by one arm and pulled her across the seat until they were pressed tightly together.

"Goddamn it!" complained Mary Lou as she climbed into Thumper's lap. "Kiss me already, you big old jock!"

48.

Snow Job

None of the women had a game plan in terms of what to do with their newfound freedom. Nan Goldberg decided she'd hang out with Poppy and Wee Gee for the day. Wee Gee wanted to eat. Poppy was not particularly hungry. Nan, for her part, remained obsessed with the notion that her life partner, Birge Hathaway, might be snowing her big time. As luck would have it, Nan knew where Birge and Mirabelle were staying in Stowe. She hated to admit she was still jealous, yet she couldn't shake the feeling that it might be prudent to drop in on Birge and Tinker Bell at their hotel, unannounced.

Nan was standing in front of the Snowbird Inn, Birge's hotel, when an idea occurred to her. The inn was definitely something Birge would have selected for a romantic getaway: a sprawling Victorian mansion that had once been the home of a New England lumber baron. The mansion was painted pure white with three-story turrets guarding each wing. Since it was late December, the evergreens that lined the steps to the entrance were draped in snowy ropes and twinkling blue lights. The place was so romantic it made Nan want to gag.

The inn supported a five-star restaurant that specialized in nouveau New England cuisine — trout stuffed with cranberry and sweet potato chutney, that sort of yummy stuff. Nan read Wee Gee the menu posted in the restaurant window, causing the novelist to bolt full steam toward the door into the restaurant.

Poppy had little choice but to follow the two older women.

The restaurant was so crowded Nan could barely elbow her way to the tiny podium where the maître d', a man wearing an expensive Italian suit, decided who would be admitted and who would be cast back out onto the icy streets to starve.

Nan, who was on a mission, was not about to leave her status to chance. While Wee Gee and Poppy hung back at the door, Nan boldly introduced herself to the maître d', assuring him they had reservations. "Check under the name Franklin," she said, as she palmed a fifty-dollar bill across the podium toward him.

"Oh yes. Here it is, *Ms. Franklin*," said the man, who wasted no time ushering Nan and her friends to a quiet table in the corner. The table was close to the front picture window, which framed a lawn that rolled in a snowy blanket toward the street. Nan could see a veritable parade of skiers and holiday shoppers as they hustled down the street. Snow had begun to fall softly. The steeple of a white church jutted above the heads of the holiday shoppers. A covered bridge lay along the cobblestone street below.

"How'd you do that?" asked Wee Gee. "The line to get in here was longer than Pinocchio's nose."

Nan shrugged. "Doesn't matter. Let's eat, shall we?"

The three women had fun selecting a smorgasbord of New England delicacies: walnut appetizers roasted in a balsamic sauce, rolled pork loin stuffed with apple chutney, and ginger squash soup. And that was just the first course.

"It okay if you eat all this stuff?" Poppy whispered to Wee Gee.

"In moderation," replied Wee Gee, who could feel herself slipping down the dark well of gluttony. This lunch would be the first real test of her ability to practice moderation when faced with a cornucopia. Locked inside Sugarbush, Wee Gee had been able to stay on an even keel because temptation was almost nonexistent, but the real world featured temptation on every street corner. Tucking a napkin into the collar of her blouse, Wee Gee hoped she was ready for the test.

Something on the sidewalk caught Nan's eye, causing her to excuse herself, pretending she had to go to the toilet. "Go ahead. Start the main course without me. I saw a pay phone by the washroom. Need to make a few business calls to Manhattan."

"Okay," said Wee Gee, who didn't want to be rude, but truth be told she'd never in her life held back from eating as a matter of manners. She knew full well where Nan was headed because she'd seen the same view as Nan out that window.

What she'd seen was Nan's partner, Birge Hathaway, arm in arm with that leggy brunette she'd had the nerve to try and pass off as a "business associate" at the farmhouse that week.

When the waiter brought the first dish, a steaming plate of walnuts, Poppy suggested they wait for Nan to return.

"No way!" cried Wee Gee, who filled Poppy in. "I bet Nan is about to go ballistic. Doubt she'll have an appetite now."

"Her partner is off shagging a tart in public like that. That's bloody awful!" groaned Poppy.

"That's nothing but life all nasty and up in your nose, baby girl," said Wee Gee as she bit into a juicy spoonful of walnuts. "Live long enough and you'll get used to it."

49.

Tinker Bell Gets Her Wings

Nan stood impatiently at the registration counter of the Snowbird Inn, not the least bit shy about lying her face off to the counter girl. "Silly me. I left my room key card in the restaurant," she said, smiling sweetly. "I'm with my partner, Birge Hathaway. She's at a business meeting. Can you give me an extra card to our room? Please?"

The young girl at the counter, who was wearing what appeared to be a green felt elf's hat, was only too happy to look up Birge Hathaway's room number and swipe a new key card for Nan. She palmed the key card to Nan, calling her Mirabelle by mistake.

So, thought Nan, Birge and her assistant were registered in the same room. Not a good sign.

Fuck that old dyke and her little Tinkertwat, thought Nan as she strode down the hallway, toward the staircase that led to Birge's private tower suite.

Birge was registered, of course, in the best room in the place: the Baron's Suite in the east turret. Nan was out of breath by the time she'd climbed the three stories to the private lair. She stood at the antique, handcrafted, double sliding oak doors, uncertain she wanted to see what lay on the other side.

Lots of people's spouses cheated on them. Most middle-aged straight women Nan knew accepted male cheating as normal behavior. They looked the other way, many secretly glad their husbands had taken up with someone else as it relieved them of sex, which after thirty years had become for many wives a fairly boring and unpleasant duty.

But Nan didn't want a relationship like that. If she and Birge were truly going to share their lives, then they had to share a bed also. All or nothing. Not some half-assed attempt at a relationship, but the real thing. Tinker Bell would have to nest someplace else.

Taking a deep breath, Nan swiped the key card through the lock unit and retracted it quickly. She had to repeat the procedure twice, as the lock didn't recognize the card on the first try. When the doors finally slid apart, Nan was pushing so hard she fell face first onto the richly carpeted floor.

Nan looked up to see Birge standing over a four-poster bed, adorned in nothing but a huge leather cock and balls. She had taken off her trifocal glasses and slicked back her short graying hair with some sort of gel.

Tinker Bell was dressed more elaborately. Like some sort of a leather-wrapped Christmas present. She was on her knees on the bed, her backside toward Birge. Her shapely ass was wrapped in a leather g-string. The string was held together by a tiny rhinestone star in the back, with matching rhinestone rings on each side. If she'd been wearing a bra, it was missing now.

Mostly what she wore was a look of surprise.

The three women stared at one another.

Birge spoke first, taking a step toward Nan, her cock bouncing. "Not what it looks like, honey."

"*Really?*"

"Really," said Mirabelle, who was off her knees, onto her feet, groveling toward Nan now. "This was all my idea."

Nan wheeled to face Birge. "That true?"

Birge nodded.

"Then you're a liar as well as a whore."

"Nan!" objected Birge.

Nan held out one hand, warning Birge away. "Please. Put some clothes on. Do you have any idea how silly you look?"

Birge grabbed a terry-cloth robe from the wingback chair at the side of the bed. "Don't get upset about this. Okay?" Birge said as she belted the robe awkwardly, and not very successfully, over her cock. "You've been out of this relationship a long time. You dumped me for a bottle of Nolet's and a bag of limes a couple of years ago. What was I supposed to do?"

"What? This is my fault?" screamed Nan.

"Mostly," murmured Birge.

Mirabelle had donned a robe and was hotfooting it to the bathroom. Nan blocked her. "Hold on there, little sister! Who do you think you are? Birge and I are married. Don't you have any respect for that?"

Mirabelle shrugged. "Talk to her. Don't blame me if you can't keep your woman happy."

Birge stepped in. "It was an accident. No one meant for it to happen, Nan."

"An accident? What, her vagina just opened up one night and you tripped and fell in?"

Mirabelle took advantage of the stunned silence to slide into the bathroom and lock the door behind her.

Birge took Nan by the arm. "Calm down!" she urged, ushering her partner into the room.

"No!" cried Nan as she shook off Birge. "I will not calm down! You lied to me. To my face. We could have talked about this in therapy, but you lied. That's sick. Here I am trying to come clean and you're playing head games with me."

"Damn it!" cried Birge. "I was lonely. You've been sloppy drunk most of the last two years. That's not very sexy, you realize."

"I realize that, but I am not drunk now."

"How do I know that?"

Nan was stunned. She had no comeback. Was this all her fault? Had she pushed Birge to seek companionship elsewhere? A chill spread through her body. She felt faint.

Mirabelle emerged from the bathroom, dressed like a normal adult rather than some fist-banged, lesbo sex slave. "I'm going shopping," she piped to Birge. "See you at dinner tonight, honey?"

Birge nodded, which sent Nan into a rage. A rage so hot and blinding she had to leave the room. She ran down the hall, knocking Mirabelle aside. She fled onto the snowy streets. The air was filled with the cheer of Christmas carolers dressed in Victorian-era costumes, making their way through the village.

Clutching her coat to her bosom, Nan broke into a run. She didn't know where she was headed. Desperate to outrun her feelings, she stumbled as fast as she dared down the slippery cobblestone street toward the nearest tavern.

50.

Ski Kitty

Candice and Dirk decided it would be fun to have lunch together in the Ski Kitty diner. The diner was the real thing: vintage New England with shiny dimpled-chrome walls and red leather bar stools and booths. The place was packed, mostly with the twenty-something ski and snowboarding crowd.

Dirk elbowed her way in, towing Candice behind her. More than one young ski kitty turned her head to stare at Dirk.

"Girls stare at you," whispered Candice as they took a seat together in a booth by the bathroom.

"Yeah, I know." Dirk sniffled as she studied the red-jacketed glossy menu.

"That happens to you often?"

"Pretty much. People can't seem to decide if I'm a girl or a boy. Can't say I blame them. I've had trouble there myself." Dirk grinned.

"I think that's very sexy."

"You do?"

"Yes."

"Then how come we're not making out?"

Candice laughed. "Because I told you, I'm not like that."

Dirk slid her menu aside. "What are you like?"

"A little bit shy, at least about sex."

"Come on!" goaded Dirk. "You're like one super-hot chick. The girls may look at me but *everyone* looks at you."

Candice blushed again. She was beginning to suspect hot flashes. She hadn't been this hot all over for years. Not since Harley, her college roommate …

The waitress interrupted Candice's thoughts with a request for an order. Dirk ordered cheeseburgers with cherry Cokes for the both of them.

Candice felt sixteen years old again. She wondered what her life would have been like twenty-five years ago if lesbianism had been as accepted as it was these days, at least in certain circles. She and her college roommate, Harley Smith, had accidently fallen in love. Away from home for the first time at the University of Tennessee, both women had been homesick that first semester. Harley was at the university on a swim scholarship. Candice was there on a national merit scholarship. Their first kiss had just sort of happened. One day after swim practice, Harley had come out of the shower naked into their tiny cramped dorm room. The light from the tall window had fallen across Harley's slim hips, making her blonde, fluffy bush glisten with drops of water. Candice remembered watching, transfixed, as Harley, realizing she was being ogled, loped across the room to kiss her full on the lips.

What happened next had felt like the most natural thing in the world. Like God had touched them both.

Until Candice took Harley home for Christmas and the Reverend Daniel Antwerp got a good whiff of her.

Candice was pulled out of her reflection by the waitress who had returned with their cherry Cokes. The waitress made a point of leaning down in front of Dirk to give her a straw.

Both Dirk and Candice got an eyeful of cleavage.

Ignoring the waitress, Candice stripped the paper off her straw. She waited for the waitress to leave before speaking. "That waitress is coming on to you."

"Yeah, I kinda noticed," said Dirk as she tugged the end off her straw, then blew the paper at Candice's nose.

My God, thought Candice, she and Dirk were dating. It was like a scene out of some quaint lesbo version of *High School Musical.* She half expected a balding high school principal to burst into the diner, forbidding them to ever see each other again.

Candice suddenly realized there was one last person she had to make amends to. As soon as she got out of rehab, she intended to look up Harley Smith. She had, she realized now, some apologizing to do for the way she had treated Harley all those years ago. As a part of her sexual reorientation treatment, Candice's father and the counselors at that awful place had made her write a letter to Harley denouncing their love. She'd also been forced to go to the president's office at the university and "turn in" Harley as a sexual invert. The university had a "morals clause" for scholarship students that made lesbian sexual misconduct grounds for immediate dismissal. Harley had been stripped of her swimming scholarship and kicked out of university, while Candice had gone on to be nominated by the faculty committee for medical school at Harvard.

"What are you thinking about?" asked Dirk as the waitress brought their cheeseburgers. "You kinda spaced out on me."

"Sorry," murmured Candice as she picked at the lettuce on the edges of her burger. "I did something a long time ago that I need to make amends for as soon as I get released."

"You hurt someone?"

"Very badly, I'm afraid."

"I'm sure they'll forgive you. You're a pretty cool person, you know."

"You think so?" asked Candice. The hot flashes were back, but this time Candice was certain it wasn't hormonal. She wanted to touch Dirk in the worst way.

Waiting until they were released from rehab was bound to be a challenge.

51.

Art Shop Angel

Though Storm had invited Dylan to tag along for Christmas shopping, Dylan chose to explore Stowe on her own. Dylan hated to admit it, but she missed Bunny. Odd, really, because it wasn't like the two women had shared a great deal. Just E and a mountain of denial.

Dylan kicked at the snow as she strolled down an alley, away from the bustle of the shopping district. Stowe was impossibly cute. Very New England. Like a picture postcard, complete with narrow streets, tall church steeples, and fieldstone walls dusted in snow. Roger would love the place, she thought. Despite his rock star persona, deep down he was such a kind, traditional, sentimental guy. Too bad he was a dude.

Dylan wandered down an alley, feeling like a kid who'd stumbled into a storybook the night before Christmas long ago. Snowflakes danced across her face. She caught a few on her tongue. She was glad to be alone. Feeling vulnerable like she did was not a feeling she wanted to share right now with any of the other women, because, well, it didn't mesh with her tough dyke exterior.

Dylan wasn't sure how she felt about her sober life, other than lost with surges of anger for no good reason. Babe kept harping on her to dig beneath the anger. Every time she did, she felt overwhelmed with sadness. Babe reassured her it was okay to feel sad. That the sadness would eventually pass. That the sadness would eventually lead to a highway of new feelings.

That all sounded hopelessly complicated to Dylan. "How long will all this take?" Dylan had grumbled, skeptical as well as impatient. Drugs had given her instant access to an array of feelings: a major reason she'd enjoyed them.

"Two years. Maybe three," Babe had assured her.

That seemed a long time to Dylan. Hell, these days twenty-four hours seemed an eternity.

Dylan stopped in front of a bay window that showcased the artwork of a number of contemporary New England landscape artists: striking mountains, meandering streams, birch trees weeping over waterfalls.

Sofa art, sniffled Dylan: stuff that would look good over the sofa in any living room. Not the kind of stuff she'd ever paint or create.

Dylan was deep in thought about her own art — she had to come up with an idea for her next monumental piece, and she was finding it hard to beat the sensationalism of *Big Pink Pussy* — when a woman creaked opened the door to the art shop and leaned out to take a long look at her.

The woman was quite a bit older than Dylan, tall and willowy, dressed in robelike layers of flowing sky-blue silk. Her white hair was cropped short to accent her high cheekbones. Diamond hoop earrings caught the faint midday sun and sparkled on her ears.

A real HOC — hot older chick — mused Dylan. Her mood immediately soared.

"Like anything you see?" the woman asked, an amused smile on her lips.

"As a matter of fact," Dylan mumbled as she kicked at a clump of dirty snow, "I kinda do."

"Come in, then!" coaxed the woman. "I just made tea. Have some while you browse. We've got a lot more art inside! Gorgeous stuff! Come! Come!"

Dylan felt herself drawn into the shop by some sort of magical string. When she stepped into the foyer, the interior glowed with the warmth of candles. A wood fire blazed in a red-tiled Victorian fireplace in one corner of the shop. Paintings were hung everywhere, even from a beam in the middle of the ceiling. Dylan had to duck to keep from grazing her head on the paintings as she walked toward an oak bureau on the far side of the room. The bureau held a tea set.

The woman introduced herself as Glinda.

"Like the good witch in *The Wizard of Oz?*" smirked Dylan as Glinda handed her a cup of steaming tea.

"Yes," laughed the woman.

Glinda's laugh was pleasant, very feminine. It reminded Dylan of water trickling across stones in a brook. As a child in Ohio, Dylan had spent a lot of time by a stony brook that ran across her uncle and aunt's farm, listening to the water in an effort to calm herself after her uncle had …

Glinda took Dylan by the arm, leading her to a rocking chair by the fire. "Sit down, honey," she instructed. "Tell me about yourself. You like art?"

"I'm an artist," confessed Dylan.

"Thought so."

"Yeah? How could you tell?"

"Your hair, mostly. You cut it yourself?"

Dylan nodded as she flipped a swatch of hair from her right eye while sipping at the hot, bracing tea. The teacup was hot in her hands, a relief since she had no gloves to keep her hands warm. "Yeah, I cut it with a straight razor. Never the same. Always changing. Uneven. Unruly. Like life."

"I like it," admired Glinda. "I really like it. I bet you make amazing art."

Dylan was going to answer yes, but suddenly felt sleepy. She sat the teacup aside. "It's kinda warm in here," she said as she cast off her jeans jacket and threw it aside. She leaned back in the rocking chair and shut her eyes. She felt warm in the painting shop. Warm and safe. Very safe. Like the first time she picked up a palette of paints on her twelfth birthday and fell into the rich magic of all those colors.

And that's the last thing Dylan remembered as she fell into a deep sleep.

Glinda retrieved a cashmere afghan from the back of a Victorian fainting couch in the front of the shop and spread it lovingly over Dylan's lanky frame. She took extra care to tuck in the sides so no icy draft would invade Dylan's peaceful slumber.

When she was confident Dylan was safely tucked in, Glinda settled into a platform rocker next to the artist. She had to work at fitting into the rocker, not because she was a large woman, because while tall she was not broad. The problem was she couldn't get her wings to bend in enough on her back so she could sit in the chair and rock comfortably.

Dylan would be asleep for some time. The young artist had a lot to dream about. The healing dreams would, Glinda hoped, help her through this dire time. Mortals were so fragile, mused Glinda, so delicate, and this one was so very lovely, deep down in her scarred soul. But so much of her beautiful female soul had been damaged. She'd never recovered from the sudden death of her parents — then that awful uncle.

Glinda blew Dylan a magical kiss before taking up a rainbow skein from the basket next to the rocker. As Dylan slumbered, the guardian angel knitted mittens at superhuman speed.

52.

Betrayal in the Bentley

Storm was standing on Main Street, in front of a furniture workshop, admiring a hand-pegged tiger-maple writing desk, when a set of warm lips slid across the back of her neck. Her hand slapped against her neck in startled defense as she turned to see who had smooched her from behind.

Scintillating turquoise eyes met Storm's gaze: the eyes of her agent, Hunter Kincaid. Hunter was standing in the snow, her slim body wrapped in a brown leather bomber jacket with a chinchilla collar and matching chinchilla cuffs. She was dressed in a skintight black ski jumper and looked lovely, per usual.

"Surprised?" purred Hunter as she slid an arm around Storm's waist, pulling her forward.

"What the hell are you doing here?" hissed Storm.

"Christmas shopping?" Hunter flipped her long, ebony hair. "Babe told me you guys might be in town today, so I hung around. Thought you might enjoy some normal company. No offense, dear, but those women you're in rehab with seem like a dreary lot of losers."

"They're okay," countered Storm, feeling defensive of the women she'd come to think of as her friends.

"Yeah, especially that little English tart. She's quite the bush baby? Yes?" Hunter's eyes sparkled with malice.

"Leave her out of this!"

"Touchy!" cried Hunter. "Thanks, you just confirmed for me that you're popping that tart."

Storm shook off her agent's grip and hustled down the street, elbowing her way through a group of carolers.

Hunter pursued her, determined to have her say. "Hold up! Look, I brought us lunch!" She held up a woven picnic basket, dangling it above the heads of the carolers who had ceased singing as they bustled toward a new street corner.

"Lunch! Have lunch with me. Okay? I've got news from the network. A raise for you!"

Storm halted. She stepped into a recessed doorway, allowing the carolers to swoop past. Hunter hustled into the alcove with her picnic basket. "I thought we'd do lunch in the Bentley." Hunter nodded down an alley where a silver auto sat, motor purring, a uniformed chauffeur slumped sleeping at the wheel.

"Okay," agreed Storm, who was worried out of her mind about her career.

The two women settled comfortably into the leather-ensconced back seat of the Bentley. As soon as Hunter had the contents of the picnic basket strewn across the built-in mahogany bar, she reached over and unzipped Storm's hooded parka. Not resisting the undressing, Storm shed the parka as soon as the zipper parted.

"You've lost weight," purred Hunter as she poured a cup of hot chocolate from a thermos and handed it to Storm. "Here. Drink this. Argentinean cocoa melded with real cream, blended with a spritz of peppermint."

Storm took the paper cup and knocked back the hot chocolate, burning her tongue. She grabbed a cold sandwich from the basket, turkey pastrami, her fave, and took a big bite, cooling her palate. After she'd eaten half the sandwich, she stopped and eyed her agent, who was neither eating nor drinking, just studying Storm as she ate.

"You said you had news from the network?" Storm mumbled as she took another bite of her bulky sandwich.

"I did say that, didn't I?"

"Yeah, you did. You said a raise."

"Well, it's sort of a raise."

"Sort of?" Storm stopped eating and set the sandwich aside. "What does that mean?"

"Don't get upset!"

"Fuck off! I'll get upset if I want. Now tell me what this news is from the network."

"They want you back early."

"Huh? How early?"

"Today, if possible."

Storm snorted. "I don't finish treatment until next week, you know that."

"They don't care about that. They're willing to look the other way. They need someone to drop inside the southern provinces. Rumor is there's an ISIS plot afoot to attack the White House on New Year's Day. Need someone in there now. Pronto."

Storm crossed her arms. "Tell them I can't do it."

"Storm, dear, this is worth a lot to the network. They'll pay a million-dollar bonus."

"A million?" Her eyes widened. "Wait. That's a mil guaranteed, whether there's a story or not?"

"Yes."

Storm stared out the window of the Bentley. The snow was falling heavily now, blanketing the streets. "I can't go. I have to finish treatment. I've been sober this long. I'm not going to stop now."

"Oh God! Don't be a little ass, Storm. No one cares if you're sober. They only care if you *test* sober. It's for the insurance."

"I do," she mumbled. "I care if I'm sober."

"Storm, this is your career. I went out on a limb to convince the execs to send you after this story. They agreed to wait another thirty days to drug test you. Frankly, they didn't want to wait for you. They wanted Christina."

Storm bolted upright in the back seat. "That French bitch?"

"Yes, *her.*" Hunter knew Storm hated Christina L'Etoille, a young French war correspondent whose appetite for risky reporting was matched only by her appetite for riding the laps of top male network executives.

Storm folded her arms. "They'll have to send her. I'm not done with rehab until the thirty-first."

Hunter pursed her lips. "I repeat: Don't be an ass."

"Look, I'm sober. I sorta like me like this. I don't want to go back to the war zone yet. I'm not ready."

Hunter shoved up the sleeve on her cashmere sweater, revealing a diamond-studded watch. She studied the watch carefully. "You're not as sober as you think, dear."

"Huh?"

"In about a minute you're going to start feeling the effects of that hot chocolate."

"What are you talking about?" demanded Storm.

"I took the liberty of mixing you a nice relaxing drug cocktail that will take away your pain, and which can't be traced by any existing drug test. It's a new designer drug from that lab in Paramus. All the sports lez celebs are using this new lab now because they create only untraceable designer drugs. I put a double shot of the stuff in your hot chocolate. You should be on cloud nine in a matter of minutes. You'll feel like your old self. And you'll pass the network drug test with flying colors.

All our problems solved," Hunter said as she took Storm's face into the cool cradle of her hands.

Storm wanted to object. Open the door and run for her life. But whatever was in that hot chocolate was beginning to take hold. She felt like giggling.

Oh my God, Hunter was right: She hadn't felt this good since rehab started. She felt on top of the world, like she could walk through a storm of bullets, and never feel a thing.

53.

Missing in Action

At six p.m., the purple queermobile spun up to the Ski Kitty diner and the women piled in, noisy and excited. Candice's arms were loaded with Christmas presents, so Dirk had to hold open the door for her.

Wee Gee and Poppy came dragging a grumpy Nan down the street. Each one had a hold of one of Nan's stiff arms. Nan was still foaming at the mouth about Tinker Bell and how she was going to rip that bitch's lovely little wings. "When I'm done with her, she won't be able to get a job managing a Kmart in Kansas City," boasted Nan. "I'll call every soul on Wall Street. That twinkle twat likes her women with big balls; well, let's see how she likes it when I hit her with some really big powerful black balls."

Thumper loped across the parking lot, only to be stopped short by Dirk. "Dude, you've got lipstick all over your face," chided Dirk as she used the sleeve of her down jacket to wipe her sister's cheek clean. "You and Mary Lou have a nice time?"

"Yeah. Thanks," muttered Thumper, mindful that Mary Lou thought she should stop being such a wuss-ass about Dirk and the whole sex-change thing.

The last one to arrive was Dylan, who showed up holding a hand to the back of her neck, her eyes bloodshot.

"Headache?" asked Wee Gee.

"Yeah, man. I mean, I don't know. I was looking at these landscape paintings with some hot old chick, and then boom! Now here I am. Really weird. I think something strange happened to me back there." Dylan cast a look over her shoulder as she shoved a load of hair out of eyes. "I feel, er, like, really weird."

"Ah," said Wee Gee, "just your brain adjusting to being clean for a change. The headaches will go away in time."

"I dunno," said Dylan as she climbed unsteadily into the van.

As she slid the door shut, she noticed for the first time that she was wearing rainbow-colored mittens: thick fuzzy mittens, lined with an equally soft interior. She'd never seen these mittens in her life, and had no idea where they'd come from. She'd arrived at Sugarbush from the fair-weather state of San Francisco with no gloves or real winter wear to her name. That she was certain of.

"Cool gloves," remarked Poppy. "Where'd you get them? Fancy them myself, I think."

"Dunno," said Dylan as she studied her outstretched hands. "I got no effing idea."

"We've got to go now, ladies!" called the driver as she smoothed her flattop. "Everyone fasten your seat belts!"

"Wait!" hollered Poppy. "We can't go! Storm isn't here." Poppy searched the back of the van again but Storm was nowhere to be found. She tossed aside some presents, certain the petite war correspondent had to be in the van somewhere. She scanned the street in both directions. No Storm.

"Got my orders!" barked the driver as she put the van in gear. "Your missing lady will have to find her own way back to the center. On a tight schedule here. After I dump you ladies, I have to pick up a load of jolly boys and girls and get them to the Pride Center in Burlington. It's queer caroling night on Church Street and I'm in charge of the volunteer van pool."

The van rolled out of the parking lot toward the lower village road.

Poppy leaned forward on her seat and stared out the frosty window, desperate for some sight of Storm. They'd not driven far before Poppy spotted something that made her heart lurch. A silver Bentley blocked an alley. The New York vanity license plates read, "KINKY K."

Kinky Kincaid. That was Storm's agent's name. That car had to belong to Hunter Kincaid. And if Hunter was in town, Poppy had a bad feeling she'd managed to shanghai Storm.

"Let me out of this thing!" cried Poppy as she tore off her seat belt. "I need to get out! Now!"

When the driver refused to stop, Poppy was on top of her, clawing at her hands on the steering wheel.

"Damn!" cried the driver, who spun the van to a stop just short of ramming into the butt of a busload of Japanese tourists.

Poppy scrambled over Wee Gee's lap, sprang open the door, and ran, slipping and sliding, down the street toward the Bentley.

"Where is she going?" asked Nan as her leather-gloved hand wiped away the condensation from a side window.

"To hell, I'm afraid," sighed Wee Gee, who had also noticed the Bentley.

54.

Back-Seat Tongue Bath

Storm sprawled on her back in the Bentley as Hunter gave her neck a lavish tongue bath. Storm loved having her neck kissed. It made her wild. Horny as a teenage toad. Knowing this, Hunter wasted no time applying her vastly talented tongue to the correspondent's Achilles' heel, sexually speaking.

"That feel good?" purred Hunter. "You like that, baby?"

"Lovely," slurred Storm who was in a dreamlike state from the huge hit of designer opiates her agent had slipped into her hot chocolate. She felt freaking great. Hunter's nimble fingers, now busy inside Storm's battle fatigues, were only elevating the war correspondent's feelings of nirvana.

Hunter expertly slipped two fingers into Storm's softness. She pulled back a little, twirling a tongue in Storm's ear before inserting a third finger. Storm was squirming out of her pants now.

And moaning.

Hunter followed Storm's near-naked lead, unzipping her ski jumper, then unsnapping her garters and expertly shedding her own silk stockings. Hunter guided Storm's hand up her creamy soft thigh to her thick bush. "Do me, baby," Hunter was urging as Storm's fist began a bold exploration.

The two women were completely intertwined, deep into each other, rocking the back of the Bentley, when the back door was flung open.

"What the fuck!" called Hunter, who, completely sober, was quick to react to the frigid intrusion.

Storm reacted slowly, not even noticing the blast of cold air at first. She pulled Hunter back down into her lap, biting at the strap of her bra in an effort to disrobe her completely.

Hunter was not so eager to return to lovemaking. Seeing Poppy standing in the snowy street, her mouth agape, she grabbed Storm's bomber jacket and pulled it over her shivering nakedness as best she could.

"Fuck off!" she called to Poppy as she reached over in a failed attempt to slam shut the Bentley's door.

"Fuck off, yourself!" cried Poppy, who climbed defiantly into the back seat, straddling both women.

Suddenly Storm was aware of Poppy's presence, and her own nakedness.

"Hello there, love," cooed Poppy. "Having a good time, are we?"

Storm didn't know what to say. She tried to get one leg back into her fatigues but missed and ended up with her agent's thong panties stuck around one ankle.

Poppy stared at Storm. "Need some help, do we?" She reached down and yanked the agent's underwear off Storm's foot and threw into the agent's face. "These yours? Yes?"

Hunter caught the panties.

Storm was so drugged she couldn't form words.

Poppy did the talking instead. "Thought you fancied me! Guess not, eh? Looks like you're off me. You off me, then? That it? 'Cause I can see you're on this whore. You're definitely on this whore. Surprised you're not on her face. Guess you would have been if I'd given you a little more time, eh?"

Storm still couldn't talk. She felt frozen, like in a night-mare.

Poppy continued. "I thought you needed my help. Guess not. Guess I'm bloody in your way here, eh?"

Hunter replied. "Yes, you are. Get lost, okay? Storm's going back with me. Tonight. We're leaving for D.C. as soon as you get your underage, twiggy ass out of my car."

That did it for Poppy. Embarrassed and dejected, she jumped out of the Bentley.

Hunter wasted no time slamming and locking the door.

Poppy stood in the street, silent, letting the snow cover her, as the Bentley roared to life and slid down the alley.

She'd thought Storm had fancied her. Really liked her. She'd obviously been deluded. Storm didn't care about her. If she did, she'd not be stoned, finger-fucking some other tart.

She'd thought Storm was special. Strong.

Crap, I was wrong.

Taking a deep breath, Poppy turned in the snow and began scouring the streets for a taxi. She stood shivering in the snow in her mini dress for a long time before a yellow cab pulled up.

"Where to, sweetheart?" asked the driver.

Poppy considered that question for several seconds. She was free. She could go anywhere. Anywhere in the world.

"Sugarbush, the rehab center," she sighed at last.

"You got it, girlie!" said the driver.

55.

Silent Night, All Is Bright

That night, back at rehab, everyone was sullen. No one could believe Storm had cut out on them. "It makes no sense!" cried Nan, who was curled on the couch in the TV room enjoying a steaming cup of soy chai tea. "We've only got a week left! Six days. Why cut and run now?"

Poppy, who'd been staring at the blazing fire, turned to face Nan. "I don't think it was her. I think that whore of an agent had everything to do with this."

Dirk shrugged. "I dunno, Poppy, Storm's a grown woman. She could have come back with us, and she didn't. Guess she had her reasons."

Candice, who was sitting across from Dirk at the card table, trying to teach the younger woman how to play bridge, threw in a comment along with two discarded cards. "Don't take this personally, Poppy. Dirk's right. Storm's a big girl. She wanted to leave. It's her life. None of us could stop her."

Poppy chewed her lower lip. She knew the women were right: Storm was an adult and could make her own decisions. Still, sadness congealed like ice around her young heart. Of course it bothered her that Storm had left treatment; but what bothered her more was that she'd let herself believe Storm had fancied her. That something special had been brewing between them. That Storm would stay sober for her, if for nothing else.

What a fool I've been.

Babe entered the room, a large ax cast over her right shoulder. The blade glinted blue steel in contrast to the well-worn blackened grip. "Christmas Eve," she announced. "Anybody notice?"

Poppy eyed the ax. "What are you going to do now, love? Decapitate us?"

Babe roared in laughter.

Nan shrugged as she wandered over to the card table to see if she might organize a real bridge game with Candice and Dirk. "I'm a Jew," she said with a sigh. "This whole Christmas thing doesn't really rock me."

Poppy sighed heavily. "Doesn't feel like bloody Christmas to me, either."

"That," said Babe, "is because none of you lazy-assed little dykes bothered to go out and get us a tree."

Candice scraped back her chair. "Tree? The stores are all closed."

Babe snorted. "Store? We don't need a store. Hell, you look out that window lately? We got a few thousand trees out there. All you girls need is this" — she thrust out the ax — "and a little girl muscle," she added with a grin.

Poppy came forward and took the ax. Even that made her sad. (She and Storm had first bonded over chopping wood together.) "You care which tree we chop?"

Babe nodded. "Partial to evergreens, myself. Scotch pine. Spruce. Take your pick. We're filthy with evergreens high up on the rock ledge behind the farmhouse. Hike up. Bring back whatever strikes your fancy."

Poppy asked Wee Gee if she'd like to tag along, but the older woman had already donned her flannel pajamas and was in no hurry to scale an icy rock ridge. "Sorry, kid. Count old Wee Gee out on this escapade."

Thumper, who'd been sitting silent in a rocking chair in the corner, volunteered to help Poppy. "Could use some exercise," she said as she pulled on her snow pants.

Babe stared at the remaining women as Poppy and Thumper headed out in search of a tree. "You all look like something the moose has chewed on. Why so glum? Hell, it's Christmas Eve. You have less than a week left!"

Candice folded her arms to her chest. "Storm. We all liked her. We thought she'd make it."

Babe shook her head. "Maybe she will make it."

Nan snorted. "Without rehab?"

Babe advanced into the room. "Look, none of you know what happened to Storm. Why she left. Stop making things up in your head. And yes, people can get sober without rehab." She grabbed a sofa pillow and tossed it at Nan's head. "Storm was here long enough to get her head filled with some good ideas. Maybe she'll do just fine. You can't know. None of us can. And, in case you haven't been listening, even if you make it through rehab there's no guarantee any of you will stay clean. One day at a time. That's all you get. All of you. One day. You're clean today, thank God. But tomorrow … every one of you will have to work at this sobriety thing all over again."

The room was really quiet now.

Candice sauntered to the upright piano by the fire. She stared icily at Babe as she rolled back the cover on the keys. "Thanks for that bit of holiday cheer." She began to move her fingers along the keyboard. It took a few seconds, but suddenly a recognizable snatch of music wafted out.

Halfway through the song, Candice looked up. All the women had gathered around the piano, including Dylan. "Any of you lezzy heathens know Christmas carols?" asked Candice, who'd once been the star pianist at her father's church.

Recognizing "Silent Night," Dylan jumped in. Then Dirk. Nan, too.

"Silent night, Holy night, all is calm, all is bright," they sang.

Candice had not played a Christmas carol for three decades. Oddly enough, every word, every note, remained tightly stored in her mind. In her heart, as she sang, a fire sprang to life. "All is calm, all is bright," she belted out; and for the first time in thirty years, she almost believed it.

56.

I Got My Sister and Me

Poppy trudged the icy hillside, the ax resting over her left shoulder. Thumper had volunteered to shoulder the ax, but Poppy had insisted she carry it. The only reason Poppy had volunteered to cut down a tree was because she feared that if she remained in the farmhouse one more second, she'd burst into tears.

How humiliating.

The night was cold, black, silent. The only sound was the light crunching the women's snowshoes made as they bit through the crusty surface of the snow. Halfway up the steep ledge, Poppy had to stop to catch her breath. She jumped onto a giant boulder that was frosted in snow. Looking out over the moon that shone through the bare limbs of a stand of larches, Poppy wished Storm were with her.

Thumper jumped up beside Poppy and stared at the moon with her. Both women waited until they had their breath back before talking. Poppy spoke first, asking Thumper about her girlfriend, Mary Lou. "She left a good bit of her lips on you, I noticed."

Thumper grinned as she rubbed a cold, rosy cheek. "That girl loves her lipstick."

"You don't?"

"I love it on her."

Poppy laughed. Thumper, like her sister Dirk, seemed to take life and love so easily. "You in love?"

"Probably," mumbled Thumper. She grabbed a fistful of snow and played at packing it into a ball, but the snow was too cold to stick so she ended up dusting it off her gloves. "We've known each other, like, forever."

"She okay with Dirk's sex change?"

"Yeah. More than me."

"What? It upsets you?"

"Yeah. Kinda."

"Why?" Poppy was curious. The twins seemed so close. Inseparable. She envied their closeness since most of the time she, Poppy, felt so bloody alone in this life.

"Selfishness, I imagine," Thumper sniffled.

"How so?"

Thumper took off her stocking cap and ruffled her blonde hair, which glistened in the moonlight. "It's, well … it's, like. Well … she was always the leader. I sort of followed."

"I get it, I think. You're afraid if she's not around to push, you might lose your edge?"

"Yeah, I guess it's like that."

"Have you told her that?"

Thumper dipped the toes of her snowshoes into a drift and played at shooting snow through the air.

"Well, have you?"

"Haven't said much of anything. She doesn't know I'm mad at her." Thumper stretched her stocking cap back onto her head and jumped off the rock.

Poppy snorted. "Of course she knows! You two are closer than anything. You're like one person. Believe me, she knows!"

"You think?"

"I know!" Poppy shrieked.

"You think I should talk to her?"

"Uh, yeah. Definitely!"

"Mary Lou said the same."

"Look," said Poppy, as she jumped off the boulder and headed up the steep slope in an effort to catch Thumper, "what you and Dirk have is very special. Most people — like me — have no one. Absolutely no one. Understand?"

Thumper stopped and stared at Poppy in the moonlight. "Uh, you have, like, the whole world. Everyone knows who you are! You're, like, hot chick number one with all the girls I know. They all want to be just like you. Mary Lou: You're her idol. And girls like me, well, we just want to do you."

"I'll take that as a compliment," said Poppy, glad to know she still had a fan base. But as she climbed the icy hill, she knew Thumper was wrong: Everyone did not know her. They knew her image. The carefully crafted star image she cast into the world like a beacon.

Only one person had taken the time to get to know her, the real Poppy, in the last decade, and that person was thousands of miles away. She'd likely never see that person again in this lifetime.

The pain of that realization was almost unbearable.

57.

Falling Star

Storm hunkered in the vibrating belly of the army helicopter, keeping her lips pressed tightly together so her teeth wouldn't chatter. Combat soldiers were tucked against her, and her network cameraman, Josh Littleton, was curled at her feet, trying to check the battery pack on the portable handheld military recorder they'd been issued at the base in Baghdad. It was pitch black inside the chopper. Josh had a flashlight strapped to his head. The wildly bopping light was of little practical use.

"Fuck!" he kept saying. "The battery's dead. Fuck!" He tossed the tiny camera, but the chopper was so jostled by turbulence and packed with men that the camera bounced back into his lap.

"Calm down!" Storm hissed at him over the pulsating whirl of the blades. Storm had a raging headache. Hunter had yanked her straight out of the back seat of the Bentley and stuffed her into the first military transport headed out to Baghdad. Out of her mind on opiates, the war correspondent had not felt much during the flight overseas. Now that the drugs were wearing off, she was hyperaware of everything: her own mortality, most imminently.

Her agent had tucked a load of opiate pills into the pocket of her fatigues, but Storm was determined to stay straight. No more drugs. She had to make it into the war zone and out again running on nothing more potent than her own courage.

The helicopter swooped to the right, then to the left. The pilot was trying to locate a cloistered target in the desert of Iraq. He was supposed to drop Storm, Josh, and a handful o soldiers at the target site, where they would be taken (in theory) to an ISIS strong hold. The ISIS rebels there were supposed to give Storm an exclusive interview on their impending attack on the White House.

Storm was struggling to stay clear-headed enough to form the key questions she'd need to ask the rebels: Whom did they represent? Why attack the White House? Were they really agents of ISIS or someone else?

Josh elbowed her. "Don't like this! Don't think they know what the hell they're doing. We've been flying in circles for hours. Think this is a trap. A trap, that's what I think."

Storm wanted to say, *The U.S. military feeding us bad intelligence? No way!* Instead, she gritted her teeth and repeated her request to the cameraman that he shut up.

The advice just seemed to annoy him. "You want to get your pert little lezzie ass blown off, be my guest! I've got a wife and kids. No way I'm parachuting into that sandy hellhole."

"Suit yourself," said Storm as she took the camera from Josh and strapped it around her own heavily padded chest. "Stay here. They'll take you back to Baghdad. I'm going after this story."

Josh caught her by the shoulder as she turned from him. "Don't be a fool, Storm. This thing smells to high heaven. You could be killed down there!" He nodded into the darkness, sweat pouring off his face. Down below, red rockets shot through the night. Yellow clouds wafted up toward the descending helicopter. The noise was unbearable.

One of the soldiers made a circling motion with his right hand, signaling Storm that they were above the target — time to jump. Storm slid across the floor of the helicopter to the open door. As soon as the first soldier jumped, she elbowed her way to the dark mouth of the helicopter and followed suit.

All the way down, Josh's warnings echoed in her ears.

What if Josh is right? What if this is an ambush?

Storm had no answer. She knew two things for certain. One: This was the only thing in life she'd ever been any good at. And two: If anything happened to her on this mission, no one would miss her. No wife. No kids. Not even a pet goldfish. Storm Waters was alone in this world.

For some reason a vision of Poppy Zigfield flashed before Storm's eyes as she fell face forward toward the earth. The image came to her against the backdrop of a vast exploding desert that rushed upward like a spinning Fourth of July celebration.

"Go away!" hissed Storm at Poppy's image. "I don't deserve your friendship. I fucked it all up. I hurt you! Big time! Get out of here! Leave me! Get out of here!"

An imaginary Poppy raged otherwise at Storm.

Storm didn't get a chance to argue. Less than five hundred feet from the ground, her chute failed to deploy. One of the soldiers who had jumped with her was trying to reach onto her back, reach the second rip cord on her safety pack.

Storm was fighting him off. "Get off me!" she screamed. "For God's sake, let me die!"

58.

Bad News BBC

Everyone scurried about when Thumper and Poppy dragged the Christmas tree into the TV room, bringing with them the fresh-cut scent of balsam fir. The room swarmed with celebratory cheer. With Nan's help, the women soon had the tree screwed into a red metal stand, ready to be decorated.

Poppy stood back and sipped hot chocolate as Thumper and Dirk fought over a badly ripped box of Christmas tree decorations. Thumper grabbed one end of an impossibly long silver garland just as Dirk grabbed the other. A tug-of-war broke out. The twins had snapped the garland in two and started a playful war over a second one before Babe managed to intervene.

It made Poppy's heart warm to see Thumper and Dirk playing like sisters again. She sighed as she realized they had no idea how rare such love was in this lifetime. Poppy doubted she'd ever find such love. In a few days she'd be back in London, inside her closed circle of musical associates. She'd have to start recording almost as soon as her feet hit English soil. Her band, the Pop Tarts, was eager to try out a new sound. Two weeks after that, she'd be on the road on an Asian tour. Her life was booked solid for months to come. Poppy would have no time to do anything but sing her heart out night after night to legions of adoring fans.

Faceless, nameless fans.

Hoping to take her mind off that sad thought, Poppy tapped on the TV remote. The nightly news blared into the room. A local weatherwoman was standing in front of a fake radar screen that boasted the outline of a red Santa in a blue sled sliding across the Adirondacks of New York toward Vermont. "Santa is only an hour out from Burlington, Vermont," declared the weatherwoman. "Better get to bed now, kids!"

Babe entered the room. "That means you, ladies. Upstairs! All of you. It's an hour past lights-out!"

Laughing like children, the women jostled past Babe, upstairs. Poppy came last, switching off the lights in the TV room. She stood alone for a while, admiring the twinkling blue lights on the stately tree. She wished there really were a Santa Claus. She was, of course, old enough to know better.

After flipping off the remaining lights, she climbed the stairs slowly, not eager to curl up alone in her bed. But when she arrived in the room, Wee Gee was wide awake. And pacing. She had her laptop flipped open on the desk. A live Internet feed was issuing a special report on the battles under way against ISIS death squads.

Poppy ran across the room to see why Wee Gee looked so ashen. There, on the screen of the laptop, flashed a photo of Storm Waters. Another female reporter, not Storm, was speaking rapidly over gunfire popping in the background. "Storm Waters has been reported missing in action. All we know for sure is that she was on an important mission into the heart of the war zone in the southern provinces of Iraq this evening when she lost communication with the network. There is a rumor - and I repeat, this only a rumor - that Storm may have died trying to parachute into the war zone after a story of immense importance to the safety of everyone in this country. We'll keep you posted as news develops."

Poppy dropped down on her bed. "My God!" she wept. "That can't be right! That has to be bloody wrong!" She ran to Wee Gee's laptop and shot the browser off CNN to the BBC station. There, a male correspondent with an English accent repeated the same story.

Wee Gee slipped both arms around Poppy and hugged her tightly. "It's all right, baby girl. They don't know anything yet. She's probably fine. You know how mean and mulish that girl is. Ain't no one taking her. She's fine. I'd bet you that." Wee Gee held Poppy, who was shaking like a frightened kitten, as tightly as she dared.

59.

Life Sucks

Christmas Day there was to be no therapy. But the women requested an ad hoc group session after breakfast, anyway. They were shaken to the core by the news that Storm was missing in action.

Even Dylan was upset. "She can't be dead. Man, that can't be right. That chick was like Rambo."

Babe stuck to her mantra: "We can't know what happened to her. We have to wait. Don't jump to conclusions. Wait for the news reports. Be patient."

Dylan wasn't buying that. "That's fuckin' cold, man."

"No," insisted Babe. "It's not cold. It's life, and it is exactly how you will get through your own lives going forward. One day at a time."

Poppy spoke up. "But we feel bad! Bloody bad. And hopeless. How are we supposed to deal with that?"

"That's fine. Feeling bad is okay. You'll feel bad. The important thing -"

Dylan jumped in: "Is what we do with those feelings."

"That's right," affirmed Babe.

Poppy glared at Babe. "This rehab thing sucks."

Babe nodded. "You'd be right about that. But your life without rehab also sucked, as I recall. It's your choice, really, which kind of suckiness you'd prefer."

Nan, who had been silent all morning, spoke up. "What I don't get is what we're supposed to do with these bad feelings. I mean, how do we keep feeling this awful and not let it eat us alive? I mean, I'll be honest with you, I have no effing idea what to do with the feelings of betrayal that are churning inside me."

Babe paced the circle of the group. "What would you have done a month ago?"

"Who the hell knows! Downed a quart of gin? Knocked Tinker Bell's head off with a tire iron?"

"And now?"

"Now" — Nan pursed her lips — "I feel angry with nowhere to put it."

"What are you angry about?" asked Babe.

"That Birge left me after all these years. Left me effing here. Then left me for real with that little slut bunny."

"Why do you think she did that?"

"Excuse me?"

"You heard me. Why do you think your partner ditched you and took up with another woman?"

The room was so silent you could have heard an elf skittle.

Babe spoke next. "Did Birge say anything to you when you confronted her in that hotel room?"

Nan ground her back molars. Babe knew full well what Birge had said, as Nan had confessed all to Babe in private therapy the day before. "She said the usual crap about how it was me who'd abandoned her. Left her for a bottle of gin."

"Isn't that true?"

Poppy tried to come to Nan's rescue, but Babe made her sit down and be quiet.

Babe turned to Nan. "Is it true that you left your partner for a bottle of booze?"

Nan inhaled deeply. "All right, maybe that's somewhat true. I get how she might *feel* like that. But I'm sober now. I'm not going to run away and hide in a bottle. I'm going to deal with my feelings now."

"How does she know that?"

"Excuse me?"

"You've been with this woman almost thirty years?"

Nan nodded.

"And how long have you been drinking gin?"

"Since seventh grade."

Everyone laughed. Nan included.

"Okay," said Nan, "I get what you're telling me. You're telling me Birge has no reason to trust me, given my record. You're telling me I have to win back her trust. You're telling me I have to be the bigger person. That maybe I owe it to Birge to discuss this thing with her?"

"A discussion? I'd say that's the least you owe her. She said she wanted to talk to you about this?"

"Yes." Nan remembered the pained look on Birge's face as she'd stood literally and figuratively naked in that hotel room. Birge had been willing to talk. Nan had been the one to flee, run from the pain.

Babe spoke again. "Look, I am not excusing your partner's behavior. What she did was wrong and hurtful and deceitful BUT unless you talk to Birge, you'll not be able to work this thing through. You can't pretend to know what she's feeling. You have to have the courage to go out and ask her. Listen to what she has to say. Do you think you can do that? Do you think you can stay present and let Birge tell you how she's feeling, even if what she has to say is very hurtful for you to hear?"

"I don't know," Nan mumbled at last. "I honestly don't know."

60.

Gold Medal Muff-Diving

After group, Candice took her feelings to the exercise room. Dirk loped after her.

Candice climbed the endless steps of the StairMaster while Dirk watched.

Halfway through her workout, Candice stopped to wipe sweat from her glistening face with a microfiber towel. "Why do you watch me?" she asked Dirk, who'd been bench-pressing weights as long as Candice had been faux-climbing.

Dirk sat up and took a swig of her vitamin water. "Because you like it."

"I most certainly do not!" protested Candice.

"Yeah, you do. You like being watched. Some chicks are like that." Dirk lay back on the bench and began fiddling with the weight locks.

Candice came over and straddled the bench. She pushed herself up close to Dirk's knees. "I got you a little Christmas present." Candice slid a wrapped package out of the pouch pocket of her zippered workout jacket. She handed it shyly to Dirk.

Sitting up, Dirk took the package. "Cool! But I didn't get you anything. Me and Thumper are on a pretty tight budget."

"Doesn't matter," said Candice, shrugging. "Go ahead, open my present. I think it's just the thing for a stud bunny like you."

Dirk grinned as she tore off the wrapping paper. As soon as the paper was off, she held up a black T-shirt. The front boasted an Olympic team insignia that looked quite official. The shirt read: "U.S. Olympics Muff-Diving Team. Head Coach."

Dirk roared with laughter. "You know me so well!" She leaned over and tried to kiss Candice, but the doctor dodged the kiss.

"Whoa!" complained Dirk. "Thought you liked me." She waved the T-shirt at Candice.

"I do like you," said the doctor as she jumped back on the StairMaster. "But I'm not having sex with you."

"Huh?"

Candice had to shout to be heard above the whirling of the exercise machine. "Not yet! Not until we're out of rehab!"

Dirk slammed herself back onto the bench and resumed pumping weights with a passion. Whatever Candice wanted, she was willing to give it a try. Besides, the idea that she couldn't have sex was making her incredibly horny. No girl had ever made her wait. Not once. Never.

Dirk cast a furtive eye at Candice, who was climbing the exercise machine like her life depended on it. Dirk pumped the weights harder, happy to imagine Candice off that machine and on her.

Upstairs, in the TV room, Poppy curled on the couch, a pillow clutched to her chest for comfort. She'd been staring mindlessly at CNN for the last two hours. She'd hoped for some news about Storm on the telly, but the news channel was instead chock-full of mindless stories: lackluster retail sales, an ice storm in the Midwest that had stranded thousands at

O'Hare on Christmas Eve. Poppy didn't care about these things; she cared about Storm.

Wee Gee strolled into the room. "Any news, baby girl?"

"Nothing about Iraq."

"Nothing on the Internet, either," sighed Wee Gee. "I checked all the news sites and blogs."

Poppy offered the writer a seat next to her on the couch.

Wee Gee took the offer.

The two women were silent for a long time.

Turning down the volume on the remote, Poppy spoke first. "You scared?"

"Of what, baby girl?"

"Leaving."

"Not so much," said Wee Gee with a shrug. "Been through this before. Several times. It's hard the first couple of days. Then you start to settle into your life again. You get busy. We all will."

"You heading home? To Kentucky?"

"Not sure. Have to be back there in fourteen days. Me and my oldest girl, Shawnee, we're checking into the fat farm together."

"Oh, God!" groaned Poppy. "More rehab! How could you?"

Wee Gee chuckled. "I need to develop a new relationship with food. It'll help if someone gets me off to a running start by teaching me to cook a bit better."

Nan sauntered into the room and threw herself halfheartedly onto the couch. "Any news, ladies?"

Wee Gee and Poppy assured her there was not.

The three women sat glumly on the sofa together.

Nan broke the silence. "I'm going to my cottage in Maine when I blow this pop stand. Just for a week. Feel like I need a decompression chamber before I go back to Manhattan to deal with Birge. Anyone want to tag along? Help me celebrate the new year sober?"

"Where's Maine?" asked Poppy, cheered at the prospect of a real holiday.

"Across the mountains." Nan hitched her thumb to the east. "I have a cottage on the shore. Usually I keep it closed in the winter. We summer there, Birge and I. But it's very quiet. Peaceful. I called last night to have my people open it up for a week. You guys are welcome to hang out with me for the new year. Got plenty of guest rooms. Great view of the ocean, too."

Poppy started to decline, but then thought about the stress waiting for her back in London. She really didn't want to face that. Not yet. Not with her heart so heavy about Storm. Her band would hate her, but she could call, beg off another week. Part of the problem that had landed her in rehab had been her willingness to say yes to anything her managers had asked of her. She needed to start taking back pieces of private time. She owed herself that much. "Count me in," she said, feeling somewhat cheered.

"Ditto!" said Wee Gee, who hated to admit she had nowhere special to go to celebrate the new year.

61.

Angelic Blow Job

Dylan strapped on snowshoes and clattered across the kitchen. She creaked open the back door and peered across the yard. Behind the farmhouse ran a series of sharp rock ledges. Granite teeth gnawed through the melting snow. Nothing for miles behind the farmhouse. Just rock and snow. More of the same.

Stepping into the yard, Dylan slipped on her new rainbow mittens.

"Effing weird!" she exclaimed to herself as she stared at the mittens. It was like her hands were on fire. Her heart, too.

"Mind if I tag along?"

Dylan looked back to see Poppy standing on the steps, her jacket and snowshoes already strapped on. Dark circles ringed her eyes. Her ebony hair was yanked carelessly back in a ponytail.

"Ah, sure," Dylan said, realizing how upset Poppy must be over Storm's disappearance. "Not going anywhere special. Just need to get some air." She flipped back a swatch of hair as she spoke.

Poppy ran jogged through the snow to join Dylan.

"Ready to rock?" asked Dylan.

"Go!" cried Poppy.

The two women were off, trudging a hill, headed to the rise of an impossibly steep rock ledge. Both slipped and slid, using hand poles to balance themselves while propelling their bodies forward. The metal cleats on their snowshoes bit like teeth into the icy rock under the snow.

Dylan lost her breath several times as they advanced up the ledge. One foot would start to slip, but then the metal teeth would bite in, saving her from a nasty fall. Common sense warned Dylan back, but she had several decades of experience ignoring that pesky little voice. She ignored it, enjoying instead the feeling she was about to do something forbidden.

Dylan felt weird these days. Lost. No drugs. No sex. Like she'd flatlined in her own life. She was starting to hate being sober. She felt desperate to misbehave. Since all the other women in the farmhouse seemed serious about this rehab thing, she'd have to misbehave on her own. Poppy tagging along was a problem, but she could deal with that. Likely the skinny little femme fluff would give out and turn back. If not, Dylan would try to entice her to join in. A couple of rock ledges more and they would be in a zone where nothing but a herd of moose could bust them.

Deep in the pocket of Dylan's jeans jacket nested a baggie of marijuana and some rolling papers. She'd come upon this stash by accident. Babe had asked her to clean out Betty's room and pack Betty's things for shipment back to her. In Betty's fanny pack, Dylan had come across the drugs. She'd started to flush them, but then, well, it seemed a better test of her strength if she kept the drugs — just to prove to herself she could handle having drugs close by.

But now a toke was starting to feel like a fine idea. Anything, really, to juice her humdrum life.

Dylan huffed up a ledge, slid down a ravine, and huffed back up another ledge. She turned her head, sure the rock star would have turned back by now, but Poppy was on her heels, her cheeks streaming sweat. Poppy's dark eyes sparked with devilish determination.

Fuck, thought Dylan. She'd have to stop and hope Poppy would be cool with her taking a toke.

Less than a minute later, atop a ledge, Dylan stopped. Exhausted, the muscles in her legs and buttocks burning, she hurled her body onto a fallen birch tree that was propped at an angle, the top stuck in the fork of a hemlock. She panted, desperate for breath.

Poppy hurled her body into a snowbank beside Dylan.

The two women stared up at a milky blue sky, their mutual panting the only sound other than a light wind that whispered through the pines above them. Dylan turned to face Poppy. "You don't give up, do you?"

"Never!" panted Poppy.

Dylan stared at the sky. "You miss Storm?"

"Yes. Terribly." Pant. "Horribly, in fact."

Dylan was impressed that Poppy would admit this. She herself never admitted to needing anything — a huge part of her problem in life, according to Babe. "You in love?"

"Seems so," sighed Poppy as she turned to face Dylan.

"You going after her?"

"After her? Hell no! That woman is in a war zone." Poppy rolled her eyes.

Dylan flipped a swatch of hair out of her eyes. "I thought love conquered all," she quipped as she fished in her jacket pocket. Finding the baggie, she pulled it out and dangled it in the anemic winter sunlight, savoring its color: celadon with flecks of forest green.

Poppy sat up in the snowbank. "Don't tell me that's dope!"

"Okay, I won't tell you," said Dylan with a wry smile as she peeled off her mittens and cast them into the snow. Her hands naked, she reached into the baggie and tweezed out enough dope to slide onto a rolling paper. Artfully, using one hand, she rolled a perfect joint.

"Don't tell me you're going to smoke that."

"Okay," grunted Dylan as she flicked a match to life and held it to the joint. "I won't tell you." She tried to light the joint, but a gust of wind blew out the match.

"Don't you dare light that thing!" screamed Poppy.

"Why not?" Dylan tried again to light the joint, but again a little wind kicked up. "Fuck!" she muttered at the wind.

"Come on, Dylan!" coaxed Poppy. "You don't need that stuff. Throw it away. Race me back to the farmhouse. That ought to juice you up."

"I'd rather get stoned," Dylan remarked dourly. Unfortunately, once again the wind blew out the match before Dylan could light the joint. Dylan stared at the joint in disbelief. Then at Poppy. "Fuck," she exhaled at last. "I've come this fucking far. Might as well stay fucking clean another fucking day."

Jumping up on her snowshoes, Dylan tossed the baggie over the ridge. It landed in the snowy ravine, disappearing immediately.

Slipping her mittens back on, Dylan propelled herself upright on her poles and shot down the slope after Poppy, who had a lead of several yards. Dylan was surprised at how fast she propelled past the rock star. The power of her own body gave her an unexpected thrill.

Glinda soared on the hillside, high above Dylan, her lips puckered as ferociously as they'd been when she'd repeatedly blown out that joint. Glinda blew at Dylan's backside, helping her speed ahead.

"You go, sweet girl!" urged Glinda, the guardian angel, who had flapped her wings on a cloud above the women each time Dylan had lit a match. Glinda blew one last kiss at Dylan's cute little ass before vaporizing back into the clouds to take a heavenly nap.

Part IV

Survivors of the Bush

Interlude

As every addict knows, the test of rehab begins the day they boot you out the front door. You stand up, bush your ass off, then immediately see Temptation lurking and smirking around every corner.

The world becomes a scary place.

Poppy was probably the least scared of all the women. She might have been more frightened about facing a world stripped of drugs and alcohol had not Storm's safety weighed so heavily on her mind.

Still no word from CNN.

Poppy was glad she'd accepted Nan's offer to join her and Wee Gee at Nan's cottage in Maine to ring in the new year on a sober note. Having company would probably help keep her mind off the thing she feared the most.

Wee Gee was relieved when it came time to back her bags. She felt back on track. Spiritually, that is. Creatively, she was still staring at solid blank paper. She hoped leaving rehab might shock her subconscious into a creative fervor. Maybe staring at the ocean off the coast of Maine would give her some romantic ideas. Nan had expressed an interest in learning how to write a novel. Maybe mentoring Nan would open some creative floodgates.

The last few days of treatment, Babe kept barking at everyone that no one was ever cured of an addiction. "One day at a time, ladies. Take it one day at a time."

What that phrase meant was finally beginning to soak in with Dylan. "What if we go out there and fuck up?" she asked, mindful of how close she'd recently come.

"Some of you will," Babe assured them. "Remember: progress, not perfection!"

Dylan squinted through her hair. "What the eff does that mean?" She was beginning to think rehab was some sort of weird religious cult. All these secret sayings. "Progress not perfection," snarked Dylan, mimicking Babe. "Progress, not perfection, ladies!"

Babe took Dylan aside the last day after group. "Don't worry. We'll always have a room for you."

"I" — Dylan screwed a finger into her chest — "am never coming back to this hellhole. No way. No how. Got that?"

"We'll see," said Babe. "We'll see."

62.

Old Lady Ass Bandit

The last day of treatment, Thumper was the first to sign herself out. Dirk was right behind her. "See ya later, you freaky old chicks," said Thumper to both Babe and Lily.

Babe and Lily just laughed.

Mary Lou was waiting outside the farmhouse for Thumper, her short-bed Ford purring like an alley cat. Thumper jumped into the cab of the truck and received an immediate smooch on her lips.

Dirk, who was clutching a snowboard, started to climb into the truck also, but found someone had her by the back loop of her jeans. She spun around to face Candice.

Candice squared her shoulders. She had a private car service, a Mercedes limo, waiting to take her to the airport. "Come with me?" she asked Dirk quietly.

Dirk eyed the Mercedes. Then Candice. Then her sister.

Not wishing to be turned down, Candice explained herself further. "If you come to L.A. with me, I can hook you up with the world's best team of surgeons for your operation. Colleagues. Real artists. The guys who make Hollywood buzz."

Dirk sniffled. "You'd do that for me?"

"Of course I would."

Dirk shifted her snowboard from one hand to the other. "Only got ten thousand saved."

"Don't be silly. You don't need money. These people owe me. It's time I called in some favors. I can do some of the work. I'll do your top surgery, your chest. Your face, too," she murmured as she ran a hand lovingly over Dirk's cheekbone.

Mary Lou shouted from the truck. "Go with her! You need her help! Thumper doesn't need you. I'll get her to the World Cup trials at Lake Placid next week. I'll keep an eye on her for you."

Cradling her snowboard, Dirk stepped away from the truck and trudged after Candice through the slush to her waiting limo. They were barely in the back seat with the door closed when Dirk draped both her arms around the doctor. "Make out now?" she whined in earnest.

"Soon," Candice muttered as she leaned over and lovingly kissed Dirk on the lips. To appease her she offered just a little tongue. "I'm not really a back-seat girl. Mind if we wait until we're at my place?"

"Sure. I can go with that," muttered Dirk, who nested herself close to Candice as the limo slid down the mountain.

Nan, too, had called a car service. A uniformed female driver in a white stretch limo loaded the luggage for Nan, Poppy, and Wee Gee. When the driver reached for Wee Gee's overnight bag, the two women's hands ended up cupped atop each other. "Excuse me, ma'am," said the driver as she let go of Wee Gee's hand.

"No worries, baby girl," assured Wee Gee, who found herself watching with new interest as the chauffer picked up the remaining luggage and tucked it neatly into the trunk of the limo.

The driver was a petite woman, her black uniform cut tight to her body, which clearly had done a good bit of time at the gym. Her strawberry-blonde hair was so short that only a few spits of it curled from under her cap. Her eyes were gray with flecks of green. She was somewhere close to sixty: just the age Wee Gee preferred these days.

Poppy nudged Wee Gee. "Stop ogling that poor woman! Get a grip!"

"What the hell are you talking about!" protested Wee Gee.

"She's talking about," said Nan, as the three women slid into the back of the limo, "the way your eyes were eating holes in that woman's delicious little ass."

Wee Gee denied such action.

"Get real!" cried Poppy. "Admit to us you'd like some of that."

"I can't believe you're talking to me like that. I'm old enough to be your mum."

"My mum," countered Poppy, "isn't some sort of old lady ass bandit."

63.

Bad Hair Day in Baghdad

Storm opened her eyes to find herself in a compromised position. (And that is an understatement.) She lay on an iron cot, her right leg shackled to the frame. The tiny room where she lay was dark. A weak light, daybreak, spilled halfheartedly through a window high up on a far concrete wall.

Storm licked her lips, which were dry and cracked like paper. Her head ached. Her right arm, also. When she tried to fist her right hand, lightning pain shot up her wrist through her elbow.

She was struggling to focus her eyes when a bare bulb flared on above her cot and the door to her room swung open. Three men stormed in, one dressed in a khaki uniform with an array of medals swinging from his chest.

Definitely not Americans.

The men began shouting at her in Arabic. Two of them poked her ribs with a bayonet, one on each side of the cot. Finally convinced she was securely held captive, the man with the medals pulled a chair next to the cot and began to shout at her in English. When he held up his hand, the other two men stopped chattering. They leaned against the wall and lit cigarettes, their rifles no longer held toward Storm in threatening positions.

"Thanks for calling off Larry and Moe," said Storm weakly. Her lips hurt when she spoke.

"You want water?" asked the uniformed man. "Here!" He raised a hand to one of the soldiers. "Bring her water!"

Storm sipped at the water. It hurt to swallow. More so to sit up. She was relieved when the cup was empty and she could collapse back onto the squeaky cot.

"Why are you here?" demanded the man with the medals, his nose almost touching Storm's. His breath was fragrant with onions and an assortment of unidentified spices. He needed a shave (and a facial, she thought).

"I got an invitation," said Storm.

The man laughed. "That is funny. This is war. There are no invitations. A war. Understand?"

"I'm with the press." Storm slid a hand into the front pocket of her fatigues searching for her credentials.

"You want these, maybe?" asked the uniformed man. He plucked her passport and press pass from his own jacket pocket. He flipped open the passport and studied it at arm's length. He squinted at the press pass. "This is you? Not a very good picture."

"Bad hair day," complained Storm.

The man roared in laughter. "This American lady is funny. You are very funny. I like that."

Storm tried to think of a comeback but her mind could not focus. She felt like she might throw up. What the hell had happened to her? Apparently her chute had opened. She'd survived the jump. But who were these men?

"Who are you?" she asked as she opened her eyes.

"You, the American press, might call us assassins."

"Is that what you call yourself?"

"No, we call ourselves soldiers. Warriors."

"ISIS?" asked Storm.

"Yes."

She collapsed back on the cot and swallowed hard. "I was afraid of that."

64.

Cottage, Castle: Why Quibble?

In Maine, later that night, the white limo bearing Nan and her friends slid to a stop at a high iron gate. A six-foot-tall bluestone wall blocked the view from prying eyes. The driver lowered the glass between her section and the back seat. "Ma'am," she addressed Nan, her voice husky. "Need a code. For your security gate."

Nan uttered a string of numbers and the driver raised the partition window back up.

Wee Gee stared out the window as the limo crunched across the snow, up a snaky drive lined with white pines. The massive trees dripped snow. Floodlights illuminated the long driveway. Wee Gee could see where previous tires had worn through the snow to reveal a yellow bed of pine needles. A four-story shingle-style stone mansion popped into view as the limo rolled over the last incline and into a tight circle drive.

Wee Gee turned to face Nan. "Girl, you said you owned a cottage."

"I do. This is it. Stone Ledge. My summer cottage."

"Really?" said Wee Gee. "Just for the record, how big is this here cottage?"

Nan shrugged. "Fifteen thousand feet, give or take?"

Poppy sprang open the back door and ran into the snow. "It's a freakin' castle!" she called as she jumped around the limo trying to get a better view of Nan's floodlit home. "A freakin' castle."

Nan stepped back and studied the stone mansion. "I guess, but to me it's a cottage. Where I've always come to get away from the world."

Wee Gee squeezed Nan's arm. "Don't worry. We'll help you with Birge."

"Help me?" questioned Nan.

"Help you decide what to say to her. You know, what to say to win her back."

Nan was about to protest that maybe she didn't want Birge back when the double front doors to the mansion opened and a troop of uniformed servants swarmed the limo.

The driver came around to the trunk and lifted the women's bags onto a handcart the doorman had ushered onto the driveway. Each of the servants greeted Nan.

"Servants?" squealed Popp as the staff moved out of earshot with their luggage. "You have bloody servants?"

"They came with the castle."

"'Course they did!" said Wee Gee with a roll of her eyes.

The women were wrangled together by the head butler (also a woman) into the downstairs library. The library, which was way bigger than any cottage Wee Gee had ever seen, was lined with framed photos and news stories about Nan and Birge. Covers from *Fortune* and *Forbes*. Features from *The Wall Street Journal.* One of the covers showed Nan about ten years younger wearing a crown some photographer had air-brushed onto her image. "The Queen of Bonds," proclaimed the cover.

Poppy made herself dizzy dancing in circles admiring the press mementos. "You really were famous. Bloody famous!"

"*Were* being the operative word, little darling," retorted Nan.

The butler returned to the library wheeling a tray laden with a bottle of Nolet's Reserve, an ice bucket, and a mouthwatering assortment of other miniature liquor and mix bottles.

Wee Gee grabbed the bottle of gin just as Nan's hand reached for it. "You'll need to pour this down the drain," she instructed the butler. "You got a bar in this little cottage?" she asked the shocked domestic.

"Several, ma'am," said the woman.

"Show me where they are. We need to dump the booze. Pronto."

The butler eyed Nan, a look of uncertainty on her face. "Ma'am, is that what you wish?"

Nan sighed as she plopped down in a wingback leather chair and lit a Dunhill. "Do what she says."

Halfway out of the library, Wee Gee hot on her tail, the butler turned to ask one final question of her employer. "Excuse, me, but you want it all poured out, ma'am? Ms. Birge's hundred-year-old Scotch also?"

"Oh, yes!" Nan's eyes gleamed. "Definitely the Scotch!"

65.

Bush Baby Goes Down

Thumper stared straight down the sheer summit of the mountain. Her feet were bound to her board, her knees bent as she readied herself to jump the slope. The wind had kicked up, and she was having a hard time, even with her goggles down, deciphering the racecourse. Sleet cut her cheeks.

Three women lined the starting gate to Thumper's right, all of them finalists to represent the American team in the snowboarders' World Cup. The best of three runs would win a top spot on the team.

So far, Thumper ranked dead last.

Mary Lou straddled the railing at the side of the gate, screaming, "Go baby! Go!" She was so loud Thumper couldn't help but hear her. In high school Mary Lou had been head cheerleader for the football team, the Mt. Mansfield Moose. Thumper had shyly watched Mary Lou perform for the boys' team from the sidelines. It felt good to have Mary Lou by her side now, cheering her on.

"Go bush baby! Go!" cheered Mary Lou as she popped up and down on the rail, eager to aid Thumper.

Thumper wet her lips and swallowed hard as the digital clock in front of the racers ticked down from ten. She had to get a grip on her ride. This was the last run of the day. Her last chance. Twice she'd failed to get close enough to the other racers to cut them off. She'd allowed them to run her to one side. As a result, she'd repeatedly lost precious split seconds. She was painfully aware that her sister would never have allowed anyone to edge her out. Dirk took every advantage. Dirk had a killer instinct on the racecourse, something Thumper had always lacked.

Thumper sucked in her breath and shot out of the holding gate as the clock hit zero. To everyone's surprise, she slid into the lead as she zoomed through the second turn. Sleet was falling like spitballs, blinding her, as she whooshed around the final turn. Shutting her eyes to the sleet, she struggled to imagine every final kink in the championship course. She'd learned this trick from her sister. In foul weather most boarders strained to see the course. Dirk had taught Thumper to shut her eyes, envisioning the course instead. On bad-weather days such a strategy gave Thumper a true competitive edge. She didn't need to see the course.

Halfway down the hill, her body swaying to keep a balance against the icy edge of the snow that threatened to dump her at every turn, Thumper was almost a full second ahead of the pack.

On track for a new world record.

But then, out of nowhere, as she jumped the last ramp, Thumper felt a body whoosh down at her right side. She looked over to see Jane Josten, from New Hampshire, neck in neck with her as they shot toward the taped finish line.

Jane was dressed in a red spandex suit with a yellow devil curled around her right thigh. (Very appropriate, as Jane was known on the pro lezzy circuit for her cutthroat moves.) Jane was so close, Thumper could see perspiration frozen in a pencil-thin mustache above her lips.

Thumper realized she had only one chance. She had to move closer to Jane, so close that the spray from her board would unbalance the other woman. Tricky, because sliding that close would mean that she, Thumper, would risk dumping her own board or forfeiting the race to a foul.

What would Dirk do?

Thumper leaned her muscled body a fraction of an inch to the right, toward Jane. In a flash, Jane went down, sliding on her right thigh across the slope into a crowd of cheering spectators. Onlookers tumbled like bowling pins.

Unfortunately, Thumper followed suit. Her break wasn't as clean as Jane's. Instead, she tumbled head over heels. She heard something snap as she landed on her back.

What the hell was that? she wondered as the world spun black.

66.

Emotional Baggage

Dirk couldn't believe Candice lived in the place the airport limo had pulled up to.

"Holy shit!" she said as she peered up at a four-story, white adobe mansion tucked into the side of a crumbing ocher cliff. Three separate porches, all glass enclosed, jutted off the main house. The sparkling porches cantilevered over the water. The Pacific Ocean licked the cliff foundation under the house.

Dirk tasted the salt of the ocean as she cradled her snowboard and licked her lips, which were chapped from the artificial air of the transcontinental flight.

"Like it?" asked Candice.

"I'll say!" said Dirk.

"Wait until you see inside. It's very cool. I designed it myself."

"You design houses?"

"Just my own."

The limo driver shouldered the bags up a steep flight of concrete-and-steel stairs. Candice and Dirk climbed to the glass abode, careful to stay back from the driver's swing of the baggage. As they stepped into the foyer, Dirk stared down beneath her feet to see cobalt-blue water ebbing far below. The

281

floor in the foyer of the house was made of tempered, pebbled glass. "Cool!" gasped the snowboarder.

The interior of the house reminded Dirk of a museum. Or a church. Nothing like the dairy farm in Vermont, where she had been raised. Two modern paintings, shocking purple and yellow, both bigger than the side of a barn, hung at angles on the far whitewashed wall of the living room, which stretched four stories high at the apex. Sunlight spilled like diamonds into the immense white room.

Candice motioned for the driver to set the bags down on an antique Chinese bench in the foyer. She tipped him generously and he was gone.

Dirk traipsed across the living room and threw herself onto a U-shaped off-white sofa that was twenty feet long.

"Shoes!" chastised Candice. Sitting on the sofa next to Dirk, she helped her unlace the black canvas high-tops.

Dirk stretched out on the sofa and grinned as she kicked off her tennies. Her Olympic muff-diver T-shirt rode up, revealing a washboard stomach and the delicate hollows of her hips.

Candice admired Dirk's muscled body. "My God, you're beautiful!" she exclaimed. "Just gorgeous!"

"Come here," Dirk said as she slipped one arm around Candice's waist, pulling her down on the sofa. "We're home. Can we make out now?"

Candice didn't answer. She couldn't because her tongue was in Dirk's mouth, teasing and playing, then teasing some more.

In response, Dirk ran her hands up under the back of Candice's silk blouse. "I really want you, baby," she whispered hoarsely in Candice's ear.

Rolling to one side, Dirk attempted to flip the doctor, gain the upper hand.

Candice fought her for it.

Dirk pulled away. "I thought you were femme."

"I am," murmured Candice. "Femme top." To illustrate, she flipped herself astraddle Dirk's lap in a split second.

"Mmm!" said Dirk, who cupped the doctor's ass as she pushed up tightly between her legs. Candice's mid-length skirt was getting in the way so Dirk reached around to unhook it. She was halfway there when a voice startled them both.

"Mind if I join the fun?"

Dirk sat up, startled.

Candice tumbled off Dirk's lap, catching the edge of the sofa to break her fall.

A petite blonde with long curly hair stood in the center of the room, wearing a pink Brazilian-cut bikini and a wide smile. A white gauze cover-up barely veiled a generous double-D cup. Her pale eyebrows had been tweezed into nonexistence. The blonde balanced a margarita glass in one hand, a cigarette in the other. She blew a smoke ring at Candice. Then Dirk.

Candice sat up and stiffened. "Get out!" she barked at the blonde.

"I don't think so," said the woman, who advanced toward Candice. The woman eyed Dirk. "Where'd you pick up this gorgeous bush baby? Rehab? If so, I'm getting sober. Pronto. Hey, aren't you going to introduce us?"

Candice took another drag. "I said get out! Get out of my house or I'll call the freaking police."

Dirk stood. "I think you better do like she says."

"You think that, do you? God, and here I thought you had balls. You do have balls, don't you?" The woman advanced, clearly intent on unzipping Dirk's jeans, a job Candice had already begun.

Candice picked up her purse and coldcocked the woman. Three blows and the woman was passed out on the sofa next to her.

"Who is that?" croaked Dirk.

"Baggage," sighed Candice. "Emotional baggage, from my drug days. Her name is Hallie. She runs Hollywood's leading makeup studio. A place called Face Off." Candice made an unpleasant face. "We used to date. Well, she called it dating. Mostly we popped pills together. She'd grope my tits every now and then like it was some big favor. I wrote her drug scrips. We pretended we were both normal het women. It was all very sick."

67.

Little Lezzy Storm Trooper

After a slow afternoon hike along the boulders above the sea in Maine, Poppy and Nan and Wee Gee decided it was time to drink hot chocolate and indulge in an old romantic movie. "Birge loves old romance flicks. We have a huge collection in the theater room," offered Nan.

"Theater room?" asked Wee Gee.

"This way, upstairs," said Nan. "Birge designed the theater room. I'll warn you, the screen is sort of large. Birge had to get trifocals a few years ago. She built this damn thing when she was in denial over her eyes and the rest of her getting old."

After riding up a mahogany-and-brass Victorian elevator in the mansion to the third floor, and meandering down own a hallway or two, Nan finally slid open double pocket doors.

The women walked into a room the size of a small movie theater with a blue silk screen any multiplex owner would envy. The decor was old-fashioned and impressive, in keeping with the rest of the residence. Carved wood panels graced the walls. A vaulted ceiling boasted an Italian mural complete with flying cherubs. Red velvet drapes hugged each side of the blue screen.

The women walked down a long slope to sit up front on a purple velvet couch.

Poppy eyed the cavernous room. "This Birge of yours has one bloody ego, yes?"

Nan laughed. "We both do. It's the primary reason we made such good partners. Nothing is ever good enough for Birge. I'm a pain in the ass at the same level. The only difference: I was born to the manner, whereas Birge grew up poor but determined."

Wee Gee settled onto the velvet sofa, enjoying how soft it was. "You call Birge yet?"

"No."

"Why the hell not?"

Nan twisted her lips. "Why is everyone on her side in this thing? She cheated on me. She's the harlot! Not me! I'm the injured party here. Me!"

Poppy shrugged as she rifled through a tooled-leather box that held DVDs of a hundred old films. "You ought to talk to her. You did just sort of run out on her. You two were together a long time. I mean, what she did was bloody awful, but people make mistakes. Yes?"

Nan rolled her eyes. "Give me that box! You guys don't need a romance movie. You're already sick with love. What do you two single dykes know about love, anyway?"

Poppy cried out. "Ouch! That hurt!"

"Sorry," murmured Nan. "Look, maybe we ought to watch some TV. See if CNN has any fresh news about Storm."

Nan plucked a remote from a side pocket on the couch and flicked on the mega-screen. A few thumb jabs later, the women were tuned to CNN. A twenty-foot-tall war correspondent yakked at them. He was dressed in battle khakis, but his hair was carefully fluffed, and he was wearing eyeliner.

"Nancy boy!" jeered Poppy.

But then the women grew silent.

The correspondent was talking about Storm. "The Pentagon received an encoded Internet message from ISIS this morning. They have Storm Waters in custody. I repeat: They have taken Storm Waters, CNN's top war correspondent, hostage. They are asking for a prisoner exchange. They want three of their key operatives released in exchange for Storm Waters's life."

The news camera jumped from the desert of Iraq to the desk of a former five-star general, now a CNN military adviser. "General," spoke the correspondent by satellite, "will the Pentagon agree to such an exchange?"

"Not on your candy-assed life," boomed the general, who, oddly enough, also appeared to be wearing eyeliner.

"You sound confident."

"I am. The Pentagon adheres to a strict no-negotiation policy. This woman is a civilian hostage. Civilians can do what they want, but the Pentagon won't waste precious resources trying to rescue them. This woman — all civilians who enter the war zone — are on their own. If this reporter has any friends watching out there, they should organize some sort of civilian release effort. If not, she'll go down as a war casualty."

Poppy stood up and sprinted up the incline toward the door.

68.

The Things We Do for Love

Wee Gee stuffed a few things into her overnight bag and hurried after Poppy, who had already ordered a car to transport her to the airport in Portland, Maine.

"Wait!" screamed Wee Gee, waving a knitted scarf and snow boots toward Poppy as she ran. "You can't do this alone! Old Wee Gee is coming with you!"

Poppy crossed her arms and tapped her foot as she waited in the snow outside the mansion for her ride. "You don't have to."

"I know that, you little English fool. I'm not coming because I have to. I'm coming because I want to. Understand?" Wee Gee was in Poppy's face now, a move that reminded Poppy that in any hand-to-hand combat the older woman might easily win simply by throwing her weight around.

"Get in the bloody car, then," snarled Poppy as the limo pulled up.

As soon as the two women were settled in the back seat, Wee Gee began to quiz Poppy. "You got a plan? 'Cause I'm thinking we definitely need a plan. Not like you can parachute your skinny English ass into the middle of a religious war and live to sing about it."

"Why not?" asked Poppy, her lips set in determination.

Wee Gee swallowed hard. She knew Poppy well enough to know they both might end up rat meat in some desert foxhole. "Fuck!" she muttered to herself. When she got back to Kentucky, she swore she was going to stop hanging out with lesbo addicts, especially the young ones. "Crazy fuckers, the lot of them," she muttered under her breath.

The limo was barely off the estate when a vintage silver-blue Jaguar sped by, nearly taking the side of the limo with it.

Poppy powered down the window, and craned her neck to see who'd just almost sideswiped them. She saw the Jaguar fishtail in the snow before slowing at the security gate to Stone Ledge. A hand shot out the window and punched in the access code, causing the iron gates to swing open. The vehicle, which featured vanity plates emblazoned "BIRGE1," spun up the private drive toward the mansion.

"Blimey!" cried Poppy. "I think that was Nan's Birge!"

"Really?" Wee Gee stuck her head out the window alongside Poppy's, but the Jaguar had disappeared.

Poppy powered up the window. "You think Birge will fight for Nan?"

"She would if this were my novel."

Poppy eyed Wee Gee. "Did you bring your laptop?"

"Laptop? Hell no, you yanked us out of there so fast I barely had time to grab my own ass!"

Rummaging in her mesh bag, Poppy pulled out a notepad and pen. "Here, take these." She thrust the items at the novelist.

"Why?"

"Because we're about to fix your bloody writer's block. Watch what I do. Take it all down. You're about to see love in action. We'll whip up a best seller. Trust me, okay?"

Wee Gee began to write as fast as she could. Some of what she jotted down was real. Some not. "What name do you want me to use for you in this sordid thing?"

Poppy crossed her legs at the ankles and settled back in the leather seat. "Prudence."

"What?"

"P-R-U-D-E-N-C-E. That's my legal name, love. Very romantic, don't you think?"

69.

Swan Song of a Lezzy Slut

Nan was just sitting down to a quiet dinner of prime rib with red potatoes sautéed in butter and fresh rosemary when Birge burst through the library door.

"Thought I'd find you here," she gruffed as she crossed the room. The steel-tapped heels of her Italian loafers resounded on the wooden floor like military marching boots.

Nan plucked up a steak knife and threatened Birge with it. "Stay away from me! You - you - you, lezzy slut!"

"Put that knife down!" scolded Birge.

Nan picked up a second knife instead (the butter knife) and began to wave it, also.

Birge halted in her tracks. "What the hell are you doing?"

"Protecting myself."

"From?"

"You."

The two women eyed each other warily.

Birge stepped forward.

Nan picked up a brass bookend and hoisted it aloft.

Birge stepped back.

"Look," said Birge. "Rehab ended two days ago. Why the hell didn't you come home? I've been worried sick about you."

"Worried? I can't see that. Why, last we met, dear, you had your face buried in Tinker Bell's sticky little sugarbush."

"That was mean."

"It was meant to be."

Birge circled Nan, wary of her weapons, uncertain of her sanity. "Can we please talk about this?"

"We did talk. In therapy. Two weeks ago. You lied. Said everything was okay."

"It was. I love you. I want to talk about this. Work it through."

"Where's your bush baby? Out in the Jaguar?"

"Fired her."

"Probably a smart move. I mean, as an employee she could sue you for sexual harassment. Now you can ball her to your heart's content." Nan rounded the library table, moving closer to Birge. "Assuming she's legal, of course. She is legal, isn't she?"

Birge crossed her arms against her chest. "This is not your most attractive side."

"Get used to it, sister. This is me, sober."

"You're not drinking?" Birge shot a glance at Nan's table setting. Sure enough, there was no frosted glass of gin, just a bottle of diet cherry Coke.

"That was the point of rehab, dear. I went to rehab to get sober. I am sober. And I have to tell you since I got sober I've discovered I'm a little bit pissed."

"About what?"

"Quite a bit, it seems."

"Like?"

"Tinker Bell."

Birge narrowed her eyes. She plucked a silver cigarette case from the inner pocket of her jacket and popped it open. She lit a cigarette for herself before continuing. "I told you, she's gone." Birge exhaled. "I had her transferred to our office in the

Caymans. She accepted it as a promotion. I'll not see her again. Anything else you want from me?"

Nan's eyes softened. "Do you love her?"

"God no!" cried Birge. "Why would you think that?"

"You were fucking her."

"Yes, I was. And for the record that was unbelievably stupid of me. The dumbest thing I've done in this lifetime, next to that time I voted for Ronald Reagan."

70.

Feel That?

When Thumper opened her eyes, a sea of faces floated above her: Mary Lou, her coach, two men in red jumpsuits, whom she did not recognize, though she recognized their uniforms as medical personnel.

"What happened?" Thumper asked Mary Lou, whose hazel eyes were wide with concern.

"You wiped. Totally," said Mary Lou, who was squeezing one of Thumper's hands. "You feel that?"

"Yeah. Feels good."

Mary Lou smiled.

One of the medics leaned into Thumper's face. "You took a bad tumble, ma'am. We need you to stay conscious, if possible. Talk to us. Work with us."

"Okay," said Thumper, concerned now that maybe she wasn't okay. Everyone looked scared. Maybe she ought to be scared, too.

The medic squeezed Thumper's remaining hand. "Feel that, ma'am?"

"Yeah," said Thumper. "But I like it better when she does it."

Mary Lou leaned in. "I'll squeeze you some more, I promise, honey, but you have to behave yourself now. Let these men finish their medical exam."

Thumper nodded, relieved to discover her neck seemed fine. More than one pro snowboarder she knew had snapped vertebrae during a tumble. "What about my legs?" she asked the medics hoarsely.

One of the medics popped into her face again. "You didn't feel that?"

"What?" Thumper leaned her neck up and stared down at her feet as best she could. She was surprised to see her boots off, her naked feet frosted with snow. "Feel what?" she asked, panic tightening her throat.

She watched as one medic ran a metal reflex rod along her foot, then her ankle. "Feel that?"

"No," said Thumper hoarsely.

The medic switched legs and repeated the procedure.

"I can't feel that," cried Thumper, trying hard to keep her voice level. She could see the fear in Mary Lou's eyes; God, how she hated that. "Take me to the hospital?" she asked the medic.

"Yes, ma'am," said the medic. "We're going to do that, just as soon as we have you strapped onto the body board."

Thumper didn't like the sound of that. Body board sounded way too much like body bag for her liking.

"Stand back!" cried one of the medics.

Thumper felt the medics grab hold of her parka and lift her onto the bright-orange board. One of them cradled her head, slipping her neck into a cervical collar. The other busied himself tightening black nylon straps around her body.

Thumper tried to bend her knees, just for the hell of it, but no matter how hard she concentrated she couldn't make her leg muscles obey her mind. Her legs lay stiff. Dead.

"I'm okay," she lied to Mary Lou as the medics loaded her into the back of the ambulance. "Fine. Okay. Understand?"

"I understand perfectly," said Mary Lou, who jumped into the ambulance with Thumper, still holding her hand.

"Ma'am," complained one of medics. "You can't ride back here, it's against the law. Your sister will be fine. You go on and meet us at the hospital."

Mary Lou ignored the medics, except for the comment about her "sister." "She's not my sister. She's my partner. Now get on that little radio of yours and call this in to emergency or whatever you guys do. I'm not going anywhere but up your ass if you don't do everything you possibly can to help the love of my life get up and walk again."

71.

Reality TV

Storm woke up, rolled onto her side, and hurled like a Scud missile over the edge of the cot. She gazed after her lunch, pita bread and some sort of mystery meat, happy to have it out of her system.

The military officer, who had by now introduced himself as Hasi Ahmad, stood up from his chair in the corner and stalked toward her cot. "You do not feel well?"

Storm wiped her lips on the shoulder of her combat jacket. "You might say that. Do you have my camera?"

"Yes, I think." Hasi pulled the camera out of a pile of equipment and firearms nested in a corner of the room. "This? Yes?"

"That's it," said Storm. "I was thinking maybe we could do an interview."

"An interview?" Hasi raised his eyebrows. "With me? For American TV?"

"Unless you have someone more handsome stashed around here. I was thinking my people would like to know about you, your men, what you are fighting for."

Hasi frowned. "We are fighting to kill you."

"I got that," said Storm. "I mean your message, your religious message."

"We sent your people a message. When you were asleep."

Storm sat up, as best she could, given her ankle was chained to the cot. "What message? What did you say?"

"We want to trade you."

"Trade me?"

"Yes, for three of our men."

"They'll never do that," scoffed Storm. "Your men are military prisoners. I'm a civilian. A reporter. The military doesn't care about me."

"That is bad for you."

Storm chewed her bottom lip. "Look, you're probably going to kill me. Yes?"

"Yes."

Storm flinched a little at Hasi's forthrightness. "So, how about we do an interview, anyway? How about you tell the American people why you're going to kill me? Then, after I'm dead you can mail the tape to my TV station and upload it to YouTube and everyone in America will hear your message."

Hasi rubbed the side of his face with the edge of the bayonet on the end of his rifle. "I think I like this."

Storm sat up and pointed at the camera, which lay in Hasi's lap. "All you have to do is turn on that red button. Set the camera on top of something so it's high enough to tape us. Release my ankle so I can come over there and sit next to you and then I'll ask you a lot of questions. You'll be famous."

"Like on *Survivor*?" asked Hasi, his grin wide.

"Something like that," grumbled Storm as she yanked at her elaborate ankle bracelet. "Come here. Unlock this thing. Let's get started. I want that tape done by the time you decide to shoot me."

Hasi scooted over and slid a key into the padlock on Storm's ankle. He did not see how releasing this little American woman could make any difference. Besides, he liked the idea of seeing himself on TV.

72.

Who Has to Ask?

Poppy threw a set of khaki desert fatigues at Wee Gee's face. "Pull these on," she commanded in a hoarse whisper.

The two women were cramped together inside a supply closet on a military air base just outside Herndon, Virginia. Poppy had used her rock star credentials, a phone call to her booking agent in the U.K., and her outrageous flirting skills to earn them special passes at the USO entrance. She and Wee Gee were booked to depart ASAP as entertainment for the troops. Poppy was to sing. Wee Gee's pass declared her a backup dancer: a Pop Tart.

Wee Gee shook her head at the fatigues. "If I put those on, I could be shot for impersonating a soldier, maybe even treason, baby girl."

"That's the general bloody idea," griped Poppy as she zipped up her own fatigues. Her uniform was a bit baggy. "Blimey!" she called as she studied her reflection in a floor-length mirror. "My ass looks like a Frisbee in these fatigues. Don't know how Storm pulls this look off."

"That girl has junk in her trunk. You don't even have a trunk. More like a shoebox."

"My ass is not unattractive!" protested Poppy.

"It is if you like a little rump in your hump."

"Ass bandit!" growled Poppy.

Wee Gee threw a duffel bag of medical supplies at Poppy's head.

A noise outside the closet caused both women to sober up. Poppy hurriedly stuck her long hair up under a duty cap. Wee Gee followed suit. "Let's board that plane."

The two women crept out of the closet toward a runway outside a hangar where two transport planes were loading soldiers for desert deployment. It was dark on the runway. All the marching women were dressed alike n khaki dessert print fatigues so it was very easy for the singer and Wee Gee to fall into step and blend in.

Wee Gee had never seen so many bull dykes in her life. She leaned over and whispered into Poppy's ear as they fell into formation: "Don't ask, don't tell. Hell, what sane sober person has to ask!"

A sergeant at the boarding door to the plane barked for silence as Poppy and Wee Gee approached. The sergeant's hand shot out after Poppy had gone into the plane, blocking entrance for Wee Gee. "Who might you be, little lady?" barked the sergeant.

Wee Gee thrust out the plastic USO pass Poppy had obtained for her. "Wee Gee Judd, ma'am. I'm here to shake my groove thing for you girls." Wee Gee wiggled a bit to illustrate her point.

The sergeant, a gray-haired Latina with cheekbones that could cut glass, and eyes as black as obsidian, made a sound deep in her throat. "This pass says you're a backup dancer. Damned Pop Tart. Kinda old for that, aren't you?" The sergeant held the pass firmly, yanking Wee Gee toward her as she spoke.

Squaring her shoulders, Wee Gee leaned into the sergeant's ear and whispered, "Honey, this girl will never too old for some of that, if you catch my drift."

The sergeant roared with laughter. "How long will you be with us?" the sergeant asked Wee Gee as she stepped to one side, allowing her to enter the plane. (Wee Gee did not miss the fact that the sergeant gave her posterior the old twice-over.)

"Long enough to get to know you better," whispered Wee Gee as she slid on by.

As soon as Wee Gee was settled next to Poppy, the rock star leaned over and whispered into her ear. "What the bloody hell were you doing back there?"

"Booking a date," said Wee Gee with a satisfied smile.

Wee Gee and Poppy fell into silence as the plane rumbled to life. Even if the two friends had wanted to turn back, they were in too deep. The door had closed. Literally and figuratively. They were a hop and a skip away from active duty.

For the first time in a decade, Wee Gee Judd shut her eyes and prayed.

73.

Free at Last, Free at Last

Dylan stripped off her jeans and stepped boldly into the hot blast of her own shower. She shook her head, flinging water everywhere. Water rained across her shoulders, down her lanky backside and legs, as she twirled in the shower.

God, it's delicious to be home again. Free at last! Free at last!

Dylan lived in the top story of a three-story renovated work/live studio warehouse midway up Portrero Hill, in San Francisco. On a clear day, she could see the downtown skyline across every window. Right now, inside her glass-block shower, she had such a view through a curtain of steam.

God. It's great to be home again. No bitchy old ladies acting like my mother. No one keeping me from having fun.

Dylan jumped out of the shower and eyed the treatment release papers that lay on a wine barrel converted into a table beside her king-size bed as she wrapped a towel around her boyish hips. She stumbled over a roll of canvas and an industrial-sized box of burnt sienna paint on her way to snatch some fresh clothes from the walk-in closet.

Dylan wasn't surprised when the Japanese temple bells she'd installed in the hallway outside her studio pealed out, announcing a visitor.

"About freakin' time!" she yelled as she loped to the warehouse door and slid it open. She didn't quite have both legs shoved into a fresh pair of black hipster jeans when her visitor stepped into the warehouse space.

Bunny Van Randolph stood there, a white Westie cradled in her arms. She was wearing a midriff-length white leather jacket accented with pink diamond-studded cuffs and collar. The dog wore a matching ensemble.

"You have a dog?" asked Dylan as she raked back a flap of hair, a look of terror on her face.

"Like, yeah. This is Mr. Yummy. And I love him to death." Bunny rubbed noses with the yapping dog. "Mommy loves her Mr. Yummy. Yes she does!"

Dylan stepped back.

"What are you doing?" chided Bunny. "Mr. Yummy won't hurt you." Bunny held the dog out, but Dylan sidestepped the squirming pet. "Hold him!" commanded Bunny. "If you hold him, he'll stop yapping."

Dylan dodged the squirming dog as she slid around Bunny. She threw herself onto an overstuffed shabby-chic sofa. "Dogs totally freak me out," she confessed as she slung one leg over the back of the sofa and reached for a cigarette.

Bunny advanced, releasing Mr. Yummy under his own volition. The dog ran to the kitchen, where he engrossed himself in a scent trail close to the refrigerator.

Dylan sat up and lit her cigarette, obviously relieved. "Uh, sorry, but dogs freak me out. I mean, I really have a thing about them."

Bunny shed her jacket and, tossing it onto the back of the sofa, sat down next to Dylan. She reached up and raked the damp hair from Dylan's eyes. "I missed you. You miss me?"

Dylan shrugged. "Hey, I don't want to give you the wrong idea here."

Bunny slid a hand to the back of Dylan's neck. "Nothing wrong about this," she purred as she kissed Dylan with a good bit of passion.

Dylan squirmed until she'd managed to slip out from under Bunny's arms. She flipped the hair from her eyes with the heel of one hand. "Sorry, I guess I should have been clearer on the phone, about why I wanted to see you."

Bunny crossed her arms to her chest. "I didn't think that needed an explanation."

"Uh, I think it kinda does." Dylan was up now. She paced to an overstuffed chair and threw herself into it before continuing speaking. "I owe you an amends," she blurted as she continued to fidget uncomfortably in the chair.

"What?"

"An amends. That's why I wanted to see you. I was thinking about it. I gave you drugs in rehab. I probably messed up your chance at getting sober."

"No biggy." Bunny shrugged.

"Yeah," countered Dylan, "I think it kinda is."

Bunny narrowed her eyes. "Oh my God, they got to you, didn't they? You've been mind-fucked by those rehab goons. Oh my God!"

Dylan blushed. "No one fucked any part of me. I just think maybe this sobriety thing makes sense. I'm gonna give it a try."

Bunny stood. "You made me fly all the way out here to hear this!"

"I wanted to tell you in person."

"How thoughtful of you. No offense, dear, but you if you were going to dump me you could have done that in a text."

"Dump you? How could I dump you, I never picked you up."

"I beg to differ!" Bunny cried, her voice escalating.

Dylan took a deep breath and counted to ten (just like Babe taught her to do). "Look, I don't want to argue. I thought maybe you and I could go on a real date. There's an installation down at Fort Mason by this woman who's really hot: this chick named Yoto, from Japan. She creates these amazing sculptures using radioactive waste, yarn, old zippers, and scrap metal from military planes."

Bunny wrinkled her nose. "Art bores me. Let's stay here and drop E. You have any more of that stuff you had in rehab? That stuff was fabbo. Really yummy."

"Bunny, you can't be serious."

"I certainly can."

"Look, I told you, I'm clean. No drugs." Dylan stood and turned her pockets inside out. "Clean. For real. Isn't that freaking great?"

"Maybe for you," said Bunny as she stood and called Mr. Yummy back to her. The terrier vaulted into Bunny's outstretched arms. "But frankly, dear, I find it a real turnoff."

74.

Thumper Gets a Halo

The next time Thumper opened her eyes, she could not move her head. While she'd been unconscious in the emergency room, the attending physician had ordered a metal halo screwed into her skull. The device sat on her shoulders, ringing her neck so she could not move her head to the right or left. It felt weird, like her neck was locked into a tube.

"The halo and brace hold her spine erect, keep her from suffering any further injury until we've assessed her neural state," Thumper heard someone say. Thumper could see three women standing at the doorway to her room, one of them her mother, Sheila. Sheila and Mary Lou seemed to be quizzing the third woman, a doctor, about her test results. Thumper did not say anything for the longest time. Instead she listened as her mom, Mary Lou, and the physician, a stocky redhead with a pert nose, discussed her status.

Sheila was talking to the doctor: "Will she be able to walk?"

"I don't know. We can't know. Right now she has no feeling from the lumbar vertebrae down. That might be permanent; might not. Sometimes spinal tissue inflammation can cause temporary swelling; and that swelling can block the transmission of feeling. When the swelling subsides, she may be fine."

"So," said Sheila, "she *might* be fine?"

"She *might*." The doctor shook her head. "I can't make any promises. No one can at this stage of the game."

Mary Lou jumped in. "What did all those tests show?"

The doctor flipped through papers on her clipboard. "Some good news. Doesn't appear to be any breaks in her vertebrae, but here" — the doctor walked over to a lighted display box that showcased a row of X-rays — "something here worries us. This could be a hairline fracture." The doctor retracted a pen from her lab coat pocket and tapped on the glass.

"*Could* be?" asked Mary Lou as her finger gingerly touched the spot the doctor had isolated.

"Could be; or could not be. We're waiting for the results of the MRI. Those images will show more. We'll see a clean break in those images, if there is one."

Thumper waited until the doctor was gone before speaking. "Hey, guys, like, what the hell is this thing on my head? I go unconscious for, like, a few seconds and you let them screw a lampshade on my head."

Mary Lou bounded over to Thumper's bedside and grasped her head. "Welcome back, hon. Your mom is here."

Sheila came over and kissed her daughter's cheek. Tears glistened in her eyes. "You scared us real bad, honey. Running the track like that, that was something your boneheaded sister would have done."

"I know, Mom. But Dirk isn't racing anymore. Just me."

"You trying to be your sister? That it? That what this foolishness is about?"

Dirk blushed. "I'm trying to win, Mom. That's all."

Sheila took a deep sigh. "You did that, all right."

Thumper tried, unsuccessfully, to sit up. "I won?" she asked, her voice high in excitement.

Mary Lou took hold of her hand. "Yes, hon, you won. A real photo finish. The judges took an hour deciding, but they ruled you won the race, and that you didn't foul. Jane isn't happy, but you won, fair and square. You've got a place on the World Cup team, honey. And you set a new time trial record."

"Jane? Oh God," croaked Thumper. "Is Jane okay? I didn't hurt her, did I? Tell me I didn't hurt her."

Mary Lou leaned down and whispered into Thumper's ear: "That old New Hampshire bitch is fine. Don't worry your head about her. She made a clean tumble. Walked away without a bruise."

"Thank God!" murmured Thumper, who had no choice but to stare straight up at the acoustical-tile ceiling, a view she now feared might be hers for the rest of her natural life.

75.

The Fire She Lights in Me

After an hour of keeping Birge at bay with a butter knife and a bookend, Nan finally decided she'd allow the woman to sit next to her on the couch in the library. "If you come near me, I'll scream for help!" warned Nan.

"Fine. I'll stay here. Nothing will move on me but my tongue."

"Seems to me that's what got us into this fix to begin with."

"Are you going to keep smart-mouthing me or are you going to be still for a few moments and let me talk?"

Nan shrugged. "Talk all you want. Yak. Yak. Yak. Be my guest, dear."

The butler tiptoed into the room. "Would you like anything, Ms. Birge? A plate of dinner?"

"Just my Scotch, please."

The butler stopped dead in her tracks.

"What?" asked Birge. "Don't tell me we're out of Scotch. We can't be out of Scotch."

The butler raised her eyebrows at Nan as she nodded toward the bare liquor cabinet in the corner.

Birge faced Nan, her eyes narrow with suspicion. "What? What did you do to my Scotch?"

Kicking off her loafers and leaning back on the sofa, Nan sighed. "I got rid of all the booze. I'm an alcoholic. Remember?"

"Well, yes, but that was *my* booze. And I'm *not* an alcoholic."

"Look at this way, dear, you really do drink too much. I've probably just saved you from turning into one."

Birge glanced at the butler, who stood waiting at the door with Nan's tray of dirty dishes in her hands. "Do we have anything else to drink?"

"Soft drinks. Coffee. Tea. Seltzer. Everything else, ma'am."

"Fine, bring me some coffee. Really strong."

"Yes, ma'am."

As soon as the butler was gone, Birge got up and threw two more birch logs onto the already blazing fire. Flames leaped in the blackened hearth. The fireplace in the library enjoyed a granite hearth six feet long, more than four feet high. It had been built to warm the shingle-style mansion back at the turn of the century, when central heat had not been an option. Birge and Nan had restored the mansion while keeping the fireplace just as it had been installed. Both preferred the raw smell of wood burning and crackling over the faint odor emitted by a modern propane apparatus.

Nan stretched her stocking feet toward the fire, enjoying the warmth. Out the French windows on either side of the fireplace she could see the moon dancing across the black, glassy Atlantic Ocean. It made her sad to remember all the times she and Birge had stretched naked in front of this very fire, enjoying each other as much as the view. "You've been unhappy in our relationship for a long time?" Nan asked her partner quietly.

"No." Birge shook her head. "I'd not say that. Mostly I've been very happy. I thought you knew that."

"I'm not sure what I know anymore." Nan yanked a cashmere afghan off the back of the couch and wrapped it around her shoulders. "I think maybe I owe you an apology."

Birge sat silent, studying her hands, which she had clasped together in her lap.

"Yes, I owe you an apology. You tried to tell me my drinking was out of control. I kept sidestepping the issue. I was in denial. I didn't listen to you. I didn't listen to anyone."

Birge looked up. "You knew you were an alcoholic?"

"I think so." Nan wrinkled her forehead. "But you know everyone we know drinks heavily." Nan rubbed a spot on her forehead. "My father drank heavily. And everything fell apart so fast on me, honey. I couldn't handle it. I couldn't admit I was failing. That I'd lost all that money for so many people, so fast." Tears came to Nan's eyes.

Birge scooted across the couch and took Nan in her arms. When Nan resisted, Birge fought back, winning, at last, the upper hand. "Get over yourself already, woman. We're in this together. Me and you. I'm here. I strayed for a few days, but I'm back. Rock solid. You don't have to do this alone, Nan. I'm here. Right here, next to you. I'm sorry, so sorry I hurt you, hurt us. Forgive me?"

Nan felt the resistance melt from her body. It felt good, so natural, to be back in Birge's strong arms. "You know," she said, looking up at Birge through teary eyes, "I've tried really hard to hate you."

"I noticed."

"But truth is, I love you. God help me, I just fucking love you." Nan reclined fully into Birge's warm, stout body.

The two women lay together in the flickering darkness, warmed by the fire, and thirty years of hard-won history.

76.

You're in the Army Now

Poppy was relieved when the plane finally skidded to a landing outside Baghdad and the staff sergeant escorted her and Wee Gee to the USO tents. "You ladies bunk in here!" barked the sergeant, who had introduced herself as Rico. By the time the women arrived at the service tents, Rico was shouldering Wee Gee's duffel bag. Much to Poppy's dismay, the two older women were flirting like Southern weasels in heat.

"You gonna dance some more for me, sugar?" Sergeant Rico asked as she flung Wee Gee's duffel onto a squeaky cot. "I mean, I've seen girls dance back in the States, but we don't get many professionals. The boys get the better entertainment. We ladies don't often get a real treat like you two coming into our tents."

Wee Gee smiled. "Maybe you'd like a private dance? Just me and you?"

The sergeant beamed. "That would be really great, sugar. Got my own tent. Lots of privacy."

The sergeant had flipped off her duty cap and Poppy could see that her dark hair, which was buzz cut, was shot through with gray. Poppy had never seen two old ladies flirt outright like this. She feared she might gag.

"Excuse us, love," Poppy said as she muscled her way between Wee Gee and the soldier, "but we were wondering if you could tell us who is in charge of press relations."

"Yeah, sure. That would be Wilson. General Wilson. Doesn't have a tent. Has her own trailer. Over behind the communications building." Rico hitched a thumb over her broad shoulder.

"Take us?" asked Poppy.

"I could." Rico nodded. "But if I did, I might get my ass chewed."

Wee Gee laid a hand on Rico's bare forearm. "I could make it worth your while. Girl Scout's honor."

The sergeant's smile was so wide it could easily have spanned her home state of Texas.

This time Poppy did gag.

"Sure. Why not?" quipped Rico. "You gals store your gear. Be back in a wink. Walk you over. But I can't promise she'll see you. Entertainment don't normally fraternize with the intelligence side of things, but seeing how you asked me nice" — Rico smiled at Poppy — "I guess I can introduce you and your little cocoa goddess sidekick to the general."

Poppy was relieved when Rico parted the flap on the tent and disappeared back into the darkness of the desert. She shivered, surprised how cold it was in a place she'd imagined as hot as Hades. "You always flirt like that with women in uniform?" she asked Wee Gee, who was busy unpacking her toothbrush and lingerie.

"Who was flirting?" asked Wee Gee. "I was just making polite Southern conversation."

"Don't get me wrong, I think it's kinda cool, flirting at your advanced age and all, but could you turn the tart factor down just a smidgen? We need to find Storm."

"Girl, you think that handsome old bull dyke is going to break the rules for your skinny cracker ass? I'm doing my best to help Storm here. I'm right here with you, ready to lay down my life."

"Oh, something's going to get laid all right."

Wee Gee tossed her toothbrush at Poppy's head.

Poppy dodged the throw and the toothbrush struck Rico instead, who'd just ducked back in under the tent flap. "Whoa! Ladies! A little order here! Behave yourselves! Both of you!"

"Guess you'll have to discipline us, sergeant," said Wee Gee.

Rico sidled up to Wee Gee. "You're one horny chocolate toad, aren't you, sugar?"

"I wouldn't be if you'd do your job."

Rico roared with laughter. "Come on, you two. Let's get you to the general before I forget myself and go hog wild."

77.

Jane Wayne Rides Again

Despite the late hour, General Wilson was awake, tapping in command lines on a computer keyboard at her desk, when Rico escorted Poppy and Wee Gee into the communications command trailer. The general was a tall, stout woman in her mid-sixties who wore gold-rimmed reading glasses with visible bifocal lines. Her dyed ash-blonde hair was pulled back in a bun.

She stood and offered her hand as the women entered her office. "Pleased to meet you gals," she said. "You in particular," she added with a nod toward Poppy. "Huge fan. Huge. Humongous."

"You know me?" asked Poppy, somewhat shocked.

"Know you?" cried the general. "Honey, you're the number one pinup girl in the ladies' locker room. Every time you come on TV in the rec room, we have to do a hand check on the ladies, make sure they keep their hands above their waistbands, at least until lights-out."

Poppy actually blushed.

The general offered the women some beer, which they declined. Wee Gee asked for diet ginger ale instead. A foot

soldier promptly delivered a chilled six-pack to the communications trailer.

"What brings you ladies to the desert?" asked General
Wilson, as Rico poured the drinks.

Poppy mulled this over. "Two things, really. First, we want
to entertain you women. Second, we were hoping you could
help us find a friend."

"Enlisted gal?"

"No," said Poppy, "American war correspondent. Storm
Waters."

The general nodded. "That's the gal they took hostage a
few days ago, down south. Yes?"

"Unfortunately," said Poppy.

The general circled the desk to come out and stand by a
wall projection screen. "She your gal?" asked the general as she
snapped on the projection system and began flipping through
maps.

"I want her to be," said Poppy, her voice meek for a
change.

The general stopped what she was doing and stared at
Poppy. "You came all the way over here to help this woman,
and she isn't even promised to you?"

"I guess that's about the size of it."

The general rolled her eyes. "You two have some balls."

Wee Gee spoke now. "General, we really love Storm —"

"Wait." The general held up one hand. "This isn't one of
those kinky ménage à trois things, is it? 'Cause if it is, I have to
tell you gals I've got a little woman and a piddle of grandkids
back home, but I'm Baptist. Don't go for none of that kinky
Orange Is the New Black stuff."

Wee Gee shook her head. "Nothing kinky here, ma'am, I
assure you. Poppy and Storm met in rehab. They fell in love.
Storm had to leave to come back here after a story. Poppy just

wants a chance to connect with her again. I'm along for moral support. I didn't want my baby girl here to get into trouble."

The general studied both women. "So happens we know where your gal is."

"What!" cried Poppy, who was on her feet in a flash. "Let's go! Get us a tank or a camel or something!"

"Whoa!" called the general as she reached out and snagged the prancing Poppy by the collar of her shirt. "Sit your cute little ass down." The general yanked Poppy back into her seat. "Let's talk about this thing like ladies. Can't just order tanks and roll on behind enemy lines. Who do you think we are? A bunch of wild Jane Waynes?"

Poppy puffed up. "Don't bloody tell us we have to do paperwork!" she cried. "There isn't time for that. Just show us where she is. We'll find her."

The general guffawed. "What are you going to do, honey? Take a taxi?"

Wee Gee jumped in. "Those maps." She nodded to the projection screen. "You can show us Storm's location on those maps?"

"Yes, I can." The general walked around and tapped a spot with a leather pointer. "Square there. Not far inside enemy lines."

Poppy narrowed her eyes. "How can you be sure?"

"Easy," said the general. "Communications. We fit every war camera with a GPS tracking device. The camera Storm is toting has a homing device. That way we can locate all our equipment via GPS. We lose a lot of these things. With night-vision gear these babies cost us upward of ten thousand a pop. With the GPS we can locate any cameras issued for use on the battlefield, get them back safely even after our cameramen have been blown to Toledo."

"We can go in after Storm?" Poppy stood again.

"Hold your wild horses, honey. We can go. I've already got a couple of Hummers ordered to leave with a supply convoy in about two hours."

"Why the hesitation?"

"Not hesitating. We need our paperwork in order. We'll have to cross three checkpoint zones. If we don't have papers in order, we'll be blood-and-gut confetti in no time."

Poppy twisted her lips. "As soon as we have the paperwork we can go after Storm?"

"Actually," said the general as she rubbed her cheek, "technically, we can't go after your gal. She's civilian. But we can go after that camera. That camera is valuable property of the U.S. military. If your gal just happens to be attached to that camera, well, we can lay claim to her, also."

Poppy was on her feet, out the door instantly. She grabbed Sergeant Rico by the arm, dragging her along. "Where do you keep your tanks?" she asked. "Show me which one to climb into."

The general and Wee Gee brought up the rear.

Wee Gee apologized to the general. "Sorry about that girl. She's in love. Young. Mighty impatient."

The general chuckled. "That lady is a real spitfire. Got to admire that. Hell, I can't get my gal to walk across the kitchen and fetch me a bologna sandwich. Great to see young love in action again."

78.

Lesbian Poker: All Hearts Wild

Wee Gee sprawled on top of a mountain of sandbags, playing poker with Sergeant Rico and a gang of enlisted ladies as they waited for General Wilson and her convoy to arrive in the lot. By consensus, the women were playing lesbian poker: all hearts wild.

"Full house!" cried Wee Gee triumphantly as she cast down her hand and raked in a mess of pennies.

Poppy was sitting on her haunches not far away, squinting at the pixilated satellite TV screen that hung on the outer wall of the mess hall. The commentator had not said a word about ISIS for almost an hour. The news was about domestic issues: some guy in a parka claimed his pet poodle was eaten by a pack of coyotes on a hike into Alaska. Poppy was not paying much attention until a picture flashed across the screen that jogged a memory.

"It's Thumper!" cried Poppy as a clip of the snowboarder and her sister competing at the last Olympics flashed onto the screen. "She made it onto the World Cup team!"

"Hallelujah!" cried Wee Gee, who'd just won another hand, this time on a bluff. She looked up to see a ticker stream across the bottom of the screen announcing that Thumper was in a hospital in upstate New York: "Olympic snowboarder injured in accident at Lake Placid. May never walk again, fears coach and family."

Wee Gee threw her cards down as she read the ticker. "God, no! Don't do that to that sweet little girl. Don't you dare do that to her!"

Sergeant Rico looked up at the screen. "You know that girl?"

"Sure do. She was in rehab with me and Poppy and Storm."

Rico whistled. "As soon as I get stateside, I'm gonna throw away my beer and give rehab a go. They got any more hot dark hens like you stashed there?"

Before Wee Gee could respond, four convoy trucks and two Hummers roared into the yard. General Wilson was seated high up in the lead Hummer on the passenger side. "Hop in, gals," she said with a wave of her hand toward Poppy and Wee Gee. "Time to get this show on the road."

Poppy wasted no time jumping up on the running board and hopping into the elevated back seat. She had to reach out and give Wee Gee a hand up as the Hummer kicked up sand, the motor revving to get out on the open road.

As Wee Gee kicked to get into the Hummer, she felt a pair of hands press suggestively against her posterior, giving her the lift-off power she needed to scramble safely into the back seat. She literally flew into the Hummer.

"I felt that, missy!" she called over her shoulder at Rico as the grinning sergeant slammed shut the vehicle door.

"You ain't felt nothing yet, sugar," promised the sergeant with a wink as the rescue convoy rolled out of the encampment into the utter darkness of the desert.

79.

What Men Fear Most

Storm was running out of questions. She'd asked Hasi Ahmad every question she could imagine, beginning with important issues, like his religious beliefs, and ending with inane things, such as his favorite pizza (goat pepperoni). The camera had run out of memory half an hour ago, but luckily Hasi was so engrossed in his own stories he failed to notice when the red light clicked off.

"Does your wife support your work?" asked Storm, who'd broken into a sweat as soon as she'd noticed the dimmed light. Her time was running out. She was at the end of the digital memory, which meant she was also almost to the end of her life.

"What wife? I told you: no wife."

"Right. Sorry. Okay, if you and your men kill me, what good will this do your cause?"

"It will show Americans we are not afraid."

"But I have no weapons. I am not a soldier. I am a woman. A reporter."

"Yes, and what you report are lies. For this we will kill you."

"Hold on," objected Storm, stepping outside her professional role. "Have you ever seen me report?"

"No."

"Then for all you know, I tell no lies."

"Maybe, but why are we talking about you?" Hasi frowned. "This interview, it is about me. Yes?"

Storm leaned back on her cot. Hasi had unchained her leg so she was free to walk about the room, but anytime she tried to walk more than a single step, one of his soldiers raised a bayonet toward her. She felt frustrated. Stuck. At the end of her wits. "Can I go to the bathroom?" she whined. "The toilet? Please? Where is the toilet?"

"Outside," said Hasi, "in the sand."

"I'm fine with that," said Storm, who'd peed au naturel a good many times. Her chosen profession demanded a lack of prissiness in this particular arena.

"Okay, but one of my men must go with you."

"Fine," said Storm. "Whatever."

As Storm sprang off the cot, she felt something jiggle in the inner zipper pocket of her fatigues. She raked one hand over the pocket and felt the rounded vial of drugs that Hunter had foisted onto her. Next to that was a small metal case that held her tampons.

Seeing her hand pressed to her thigh, Hasi demanded to know what she was doing.

"Looking for a tampon," she lied.

"Do not say that," said Hasi, his face stern. "We do not talk about these things."

"What? Menstruation? You're telling me you don't talk about menstruation?"

"That is enough!" warned Hasi, his face reddening.

"Because I'm having my period," remarked Storm casually as she pulled a super tampon from her pocket and waved it in the air. "And I need a new one of these inserted as soon as possible."

Hasi and his men stepped back from the tampon-waving correspondent, clearing a path to the door.

Storm had what she wanted now: Hasi and his men unbalanced. *Tampon! Tampon! Tampon!* she felt like screaming as she walked toward the door unencumbered. She'd forgotten what wussies men were about women's periods. At last, she had the upper hand.

"Let her go," croaked Hasi to his men, who could not have retreated any farther into a corner if they had tried. "There is nowhere for her to go. Whether we kill her or the desert kills her, makes no difference. Yes?"

"Thanks," said Storm, who was out the door before Hasi and his men could change their minds.

80.

Her Healing Touch

Mary Lou was reading a tattered copy of *O, The Oprah Magazine* when Thumper awakened. Casting the magazine aside, she climbed into the elevated hospital bed with her girlfriend. "You've been asleep for, like, hours," murmured Mary Lou. "It's three o'clock in the morning."

"Miss me?" moaned the snowboarder.

"Like the dickens!" proclaimed Mary Lou. "Dirk called when you were asleep. She saw your tumble on CNN. She called to congratulate you, and to ask if you were okay."

"What'd you tell her?"

"That you were fine and dandy."

"Good. Thanks. She like California?"

"Loves it. Candice has her back on testosterone and she's taken up surfing. Says it's just like snowboarding, except you can do it naked."

"Cool!" said Thumper, who at the moment envied her sister her physical freedom. "Any news from the doctor?"

Mary Lou snuggled against Thumper's side as best she could, given all the apparatus and wires they had tangled around her girlfriend. "No news," she sighed.

The two were quiet for a while. It was dark in the room, except for a single bedside lamp where Mary Lou had been sitting reading. The machines around Thumper hummed and bleeped.

"Think we can make out?" asked Thumper.

"I think we should try," insisted Mary Lou.

"Can't really move much," complained Thumper.

"How about I get up and straddle you?"

"Cool! If you do that, I can move my hands, give you something to ride."

Mary Lou, who was wearing a skirt, slipped out of her panties and kicked them across the room before straddling Thumper.

Hiking her skirt, she was soon at home on top.

"Can we, like, do this in here?" whispered Thumper.

"They're charging us, like, five hundred dollars a day for this bed. Honey, at those prices I say we can do anything we damn well please."

Mary Lou slid apart Thumper's gown and began to slide her tongue over her washboard abdomen. "Feel that?" she purred.

"Ah, yeah! Definitely!" giggled Thumper.

"Good," Mary Lou murmured as Thumper's hand slid between her legs and she mounted two fingers, then three. "Mmmm! I feel that, baby!"

Mary Lou was soon biting her bottom lip, trying to keep her panting to a dull roar. The harder she rode Thumper's hand, the harder Thumper pushed back. When she came she had to bite into Thumper's shoulder to muffle her scream. She rolled off Thumper onto the side of the bed, perspiration glistening on her rosy cheeks.

"Mary Lou?" whispered Thumper in the darkness.

"Yes, honey."

"I felt that."

"Course you did," snickered Mary Lou.

"No," said Thumper. "I mean I *really* felt that. Down there. In my, er, clit."

"Oh my God!" cried Mary Lou. She peeled pack the sheets and stared at Thumper's bulging muscular thighs. She ran a hand along one thigh. "You feel that?"

"Oh yeah!" cried Thumper.

Mary Lou leaned down and kissed her girlfriend's mound through the thin cloth of her tighty-whiteys. "How about that?"

"Dunno. Try it again. A little harder?"

Mary Lou was only too happy to oblige. Less than a minute later, it was Thumper who had to bite the air to keep from screaming.

81.

Lull in the Storm

Storm was not far from the shack where they'd held her captive when she dropped her fatigues and began to urinate. She had not lied about that. She wasn't on her period, though. That had been a bald-faced lie: a very effective one, it seemed.

Storm sighed as she relieved herself. At least she was outside. Free for a few of the last moments of her life. She stared up at the stars as she wiggled back into her fatigues. The sky twinkled with a different pattern of constellations than the ones she'd viewed only a week ago. The last time she'd really looked at the stars had been with Poppy in Vermont. That seemed a long time ago. A lifetime ago. Storm kicked at the wet sand, ashamed of how she'd last treated Poppy.

Poppy was special: Storm had never allowed anyone as far into her heart as that little tart had managed to climb. She wondered where Poppy was now. Had she completed rehab? Storm was certain she had; she wished she could see Poppy one more time. Say good-bye. Make amends. She hated the idea that she was going to her grave without letting Poppy know how much she really cared for her.

The door to the shack creaked open and Hasi Ahmad stepped out into the hazy starlight of the desert. "Come back now!" he pleaded. "We must finish the interview."

Storm kicked more sand as she walked toward the shack. It was no use, really. She shoved her hands deep into the pockets of her fatigues, only to jam her right hand into the vial of pain pills Hunter had forced on her.

The pills. I can swallow them all. Take my own life instead of giving it to them.

Storm realized in an instant this was the only way she might die with dignity. She slowed her pace as she shuffled toward the hut, popping first one pill, then another. She had difficulty swallowing the pills. Her throat was dry. She tried to work up some spit, but the pills kept sticking to the roof of her mouth. They dissolved against her tongue as she walked, bitter and hard. Storm kept swallowing pills right up to the door, where Hasi ushered her roughly inside using the butt of his rifle.

By the time she was back inside, she felt sleepy. She lay down on the cot. The muscles in her legs felt like jelly. Even her tongue felt numb. When she tried to talk, her tongue wiggled like hot rubber against the roof of her mouth. Her lips felt swollen and heavy. She felt she might choke on her own tongue. On the bright side: She felt too dreamy to care one way or another. A haze hung over the room. Hasi and his men appeared to be wearing halos.

She lay back on the cot and shut her eyes, confident hers would be a pleasant death, after all.

82.

A Different Kind of Fox Hunt

Poppy chewed her cheeks as the military supply convoy stopped at the third and last checkpoint on its way into the war zone in the southern provinces. It seemed to Poppy like the Hummer and its escort tanks were lurching as slow as giant scorpions across the sand.

The rock star wondered again why the Americans were at war in this godforsaken place. Normally she paid little attention to politics. A month ago she could not have dreamed she, too, would be at war. She'd never loved anyone enough to risk her pride, let alone her life.

Wee Gee squeezed Poppy's arm, bringing her out of her trance as the Hummer lurched forward, toward an arc of lighted missile fire that spread like a halo over the eastern sky ahead of them. "The general said that's where we're headed. Over to the right of that light," said Wee Gee.

Poppy frowned. "That looks far away."

General Wilson turned around in her seat to address Poppy. "It ain't far, honey. About five miles. We'll be there in about the same amount of minutes. I have to tell you gals we could hit some fire. Or roadside bombs. If we take fire, I want you two to get down on the floorboard, as flat as you can.

French kiss that goddamn floorboard. This thing is bulletproof. The bottom is steel plated. Just get down and stay down. Understand?"

Wee Gee, who was already on her knees halfway down into the recess, replied, "Yes, ma'am!"

But Poppy remained seated. "May I have a gun?" she asked General Wilson, her voice as steady as if she were asking for a cup of tea.

"Can you shoot?" asked the general.

"Of course."

Wee Gee snorted. She looked up from her cubby on the floor of the Hummer. "You know how to shoot a gun?"

"Of course. I'm English. I've been on duck hunts and fox hunts."

"Fox hunts?"

"Yes."

"You ever kill any foxes?"

"Not the furry red ones, no. Though I have to say I have knocked out a few of the lesbian kind in my time."

Wee Gee chuckled.

The general's head disappeared from the seat ahead of Wee Gee and Poppy. When the general reappeared, she was hoisting a machine gun over the seat of the Hummer.

Poppy took the gun, along with a belt of ammunition. She strapped the ammunition around her chest and sat back in the seat, lowering her eyelids.

Outside the Hummer the noise had picked up. As long as Poppy kept her eyes closed, it sounded like a celebration, like fireworks across the Thames on a hot summer night. *Pop! Pop!* Then a low rumble.

"We there yet?" asked Poppy, as the Hummer slowed to a crawl.

In the front seat, General Wilson had been tracking the GPS signals in Storm's camera. A green dot pulsated on the screen. "Almost there, ladies," said the general. "That shack up there just off the road seems to be the place."

Poppy squinted in an effort to better decipher the tin-roofed edifice in the shadowy distance. Light leaked in thin rays out the cracks around the front door. Two windows glowed with yellow light, one on each side of the door. In the far distance, by moonlight, she spied a group of armed men scrambling like scorpoions over the ridge of a sand dune. Poppy gripped the barrel on her gun as the Hummer slid to a stop not twenty feet from the shack.

General Wilson turned in her seat to instruct Poppy to wait, let her soldiers secure the shack, make sure it was safe. But by the time the general had her neck craned around, Poppy had opened the door to the Hummer and tumbled into the night. She ran as fast as she could toward the shack. The weapon bounced against her chest, an event that would have been painful if Poppy had been in her right mind.

But Poppy was not in her right mind.

"Goddamn it!" yelled the general after the rock star. "After her, ladies!" she called to a platoon of soldiers who spilled out of the Hummer next to them.

83.

Operation Desert Storm: Code Blue

Poppy burst into the shack, relieved to find Storm alone, face down on a cot. She rushed to the cot. Kneeling, she grasped Storm's head, gently rotating it until the correspondent's cold face fell into the cup of her hands. When Poppy saw Storm's face, her relief turned to panic. The war correspondent's normally creamy complexion was tinged blue.

"Storm!" she cried. "Can you hear me? You all right, love?" Poppy squeezed Storm's right hand, which hung cold and lifeless off the side of the cot.

A pair of medics struggled to drag Poppy aside. "Let us have a look at her, ma'am," said the first medic, a tall, gangly black woman. "Please, let us see her."

Wee Gee, who was now in the shack alongside General Wilson, grabbed the grieving Poppy around her waist. Struggling, she pulled Poppy backward, off Storm's body. "Get back, baby girl! Let these ladies have a look."

Poppy kicked and screamed. One well-placed kick of her combat boot and she was free of Wee Gee's grip, back on top of Storm's seemingly lifeless body.

While Wee Gee regrouped, trying to catch the breath Poppy had kicked from her, the general sauntered up behind Poppy. She made a small jabbing motion with one hand to one of the medics. Understanding the motion, the medic pulled out a syringe, which was already loaded with a clear liquid. She thrust the needle into Poppy's posterior.

The rock star's knees buckled. General Wilson caught her and swung her to the ground softly while both medics busied themselves over Storm.

The general studied Poppy's limp form. "Sorry about that," she said to Wee Gee. "But she's not helping her friend. The medics need to make an assessment, and they can't do that if they can't get to the body."

Wee Gee licked her lips. She did not like the term *body*, which the general had used to describe Storm. She held her tongue, though, and cradled Poppy in her arms as the medics performed a series of maneuvers involving tubes and bags over Storm's limp body.

One of the medics turned to face Wee Gee. She held up a plastic vial. A pair of large, blue tablets clinked softly together in the vial. "You recognize these?" she asked Wee Gee.

Wee Gee shook her head a virulent no.

"Your friend have any prescriptions she took regularly that you know of?"

"She was an addict."

"An addict? What did she use?"

"Pain killers. She loved the things. Anything with opiates."

The medic rattled the vial again. "But you don't recognize these?" The medic spilled the pills into her palm and fingered them, searching for the coded numbers that would tell her, perhaps, what kind of drug Storm had taken. The tablets had no code. They appeared to be a private manufacture of some sort. Desperate for some identifying data, the medic bit into the bitter end of one pill.

The other medic popped her head up. "What is that stuff?" she asked. "She had to have taken it. Look at her shirt."

The front of Storm's fatigues were stained a milky blue. Clearly she had taken the drugs, or been fed them, then vomited.

Wee Gee leaned forward. "That's vomit? That's good? Right? If she vomited she didn't get the full effect? Right?"

Ignoring her, the medics resumed work on Storm. One of them filled another syringe and injected the medicine directly into Storm's chest, close to her heart as near as Wee Gee could tell.

"What was that?" Wee Gee asked. "We don't know what she's taken. Do we?"

The medic shrugged. "Assume it's an opiate. See if we can get a heartbeat. Anything at this point."

Wee Gee watched in horror as the women cracked open the dented red metal case on a portable machine. Ripping open Storm's shirt, one medic slapped the small red paddles to her blue chest. Storm's booted feet jumped as the medic applied the charge of the machine.

Then again.

Wee Gee held the unconscious Poppy tight to her own chest, smoothing her hair, as one of the medics leaned back and adjusted the dials on the machine.

"Got a beat!" one medic cried. "She's back!"

Wee Gee didn't have to ask what that meant. Storm began to moan. The medics rolled her to her side on the cot as a steady stream of what looked like blue milk leaked from her chapped lips.

84.

Coming Home

The doctor shook her head as she slipped the black cuff around Storm's arm and took her blood pressure. "You're damn lucky. That's all I've got to say." She rounded the bed and checked Storm's pupils with a silver penlight. "Damn lucky those field medics knew their stuff."

Storm was sitting up in a hospital bed, in Herndon, Virginia. Though a civilian, she'd been brought into Baghdad central military ER, then promptly airlifted stateside. Purple crescents floated under her ice-blue eyes. Her lips were so badly chapped and cracked, the hospital doctors had applied a white salve to stem off infection.

Wee Gee crossed her arms as Storm adjusted the tubes that snaked around her chest. "Girl, you look like something the dog's been keeping under the porch all summer."

"Really?" said Storm. "Well, don't hold back on my account, dear. Tell me what you really think."

Poppy sat silent in the far corner, curled in an orange plastic chair, reading a fashion magazine. Since arriving stateside with Storm, she'd been unusually subdued.

Storm crooked a finger toward Poppy. "You!" she croaked. She pointed to a spot on the edge of her sterile white bed. "Here. Next to me."

Poppy laid aside her magazine and trounced over to Storm's bed. "Do I look bad?" Storm rasped weakly as Poppy perched on the edge of her bed.

"Bloody awful," said Poppy.

"I guess you won't kiss me, then?"

Poppy wrinkled her nose. "Bloody right about that!"

Storm curled a hand around Poppy's own hand, which rested at the edge of the bed. "Thank you for coming after me."

"You don't need to thank me."

"Yes, I really do. No one ever did that kind of thing for me before." The emotion was apparent in Storm's voice. The rasp in her throat wasn't caused by cigarettes now but by the deep feelings Poppy had evoked in her.

The two women were silent for a moment. Storm spoke first. "I'm not good with this talking about feelings thing, but I want you to know that when I was in that desert, certain I was going to die, all I could think of was you. I didn't want to leave this life without telling you how sorry I am."

"Sorry?" Poppy furrowed her brow. "About what?"

"Hunter," rasped Storm. "That thing I did to you in Stowe. You finding me like that with Hunter." Storm averted her eyes in shame. "I hurt you. I could see it in your eyes. I'm so, so sorry."

"That was a shock. I thought you fancied me."

"I do fancy you," whined Storm, her voice rising. "I did then, and I still do. I, like, really love you. I want to be with you. Don't you get that?"

"It would have helped if you'd told me that, like, in words," mumbled Poppy, a little embarrassed that Wee Gee was listening to every word, her ears perked and her pen poised.

Storm shut her eyes and sighed. "I couldn't tell you back in rehab. It scared me."

"I?" Poppy poked a finger into her chest. "I scare you?"

"Duh? Yeah."

"You scare me, too," Poppy confessed, her voice a whisper.

"How come?"

Poppy squeezed Storm's hand. "I get this feeling that if I ever fall into your arms, I might not come out again. Might not want to."

"Is that bad?" croaked Storm.

"No, I imagine it could be quite good. It's just …"

"What?" asked Storm, attempting unsuccessfully to sit upright. "Just what?"

"I never fancied anyone the way I fancy you."

"I think I feel the same way."

"*Think?*" shrieked Poppy.

"Erase that," said Storm. "I *know*. Look, I was thinking as soon as I get out of this place, maybe you and I could go on a damned date."

Poppy twisted her lips. "A date?"

"Dinner, maybe?"

"You buying?"

"Of course I am. I'm the butch, right?"

"You better be."

"It's settled, then. We'll date?" Storm squeezed Poppy's hand in a way that made both women wish Storm wasn't restrained, slathered in medical creams.

Storm wasn't much for words, but then Poppy didn't feel she needed a lot of words. One look from the depth of Storm's ice-blue eyes and Poppy felt, for the first time in her life, as though she understood the universe, and her place in it.

Epilogue

Life passes one day at a time. Some days shimmer with promise while others hang dim with despair. Most days are mediocre, passing quickly, forgotten ripples in the ever-flowing river of time. That said, the future can sometimes be forecast with alarming accuracy. The women of Sugarbush did all right for themselves as time slid by.

Dylan Redford received an unexpected two-million-dollar licensing offer from the French government to turn her *Big Pink Pussy* art installation into the world's most memorable carnival ride in Sexland, the world's first X-rated theme park for adults, now under construction south of Paris. She's still single, and still sober.

Nan Goldberg and **Birge Hathaway** took time off from work to travel around the world on a yearlong recommitment honeymoon. They were last seen chain-smoking expensive English cigarettes together outside the Taj Mahal. Birge was complaining about her festering bunions and bad back, and Nan was letting her.

Wee Gee Judd recovered completely from writer's block. Her latest novel, *Desert Hearts Gone Wild* (wink-wink) takes places on the battlefields of Iraq and involves the undying love of Prudence (a tough British army nurse) for her handsome, swaggering, Yank war hero, Sergeant Storm, who loses one leg but wins Prudence's heart in his noble fight for freedom. (And yes, Wee Gee did get laid by you know who.)

Dr. Candice Antwerp got to keep her medical license, which is good considering how much time she donated to help Dirk through her transition. One of Hollywood's leading lezzy spokeswomen, she no longer lives in the closet. Her mother, Ellen, left her father the reverend, and now lives with Candice in California where, to make amends to her daughter, she administers the Hollywood chapter of PFLAG.

Dirk McGraw is now living as a man, a world-class surfing instructor, with his own branded line of boards, clothing, and sports products for women. A reality TV show will soon feature Dirk bronzed and practically butt naked on the beaches of Malibu teaching a gang of adoring Dallas Cowboy Cheerleaders to ride the wild waves.

Thumper McGraw and **Mary Lou Lippenfield** were married in a civil ceremony in the rose garden on Thumper's mother's dairy farm in East Hardwick, Vermont. Everyone cried a lot (especially Mary Lou). Mary Lou is now pregnant with twins (turkey-baster babies) and will accompany Thumper to the World Cup.

Bunny Van Randolph is, sad to say, just as we left her. Flirting, drinking, and doing drugs. (We can only hope she'll find her way. Perhaps in Sugarbush II?)

Betty Frump still tokes her old friend, Mary Jane. She had a close call when, during the divorce proceedings, her ex-partner, **Alice Everwright**, tried to run her down in an environmentally correct Toyota Prius hybrid. (The Prius lacked the acceleration needed to take Betty down; the stoned activist crawled out from under the Toyota with little more than a bruised ego.) In the end, the public sympathized with Alice as a battered woman, awarding her full custody of all adopted children along with generous child support. Alice, her thirteen children, and her new partner, Frances-Wearer-of-Dildos, live together in one obscenely large yurt in the middle of an organic flower field outside Northampton, Massachusetts. (They have started a womyn's drumming circle, to which all are invited.)

Oh, and **Poppy Zigfield** and **Storm Waters** live and love together in well-feathered nests around the world. Both travel a great deal, so instead of buying one big home they purchased several cozy little bungalows at strategic locations: one in the Seychelles, one in the Shetland Islands, and one in the British Virgin Islands. Storm gave up war reporting in exchange for her own travel show on the National Geographic Channel. *Taking the World by Storm* is a huge ratings hit. Poppy and the Pop Tarts are hotter than ever, especially in America, where a carefully orchestrated wardrobe malfunction during a performance on *Saturday Night Live* earned Poppy the jaw-dropping adoration of a new generation of late-night bush babies.

— The End —

Want to read more Sugarbush novels? Go to Ana's blog, www.thebigsugarbush.com and make suggestions for new characters and plotlines. Subscribe and receive weekly doses of humor, lesbian wit and culture, book reviews, cartoons, and other cool stuff for free. You'll also receive advance notice when Sugarbush II hits the street.

About the Author

Ana B. Good resides in the Green Mountains of Vermont. Her stories and essays have appeared in *Salon, Out, On Our Backs, The San Francisco Bay Guardian, San Francisco Bay Times, Berkeley Fiction Review*, and several literary anthologies, including Penguin's *Storming Heaven's Gate: An Anthology of Spiritual Writings by Women*, and the Crossing Press's *Breaking Up Is Hard to Do* and *Love's Shadow*. Her articles and essays have appeared in over three hundred markets ranging from CNN Online to *Home Office Computing. The Big Sugarbush* is the result of Ana's efforts to ward off cabin fever one particularly long New England winter. This is her debut novel. She loves to snowshoe and disappear into deeply superficial pulp fiction. She wrote *Sugarbush* so people would know not all lesbians live in Los Angeles or San Francisco (though Ana herself spent her twenties learning how to be gay in the Baghdad by the Bay). She can be reached anytime at www.TheBigSugarBush.com.

www.TheBigSugarBush.com

Chick Lick Books, an Imprint of Hot Pants Press, LLC